Changeling Press, LLC

ChangelingPress.com

Reaver of Souls

Stephanie Burke

Reaver of Souls
Stephanie Burke

ISBN: 978-1-60521-846-5

Publisher:
Changeling Press LLC
315 N. Centre St.
Martinsburg, WV 25404
ChangelingPress.com

Printed in the U.S.A.

Editor: Martha Punches, Karen Williams
Cover Artist: Bryan Keller

Reaver of Souls has been previously released in E-Book format.

Table of Contents

Chapter One

"You don't have to do this." His father sighed as Torn stood in front of the tall mirror and examined the cut of his white ceremonial uniform. "You know, you are quite young for a joining, and it's never too late to say no."

"I need her, Father," he calmly replied as he brushed the long, dark, curly hair away from his violet eyes. "She makes me feel... not as alone."

He turned his great, liquid eyes to his father, eyes that had seen more than their fair share of pain and misery. He absently nibbled on his bottom lip as he looked at the taller form of the man who had sired him, had raised him to know right from wrong, who had ultimately cursed him.

"Torn," his father began, but stopped short when his son wrapped his arms around him in a loving embrace.

"I need to do this for me," he said quietly in the silence that fell between the two of them.

His father stood stiff in his embrace, but now he was listening.

"I am tired of being alone, tired of that emptiness inside of me. Father, there is a hole where my heart should have been, and it aches for fulfillment."

"And you expect to find fulfillment in the arms of that she-witch?" his father asked as he closed his eyes in pain.

It was his fault his son was so alone, would always be alone. Even now he was terrified of wrapping his arms around his only child, the child of his flesh, his blood. He still didn't know if his reluctance to embrace his son came out of guilt or fear.

"Father, Zultha is not a witch," his son's amused

voice breathed in his ear. "She is a bit undemonstrative --"

"Cold!" his father interrupted.

"And shy, but her heart is good."

"She has a heart?" His father's gruff voice was filled with contempt as he contemplated the woman his only child would join with. Damn it, he still couldn't bring himself to embrace him.

"She has a heart, Father, a big one. The sex is not so important in a relationship. But the caring is."

"Sex is not important?" His father took firm hold of his son's shoulders and moved him back so that he could take a good look at his face.

He had his mother's eyes. His son rarely smiled, but when he did, he saw his beautiful Nello in the joy that lit up his face. He had the height of his mother's people, not quite as tall as his sire, yet he was powerfully built. That, Terror thought with pride, came from him. That and his unruly long, curly, jet-black hair. These were the loving gifts he had bestowed upon his son. The *only* gifts.

"Young man, sex may not be what you base a life joining on, but it certainly can make or break a relationship."

He held in a smile as a bright red flush of embarrassment filled Torn's face, highlighting his high cheekbones and his well-formed nose. His lips were full and wide, a mouth that would make any woman melt, but not this Zultha.

"Well, it was not all bad," he said as he looked up into his father's eyes.

"Not all… Save me from blind fools who don't know their asses from a hole in the ground!" Terror sighed as he tightened his grip on his son's shoulders. "You had sex with her," he began.

"Right."

"And I mean the whole thing, penetration and movement."

"Yes, sir," Torn replied, his blush deepening.

"And it... didn't move you?"

Torn closed his eyes and thought back to the sweaty grinding that was sex. Oh, he loved the feel of a woman's soft skin beneath his hands, the smell of her lush femininity, the sounds she made when penetrated, the gasps and begging moans, but it all seemed... different with Zultha.

Zultha had invited herself in one evening while he was reading by the fire, all long red hair and dulcet tones.

"I have what you want, Torn," she'd purred, dropping the enveloping cloak she wore and exposing the pale, naked body beneath.

His breath had caught at the perfection of her form, from the bright pink nipples to the lush thatch of hair that covered her woman's secrets.

Almost as if in a trance, Torn rose to his feet, nostrils flaring as he fought to control that small voice in the back of his head that warned of caution, and strode toward his intended.

Grinning, she stepped forward, allowing one hand to brush his chest as she stared into his purple eyes, reading the hunger that dwelled there.

"I have what you need."

Then her hands were pulling his loose tunic over his head, her nails scratching at his nipples as she ripped the hapless garment from his body.

"You know what I need?" Torn questioned, a smile in his voice.

Torn was no virgin, untried in the ways of love sport. But he had held his urges back with his mate, both to quell the small warning voice that was always with him and to honor her parents. He would show she who would be his mate all due respect.

But apparently, Zultha was more than ready to take this step.

"I know what men like," she whispered, her tongue lashing out to lap at his lips. "I know what men need."

Startling a gasp from her, Torn wrapped muscular arms around her body, pulling her abruptly against him, smashing her bare breasts into the skin of his chest, a low growl erupting from his throat.

"Then show me."

He blinked as he realized that the memory did not really turn him on.

Oh, it wasn't the performance or the lack of willingness on either of their parts, but the whole thing just seemed forced to him, that even when he was slamming into her writhing body on the tangle of furs that made up his bed, there was something missing.

"Well, she enjoyed it," he said, looking more than uncomfortable under his father's scrutiny as that particular memory flared through his head.

"I am glad my son is capable of pleasuring his woman." He sighed. "But what about you, Torn? Will merely adequate be enough? Can you exist on a lifetime of merely pleasant? Will that be enough to sustain you?"

Hearing that, Torn nibbled on his bottom lip again, tearing the soft skin with his sharp fangs.

"Well, it's a start," he hedged after a moment of contemplation. "She will learn what to do to please me, and I will learn to please her better."

"Torn, you don't have to do this!" Terror said again, running his fingers through his own long dark hair. "This is not what your mother would have wanted for you."

"Then you can thank Grandfather for what I have to do to ease the longing in my heart!"

Terror blanched and looked away, devastated.

Torn looked shocked at what he had said, his face showing the pain he felt at the thoughtless words that had so injured his father. The rift in his heart, in his soul felt wider and more painful than ever.

"Father," he began reaching out to him, "I did not mean that." He sucked in a deep breath as his father pulled away from him. "Father?"

"Then you may as well blame me too, Torn," he said sadly. "And you would be correct. *If* I hadn't angered her father, he never would have laid that curse upon my head. But I loved your mother so much, son. I would die for her. That is what we both wanted for you. An undying kind of love."

Terror turned to face his son again, noting the tears of sorrow now filling their deep purple depths.

"I don't blame you, Father, or Mother!" he explained. "Or even her father! Those were unthinking callous words that I meant not to utter."

"But you still suffer for our actions, Torn. And I never wanted that for any of my children."

"Father…"

"And I don't want my only child to suffer in a joining with a woman who does not deserve him, Torn, please. There must be another way!"

Torn sighed tiredly and lowered his head for a moment. Then as if gathering his thoughts, he cocked his head to the side and eyed his father from beneath curious lashes.

"What woman would have me?" he finally asked. "What woman could put up with the knowledge of what I am and not break under the strain or the fear? I hate being feared, Father. It burns more than the loneliness, and the loneliness consumes what is left of my soul."

"Torn," Terror began, but the slow smile on his son's face quieted him.

"I may not have this all-important love, Father, but I will at least claim a little bit of contentment."

Terror could say nothing to that. He sighed deeply and examined the man who stood before him dressed in his finest leathers. Torn needed something, anything to ease the pain of his soul.

"You know you can always return home," his father reminded him, and felt lightened by the joyful smile that lit his son's countenance.

"I know, Father," he replied.

That was the closest that his father had ever come to admitting love for the creature that he had spawned. And for the moment, that was enough -- more than enough; more than he'd had his entire life.

*   *   *

The room almost glowed, so brightly was it lit with the light of a thousand candles in their high holders. The calming fragrance they gave off soothed the nervous bride and her parents.

Zultha stood at the altar, dressed in the ceremonial white of her beloved's house. The tightly laced sack she now wore came courtesy of her future new-father and his heir, her future mate, Torn.

If this joining ceremony wasn't going to deliver her father's worst enemy into their hands, she wouldn't have bothered with young Torn and his ideals. They were based on outdated beliefs, like love and fidelity.

Fidelity? Ha! Not with the body she had, or the

power she possessed through her father.

Zultha's black eyes winked and glittered in the candlelight at the thought of what would take place next. Hidden in her flower arrangement, those smelly things that Torn had presented her with earlier, lay a special surprise for her lover boy.

"He will show?" Her father leaned down and murmured into her ear. To the people watching, it looked as if he was praising his daughter's beauty, or offering words of encouragement. But Zultha knew that her father had no room in his heart for the kinder things in life.

"Your frostiness hasn't driven him away, Daughter?" he asked. Which of course meant, "You had better not have driven my pawn away, young lady, before I had a chance to use him, or you will be sorry!"

"He will be here, Father!" She laughed. "Who else would have that fanged-toothed half-breed anyway?"

"There are a lot of reasons a man will prefer his own company, Daughter, than to be frozen out of his bed at night!"

There was a discreet look at her mother, the coldest woman on their continent, before he turned his searing gaze back to his daughter.

"Relax, Father," she replied. "He will be here. Last night saw to that!" She quickly turned away from the doubt in her father's eyes and snorted.

Torn would show and he would make the perfect bait to set a trap.

Before she could contemplate her future mate any further, the rear doors opened and Terror, ruler of the Magical holdings, entered the room, looking gloomier than usual. He took his place at the rear of the room, followed by his armed escort of five men.

Terror was still a man of great importance and strength, and his strong physique showed that his age was no deterrent for his skills.

Around the room, female hearts fluttered at the sight of the man in his full warrior's garb. The tight, black leather vest and matching pants showed every bulging muscle to advantage. The mantle of leadership wore lay heavily on his broad shoulders, but it was a weight he gladly bore. He alone stood between two worlds, the Magical kingdom of his mate's people, and the violent world of the savage Swordwielders that he now ruled.

"Zultha, Zoot," he called down the aisle. "I present my son, with all of the blessings that I could muster."

The waiting witnesses clapped, not hearing the barb that struck home with unerring accuracy. Terror was not a man to be toyed with. They had only one chance to make this plan happen, or they were all dead.

Zultha tightened her lips and tossed her bright red hair behind her shoulders. *Blessings he could, and should muster*, she thought. Soon he would be begging for mercy.

Further conversation was stilled as the doors swung open, and Torn stepped into the room.

Many a woman showed shock at the muscular build of the quiet son of their ruler, the one born of two worlds. Although he was the son of a great leader and warrior, no one expected the quiet, intellectual son to have the superior build of a fighter.

The sleeveless white vest he wore exposed the thickly muscle arms and plainly marked their strength. The tight leather pants accented the long cords of rippling muscles that moved with grace and ease as he stopped, bowed to his father, then walked down the aisle toward his mate. Many women commented that if they'd known that Torn, quiet, studious Torn, that strange man Torn, had a body like that, they would have paid the shorter man much more attention.

It was apparent to all the warriors present that the sword, which rested comfortably on the man's side, was no mere ornament, but a weapon he'd been well trained to use. The way he moved bespoke of confidence and experience from proper training. That and the staff at his back were all the weapons any warrior needed. They nodded their heads in approval. He might be a poet and an intellectual, but he was still Terror's son.

"Are you sure you can do this, Daughter?" her father asked, looking at the man who now approached, exposing his strength for the first time. "You will have to do this right. You will not get a second chance."

"I can do this, Father," she replied, and pasted a wide smile on her lips for her future mate.

"Zultha, how beautiful you look," Torn said quietly as he stopped before his joining mate. "Zoot." He nodded politely to her father. His courtly ways in the face of the usual sword wielding warriors had always embarrassed her in the past, but now with his body exposed for the well-maintained machine that it was, Zultha smiled. Then again, she knew what that body was capable of firsthand.

Torn stood a few inches shorter than Zoot, as with just about every male on this planet, but proudly presented himself for the ceremony. His dual blood showed in his pointed ears and purple eyes as well as his height, but his demeanor said that he was a man of purpose.

Several people whispered that he had the magical abilities of his mother's people, but that was never proven. In fact, Torn led a very quiet life, serving the people around his father's castle, working with their prized horses, and contemplating verse more than warfare. That Zultha, daughter of the second most powerful family on their continent, was interested in the quiet man, was a shock. But now, they all saw what she saw in him, the strength, beauty, and purpose in him. They were amazed at her cunning, for seeing what lay below the surface of the man. But then again, he was Terror's son.

"Will you care for her, poet?" Zoot suddenly asked, and Torn's eyebrows shot up in surprise. The man had always given his support to their relationship and his intentions before.

Torn looked at the tall, robed man, and tilted his head a bit to the side, as if facing some strange puzzle.

Zoot had not the build of his father's people, nor the magical properties of his mother's people, yet there was cunning about the man that had often made Torn uneasy. He would ponder that line of thought later, he decided, as he gazed upon the anxious face of Zultha.

Zultha, beautiful Zultha, with her sunset hair and black eyes. Never a more beautiful creature had he seen besides the maidens who dwelled among his mother's people. He was proud to call her his mate, even if his heart could not feel true love. He would make her happy.

"Of course," he stated as he cocked his head to the side again, as if that would give him a better understanding of this man's question.

"Then, will you kneel before her and offer her your pledge? It is… a family tradition," he said in explanation, and the female witnesses sighed at such a romantic gesture.

Zoot's people were known for their excess of emotions, so dangerous a fault in a true warrior. How could one fight effectively when one's head was clouded by anger? That was why his people had become the scholars of their land. Another reason why the beauteous Zultha found Torn so attractive.

"Of course," Torn replied as he adjusted the sword so that he could kneel at his beloved's feet. Easily he dropped to one knee and gazed up at his mate's face, his admiration for her plain to see.

"I promise to keep you and protect you, Zultha," he said, his deep, midnight voice sounding clearly throughout the hall. "I promise to care for you and to provide for your every happiness, even at the forsaking of my own life."

There was a hush as the romantic words filled the room. The emotion, the strength, the intensity of his words rang clear and true.

Zultha stepped forward, collecting her flowers in her right hand and leaned into her lover's shoulders, her left hand cupping his chin, lifting his eyes to hers.

He had such beautiful eyes. Pity.

"Then die," she breathed, a moment before a brass collar slid from the bouquet in her hand. It flashed brightly in the softly lit room, a hint of dark magic in the eerie light. Before Torn could move or his father could react, she slid the cuff around his neck. As the pretty flowers fell around them, falling like leaves in the wind, softly beautiful and heralding change, the collar snapped around his throat with a loud, sickening *click*.

The witnesses began to mutter uncomfortably, wondering why the groom was suddenly gripping his throat. Then there were screams of outrage as the heir was left gasping and choking.

It was the kick that Zultha delivered to his chest that exposed what she had done and caused panic to set in.

"Zultha!" Torn gasped, falling flat on his back, his eyes going wide as his face paled.

"I want the Reaver!" she screamed as her father's armed guards stepped forward, pushing people forcibly back toward the exit.

Suddenly there was a mass exodus as the people inside the room decided retreat was the better part of valor and ran for the rear door, en masse.

The women screamed and the warriors, not wanting to see the sword of one of the fighters descend upon Torn's unprotected body, formed a line behind the fleeing women protecting their retreat.

"Torn!" Terror screamed as he attempted to race forward, to protect his son.

But he was tackled by several members of his guard and pulled backwards through the screaming bodies and nervous men, toward the rear door and safety.

"The Reaver will come and save you, Torn, dearest." Zultha laughed as she stood above him, shoving one of her guards away. "But he needs to be dealt with. He is the one thing standing between my father and the throne!"

"Zultha!" Torn gasped as the ring tightened around his neck. He tugged and pulled at the metal to no avail. It merely tightened its hold on his flesh, buzzing with some unknown but dark spell.

"Oh, stop struggling, Torn," she huffed as she tossed what was left of the flowers aside and nodded to the wide band surrounded his neck. "It will only get tighter."

"Why, Zultha?" he gasped as he continued to struggle with the collar. He turned huge purple eyes in her direction, pleading for understanding.

Zoot stood beside his men and his coldly smiling wife, looking down at him, and shaking his head, before he stepped forth to answer that question.

"For power, young Torn," he replied as if his answer was obvious to anyone. "You were never any threat to me or my power, Torn, but I needed a pawn. The Reaver always acts in the best interest of the Ruling house, conjured by your father. So the perfect pawn is you."

He took a step back, observed the young man who had made the mistake of loving his daughter, then shook his head. His wife stood by his side, unmoved by the tragedy and angst in the fallen man's plight.

"My father --" Torn began, but Zultha cut him off.

"Too well-guarded, Torn, and protected by your mother's magic. Have you any idea how many death spells were canceled by that whore's magic? You were easier to get to, and much more enjoyable. When the Reaver is destroyed, no one will be there to protect your father or those simpleminded fools who support him. The throne will be ours."

"Power," Torn spat, pausing in his mad struggles to free himself. "All of this for power."

"And to rid ourselves of the Reaver," Zoot added. "What good is it being evil if that dark angel always comes to defend the people and right the wrongs?" The last was said in a singsong voice, the sarcasm unmistakable. "Your father's magic, stolen from your mother as it may be, is too powerful for us to overcome. Therefore, the rules of strategy dictate we remove his next greatest offensive device. His main weapon must be destroyed, Torn. Even someone as lacking in intelligence as you should understand that."

"Cleansing hearts and eliminating evil souls." Zultha rolled her eyes as she shook her head in disgust. "That job is overrated, Torn. He has to go, and you, being the innocent party in this power struggle, will force your father to call him. And call him he will. The Reaver will arrive, my love, but he had better show soon. That collar is set to perform a specific function."

"What?" Torn asked as he rolled to his hands and knees, and when that move wasn't objected to, he moved to his feet.

His anger had begun to grow, taking away the chill of a painfully shattered heart. Heart? No. He had no heart.

His sudden cool assessment and detachment from this situation was proving that beyond any doubt. He was a man, betrayed by one he thought to trust, but he now only felt nothing but a mild curiosity about the whole affair.

"It's magic, Torn. It is set to send you to a place far from the reach of your people. Death is simply too far a place for anyone to grab at you, Torn. And the irony of this all -- you will love this one, beloved -- is that the spell and the collar were made by your mother's people."

"Mother?" he gasped as the buzzing increased in intensity. That would explain how the collar could affect him, but why?

"No, Torn, not your precious mother. Her father."

Zultha shrieked in laughter as she watched the disbelief on Torn's face.

"He decided that Terror hadn't been punished enough for stealing away his daughter and her virtue.

He wants him to suffer. He wants all whom he loves to suffer. That means the people of this land, and you, beloved."

Torn's head dropped at her words, but then, just as emotionless as his former bond-mate, Torn raised his eyes, cocked his head to the side and smiled.

"What is so funny?" Zultha demanded as she stepped closer to Torn, angered that her words had not broken the proud man.

"Death, my love," he replied with a chuckle. "I guess I will have to die here and now, for the Reaver will not show his face."

"Wrong, my son!" came a voice from the rear doorway.

A short, purple-haired woman stood there in a long flowing gown. She smiled at the man with the choking band around his neck.

"Nello!" Zoot gasped as he took a step back. "I thought you dead."

"So you decided to visit my father and spin your lies about my mate," she stated, her soft voice ringing with the sound of thunder.

"Mother?" Torn gasped, as he widened his eyes in wonder.

"Oh, my son!" she breathed as she stepped forward. "I came as soon as I heard!"

"Torn!"

Torn raised his head to see his father standing there, horror written on his face. "Father," Torn gasped, momentarily forgetting the buzzing collar around his neck. "Mother has returned."

"To stay, my son," she decided as she finally reached Torn, disregarding the enemy warriors who stood staring at her and her child as if they were bothersome insects on the ground. "To stay."

"But you can't save him," Zultha declared as she stepped further away from the magical woman who seemed to have arrived from the dead to join them. But then, that was not so surprising in a woman who'd defied the wrath of her father, one of the most powerful magical beings to ever exist, to be with Terror. The same woman who then fled her home and her young son to save the family she loved. "Your father said that once magic has been set, no one could undo it!"

"That is true," she decided quietly as Terror, flanked by his men, stepped forward.

"Nello?" he whispered, before his arms went around the woman he loved more than life. Expressions of joy, disbelief, fear, and an undying love, crossed his face.

"I ran away to spare you my father's wrath," she explained as she stared into her Terror's beautiful eyes, one hand reaching up to trace the solid lines and planes of his face. "And when I finally get the chance to behold my son, he is soon be taken away from me."

Then she lifted menacing, glittering purple eyes to Zultha and her parents. "This will not go unpunished."

"You can't hurt us," Zultha said with a decided smirk. "We have a talisman for protection from your father. Your magic is useless against us."

"But the talisman is useless against the Reaver." Torn chuckled around the tightness around his neck. "The Reaver is of magic, true, but is also of this realm as well as the magical one, Zultha. He is beyond my grandfather's influence."

"What?" Zoot asked as he reached out and pulled his daughter closer to him, closer to the dubious safety that his warriors represented.

"Magic does not affect him, Zoot! He is the curse and the scourge of my mother's people. He destroys the wicked and absorbs their dark souls into himself. He was supposed to kill my father once he was released into this plane, but refused. There is no evil in my father or in his supporters. So instead, he cleanses this land of evil, Zoot. All evil. Evil… like you."

"What do you know?" Zultha shouted as she stepped further away from the man, now standing quite easily despite the collar, the man who had begun to unnerve her. Where did Torn gain such command? It made her nervous, like there was more to him than she estimated. "What do you know of him, Torn?"

"I know that he is coming," he purred, his voice growing light yet menacing. "He is not very far now."

"He has blood of the Magic Realm," Zoot breathed as he stepped back amidst the protection of his men. "He would know. But when the Reaver does show, it will be for the last time! Magic may not touch him, but hard, sharp steel will! Let him come! My men are at the ready. And there is nothing, nothing that you or your father, or your magical mother can do about that!"

He looked back at his specially trained men, at the smug grins on their faces at the words of praise from their commander. His lips spread into an almost childlike smile.

"But Zoot," Torn breathed, catching the man's attention, "he is already here!" Before anyone could move, Torn dropped his head and began to laugh.

Louder and louder his laughter grew, until it filled the room, echoing off the walls and striking fear in the hearts of those who would murder and maim for their cause. Anyone unlucky enough to hear that laugh would never forget it, its low manic quality, and the undisguised undercurrent of danger.

Torn raised his head and watched as they all stood back from him, staring at the changes in his face. His purple eyes swirled and changed until they went bright scarlet, pulsing with anger and menace. An unseen mystical wind began to blow his long hair around his face as it carried the faint warning, *Beware*!

The sound of snapping seemed to fill the air as his clothes began to rend and tear from his body as his physical structure began to change. His arms flung out to his side and he tossed back his head with laughter as the muffled wet sound of tearing flesh caused the watchers to jump, and suddenly two obsidian wings exploded from his back. Dark and leathery, they slowly unfurled, increasing his mass, and striking fear into the hearts of those who had sinned.

Still laughing at the shocked faces of those before him, Torn snapped his wings to their full breadth, casting eerie shadows on the walls, before raising his hands in front of his face.

"Torn?" Zultha gasped as she scrambled backwards, almost tripping over her father in an effort to get behind him.

"No, Zultha," his midnight voice answered, deeper than before, darker, scarier, as he lowered his hands from his face. "The Reaver is here."

Zultha bit back a scream as Torn exposed his face. He was completely changed! In place of the almost beautiful man, stood a fierce demon with black angel's wings, and the changes that kept growing!

His eyes glittered bright blood red and his skin slowly darkened to a shade of the deepest black. Where once his strong yet gentle hands had hung at his sides, now existed two strong, powerfully clawed paws, their sharp talons glittering silver at their tips.

His body grew until it more than doubled in size, his heavy breathing drawing attention to the massive chest that rose and fell rhythmically, as he cocked his head to the side and examined those who would have murdered him to gain his alter ego. He stood nearly nude, the scraps of his white leather pants all that protected the thick length of flesh at his groin from public view.

"*No!*" Zultha screeched as this startling apparition stood, grinning at her, exposing its elongated fangs. "It *can't* be true!"

"Oh, but it is." That midnight voice seemed to echo in three different tones as he answered her cry of disbelief. "Are you ready to pray for redemption? Are you ready to be cleansed?"

Growling low in his chest, he narrowed his eyes at the woman he'd sworn to love and protect. Those eyes that once stared at her, naming her his salvation and his freedom, now stared at her... filled with disgust.

"*Nooo!*" Screaming, Zultha turned to flee by way of the rear doors that let her father's soldiers in, and barely made it through the doorway, before her father's men attacked.

But the Reaver met the challenge head-on, easily dodging their cuts and jabs and ripping out throats where he'd made an opening.

Zoot's wife, freed at last from her paralyzing silence, screamed and tried to rush past the beast murdering her mate's men, but she was met by an angry, purple-eyed woman.

"Repayment!" Nello shouted as with a wave of her hand a purple glowing wall surrounded the woman, preventing her escape.

"I did nothing!" the woman cried.

"Nothing but keep quiet about this action against my son and husband. After hearing all of the lies that you spouted about my Terror, my father is anxious to meet you and your husband. He wants to have words with you. He is especially anxious to meet your lovely daughter."

The woman's eyes grew as wide as dishes before she gave a queer whimper and passed out in a dead faint, which was probably the only real emotion she'd showed in years.

By now, the Reaver had destroyed Zoot's men, becoming a spinning, whirling dervish of death.

Heads fell, severed limbs lay twitching on the ground at his feet, men screamed and died until there was none left.

And then, only then, did he turn to face the man who had wrought all of this blood and destruction himself… Zoot.

"I should kill you," the multi-toned voice taunted as the man cowered and ran away from the carnage, escaping in a way that was not taken by his daughter or his wife. He cowered in the nearest corner and watched his plans fall apart. But at his words, Zoot looked into the eyes of death himself, and he feared. "I should tear you apart, piece by piece, and scatter your parts all over this realm!"

"Torn!" his mother interrupted, shocked at the strange tone in her son's voice. "Torn, no!"

"And should I cleanse him, Mother, take this bad, this evil, unto my body and purge his soul?"

"No!" Nello cried as she stepped forward, a pleading look in her eyes.

"Why not then, Mother?" he asked, his eyes never leaving the frightened form of the man who was responsible for his latest misery. He could smell the taint of his fear.

"Now we go home!" she said as she reached up and cupped her son's face, hoping to ease his pain and confusion, and stared into his scarlet eyes. "Now we start over."

"Start over?" He laughed, his voice filling the room with echoes. He slowly, almost reluctantly, pulled away from the caress of the woman he had dreamed about feeling. It pained him, yet he pulled away. "There is no time to start over, Mother."

He pointed to his father's men, noting the frightened looks on their faces as they viewed the monster in their midst and the death he so easily delivered. "Start over, go where there is nothing but the fear, loathing, and disgust that I am sure you feel? I can't even go back to being invisible like I was before, Mother. And you know what? It doesn't even matter anymore. Nothing else matters. Your father's neckband will kill me soon anyway. Can you not hear the humming, Mother?" As he spoke, the buzzing around his neck increased, growing louder and more frightening. "My time here is short."

"No, my son. I can't break my father's magic," Nello said, her eyes wide and tragic, but filled with confidence. "But I can alter it."

"Mother," he began as he looked around at the destruction he had wrought in such a short time, at the death that seemed to surround him like a shroud.

He furled his wings and dropped his head. "I would rather die than to live the rest of my life feared and alone."

"Never alone!" his father said finally as he stepped to his wife's side and enveloped her small form in his embrace. "You will always have a place with us!"

There was an unnamed fear in his father's eyes, but for once, Torn felt -- no, he *knew* that it wasn't fear of him.

"No, Father," he decided as his eyes began to slowly dull into the more familiar lavender shade of his mother's eyes. "I am tired, so... very tired. I have the weight of a thousand souls within me, Father, evil souls. They consume me. I can no longer... feel my own emotions, and what I do feel, I am not sure of. I would rather cease to exist than to live with this... emptiness."

"I will not allow you to die!" Nello cried out as she broke free from her husband's arms. "I refuse to give you up for lost!"

"And you," Terror said quietly, his rage focused on Zoot. "I want a few moments of your time before you go to face the ruler of the Magical Realm."

Zoot whimpered in abject fear as Terror latched onto him and pulled him from his corner. After shaking the man, he hurled him to his men with curt orders to toss him in the dungeons until he had time for him. He was afraid that if the man stayed in the room with him, he would give in to the temptation to crack his spine in several places. "Let me go, Mother!" Torn begged, feeling the weight of his existence as well as the truth of his name. "Let me die, let me find peace."

"You will have peace, my son," Nello said as tears began to run down her face. "But not here. The spell was to send you far away in death, but I can change that."

Before he could even think to avoid her sudden move, Nello reached up and grasped the copper band around his neck.

"Mother!" Torn cried as the buzzing increased

and seemed to snatch the strength from his body. His arms wrapped around Nello instinctively as he felt the power flash from her to his adornment, and he fell to his knees. "Mother… What have you done?"

"I will not lose you to death, my son! But I have sent you far away… from me," she cried, shudders racking her body as she forced her hands to move, to wrap around the baby she had not been able to rear.

"Where?" he demanded before the buzzing grew louder, the world began to spin and twirl, and he held onto his mother like she was the only stable thing left in his universe.

"Far away, my son," she whimpered, the tears falling fast and furious. "But you will be alive!"

So be it, he thought as he turned to face his sire.

"Father," he desperately called as his body began to flicker and fade, to go transparent. "Thank you, Father! You were right!"

"Torn!" Terror called as he reached forward to touch his son, to say he loved him, to show him that he really loved him.

But then he was gone.

Terror stood watching the place where once his son had stood, where once the Reaver had protected the realm, for the last time.

It took him a while to notice that he was on his knees and that his wife cradled his head against her bosom as he cried like a child.

"I never even hugged him, told him that I loved him!" he sobbed, unashamed.

"He knew," his wife murmured in return, her own small body quivering with her grief.

Chapter Two

"Terror!" Nello bellowed as her hands fisted in the sheets, her hair flying wildly around her head as she clamped her teeth onto her bottom lip. *How could she have given this up*?

Pants and small screams erupted from her throat as Terror took fistfuls of his long, soft, straight hair to caress her nipples, causing her to buck against the caress.

Terror chuckled, his hot breath wafting over her moist skin, sending shivers down her spine and wrenching another sharp cry from her throat.

"Terror, please!" One hand left the twisted sheets to tangle into his hair, all pretense of gentleness gone as she tried to force his head lower, to her wet heat.

"You smell so damn good," he purred as his tongue lashed out at the muscles of her stomach, tracing down to her navel where he dipped his tongue into the small indentation.

He shuddered as he buried his face into her soft skin, kissing the small pink stretch marks, the badges of honor that came with carrying his child.

Suddenly, desire to see her body trembling beneath his tool took a backseat to just the plain desire to have her in his arms once more. He settled his head over her stomach, his hands gently caressing her waist, as he pressed as close to her as he could.

"Nello..." he began, but his voice broke.

Tears burned the back of his eyes then made silvery trails down his face as sadness and loss warred with elation and joy.

"Nello, I missed you so much. I love you so much. How could I ever give you up? Why did I let you leave me?" His massive shoulders shook as he struggled to hold in his emotions, to keep them from swamping him totally, but it was a wasted attempt. Tears began to flow as tearing sobs broke free.

"Terror, I am here," Nello whispered as she wrapped her hands around her man, determined never to let him go again. "I am not going anywhere."

"I know in my head," he managed with his tear-ravaged voice. "But you promised me forever before, and then I had nothing."

"I'm so sorry, Terror. It was the only thing I could think of to keep you safe, both of you."

"I would rather have death with you than face eternity without you," he whispered as he pulled free of her grasp to rise up and stare into her purple eyes. "I don't want to be without you again."

He stared at her beautiful face that he thought he would always wake up beside, and carefully examined it for changes.

Twenty-nine years had brought few changes to her features, but there was a decided lack of youthfulness and innocence in a face that had seemed eternally young. Not that she looked old, but her eyes had aged.

The years of pain and anger were there in the depths of her eyes. The years of separation from her loved ones had stolen the life from her.

"I'm going nowhere, Terror," she whispered as her tears began to flow. "I would rather face whatever tortures my father would force onto me than to leave you again. I died so many deaths, Terror. I wanted to end my existence…"

"NO!" Terror rose up and clasped her to his chest, to his heart, pulling her head to rest under his chin, safe. "Never even think it, Nello. Never!"

"But I couldn't," she continued, snuggling in

deeper. "I could not when I had a chance to be with you again, with you and Torn."

She shuddered and pulled herself in closer to her mate, listening to the slow, steady beats of his heart, breathing in his scent, feeling his masculine heat surround her.

"And then I heard what my father had done. When I heard, I crawled out of the hiding place I'd made for myself and confronted him face-to-face. And when I discovered what he had done to my baby… Terror," she cried, her body stiff with tension, "I wanted him to die."

"No, Nello. That is not your way, love. Murder is not in you."

"It is in any mother who discovers her child has been harmed, Terror. He did this to us after I left you, after I took myself out of my child's life to protect him. How dare he harm my baby? He did not have the right!"

"Shh, Nello," Terror soothed as he began to rock her side to side, gently comforting his mate. "Nello, you are not responsible for what he did. No one is responsible for his actions but himself."

"I know it in my head, Terror. But like you say, the heart refuses to believe."

"I know, Nello," he breathed. "I know."

"And now all I have left to hold on to, Terror, is this body that feels like a mother's, yet it has no baby to hold in its arms. I am in a body that has been denied what it naturally would have. I am useless, Terror. I'm a useless waste of a body that clings to hold on to what I gave up."

"Never, Nello. You are not useless, woman. You are my mate, my one and only true love. There has been no one but you, Nello. You own me mind, body, and spirit. There can never be another."

"You never…" The shock made her pull back to stare into his beloved face, caressing the knife-sharp cheekbones and the strong stubborn jaw. "Never?"

"How could I?" he asked as his own tears dried up and a new heat began to pulse within his body. "How could I even think about taking another when you are imprinted, no, burned into my mind?"

"But… but it is your right. I left you and Torn! I…"

"You did what you thought was best for protecting your family. But you are the only one my body quickens for, Nello."

He pulled her in tighter as the warmth in his belly blossomed and expanded low to the base of his spine and then even lower. He felt the tingling in his balls that signaled his erection was returning.

Smiling, he breathed in the fresh scent of her. She smelled like moonbeams, and magic, and woman. There was no greater smell in the world, he decided, no more arousing scent than his Nello.

Nello gasped as she felt his renewed interest as his cock swelled against her stomach. Her breathing became low and wispy as she felt the heat from his cock grow and grow.

She leaned back so she could force one hand between their bodies, to touch and caress the thing she had dreamed about for years, the thing she coveted even though she had been far away from him.

"Make this body sing, love," she whispered as her gaze dropped down to the swollen purple head of his sex. "Make this body worth something again. Bring me back to life."

"Nello," Terror said softly before one hand slipped down her back to caress her ass, to pull her deeper into his body as he began to thrust his hardness into her stomach. A low growl emerged from his throat.

The stimulation of her soft skin on his hardening cock was unbelievable. It was a sensation he thought never to have again.

"Oh Creator, Terror!" Nello gasped, arching into his touch. "Now, take me now!"

"No, you are not ready."

"I've been ready for twenty-nine years." Her heart beat wildly in her chest and her breathing grew rapid as her senses were overwhelmed with the touch of her mate.

Her juices flowed freely as his hands dipped lower, pressing the sensitive skin of her rosebud before encountering the weeping well of her vagina. She shuddered as one broad finger invaded.

"If I took you now, there would be pain," Terror explained, his fingers circling her lower lips gently, pushing in slightly, feeling the drawing heat and moisture that told so much of her desire for him. "And I will never cause you pain, Nello."

That said, he urged her back among the pillows, mounding them up behind her to hold her in a sitting position.

"Watch me," he purred. "Watch me love you." And his lips attached themselves to her right nipple.

"Ah!" Nello gasped, arching up as his teeth took a nip of her swelling flesh, awakening it, making it sensitive, before his tongue laved away the minor hurt.

"Watch me," he urged again, lowering his body between her legs, grinding his hard cock against her thigh.

His lips left one nipple and traveled to the next, his fingers plucking the shiny one his mouth left free.

A keening wail filled the room as Nello struggled to keep her eyes on her mate, struggled to watch as he aroused her body, made her hotter than she had ever been.

He drew in her nipple, suckling it, lashing it with his tongue, filling his mouth with the flavor of her.

Almost unconsciously, his free hand dropped to his crotch, adjusting his long, thick, aching cock, then fisting it lightly to heighten his pleasure. The head rapidly moistened as liquid drops of his essence bubbled to the surface.

"Creator, Terror! More!"

His mouth left her nipple with a wet *pop* before he lapped the sweat that sheened the skin of her stomach. He trembled as he felt the heat and energy from the center of her core churn and roil with his caresses.

"It was always beautiful with you, Nello," he rumbled as he dipped his tongue into the indention of her navel once again.

Her hands tangled in his hair, pushing him down as she began a litany of pleas. "Please, Terror," she panted. "Please. Put your mouth on me. Lick me. Please…"

Unable to ignore her voiced commands, Terror slid his hands between her thighs, pushing them further apart with his sword-callused hands, making a wider space for himself in his paradise.

"When you ask so sweetly," he purred before he dropped a kiss at the top of her slit, his tongue peeking out to caress the hood of her clit.

Nello felt that burning caress as a lightning bolt, almost delivering a powerful shock to where she needed it the most. "Please!" she gasped, then screamed as his tongue traced the lips that protected the seat of her pleasure.

Terror growled as the taste, the smell, the sight of the swollen pink folds surrounded him. His senses were on high alert as he saw how delicate she was to him, how fragile. Then his hunger took over as he peered at the liquid readiness that poured from her, fragrant and thick.

With his thumbs, he spread her lips apart and feasted his eyes on her glistening treasure. "Mine!" he growled, and then dropped his mouth where she most needed.

Nello arched off the bed, a wailing cry erupting again from her throat as his heat touched her, the furnace heat of his mouth. She shuddered as those soft, full lips took her clit between their hungry folds and began to suck.

"Unnn," she hissed as one hand left off holding her thighs apart and two fingers slid into her wet opening.

"Terror," she managed as they slid deep, scissoring to stretch her inner walls to accept an appendage that was significantly bigger.

Terror moaned, the vibrations going straight to her clit, as he felt the heat of her enfold him and tried to suck him in deeper. The thought of those sugared walls gripping his cock made him shudder and flooded his mind with erotic imagery.

He wanted her. She was his. He would claim his mate and take what was his by right but had been denied him by circumstances and human sacrifice.

With one final lick to her swollen and reddened clit, he pulled his mouth back, licking her juices from his lips as he added a third finger. He watched as she jumped and bucked on the bed, dislodging the pillows from behind her as her passion took control of her body.

He slowly began finger-fucking her, watching as her temperature rose and the red flush of desire covered her body.

He watched, maintaining his control while he slowly stripped hers from her. "Are you ready for me?" he asked, his voice little more than a growl.

"Yes," she panted, still lost in the feelings but knowing something greater was going to befall her.

"Then take me!" Terror pulled his fingers out of the sucking heat and replaced the thickness of his fingers with the purple head of his dripping cock. He held himself motionless there, just for a moment, until purple eyes maddened with desire looked into his. "Mine, forever," he whispered, then he began to push his thickness into her body.

Heat! It exploded over his senses, clouding his mind with pleasure. He felt a tingling at the base of his spine and had to drop down over her to try to find his balance in the overwhelming storm of emotions.

Nello gasped as his large cock filled, and filled, and filled her to the breaking point. Oh, Creator, how could she have forgotten it, forgotten the feel of his thickness parting her, making a home for himself within her?

"Terrrorr," she moaned as his legs slid up along her thighs.

Her eyes closed as sensation swamped her, her hands reaching up to grip his forearms. Terror became her only port in this wild storm of erotic sensation.

Terror felt his muscles lock as he reveled in the feeling of her tight wet heat. He fought the urge to give in to his needs, to slam and pound into her until his soul found the release it had sought for so long. Instead, he eased out about an inch, testing her readiness, before easing that length back inside.

"Terror, take me," Nello managed. Now that the first wave of pleasure had flown through her body, she wanted more, she needed more; she had to have him moving deeply inside her pussy.

Pulling out slightly, Terror eased more of himself inside, feeling her body adjust around him, softening to welcome him deep inside. Then he was moving, pulling out and pushing back in, the symphony of her cries music to his Nello-starved ears.

Slowly, he created a rhythm for their bodies, and then increased it, playing on both of their reactions, making the screams and gasps increase in frequency and volume.

Then his tension became too much.

He looked down at Nello, her legs now wrapped around his waist, her heels digging into the flesh of his ass, urging him to move faster, harder, stronger. He gave in to her desires.

Pulling out so just his head remained inside, he slammed forward, filling her with his power and energy, creating a magical flow that traveled from him to her.

"Ahhh!" Nello screamed, arching up into his thrusts, demanding more.

The pounding rhythm he set could not last, and before long, he felt a stinging in his balls that told of his impending release.

Not wanting to leave his lover behind, he slid his hand between their heaving bodies, his thumb finding and pressing onto her clit.

"Terr… Creator!" Nello screamed as this extra stimulation dragged her over the precipice.

"Nello, Nello!" Terror bellowed as his balls churned, then slammed against the base of his cock, sending their milky fluid exploding through his cock. "Ahhh!"

Seeing his trembling form, feeling his release course through his cock, he suddenly became harder, feeling that extra thickness rub her sweet spot in just the right way. Nello arched up and a gasp escaped her tight throat as spasm after spasm shook her body.

Her inner walls rhythmically clenched around his cock, her nails dug into his skin as an almost painful pleasure swamped her senses.

"Nello," Terror gasped again as he settled carefully on top of the trembling body of his mate.

As he watched her enter into the sexual afterglow, tears filled his eyes, and his vision of her became hazy, ethereal.

"I love you," he whispered as he eased his still swollen cock from her grasping heat and turned her to her side, pulling her protectively against his chest. "You are my life."

Nello nestled back against her mate, wrapping his arms tighter around her. Silently she echoed his sentiment. She was safe; she was in his arms. She was home.

* * *

Later that night, back in their rooms, after the confusion had settled somewhat and she was allowed to be alone with her husband for a time, she asked him, "What were you right about?"

"Hmm?" he asked as he raised his weary head to glance at his mate. He had never before felt so tired, so old.

"Torn," her voice cracked as she said his name. "Torn said that you were right." Terror looked down at his mate, the woman he loved more than life, and smiled.

"I told him that settling was not enough to hold a man, and that only true love will fill the void inside of him," he said, praying that wherever his son was, he would find a woman to give him the love that he had been denied his entire life.

"Terror," Nello said and hugged him tightly. "You were right."

* * *

"*Life in the fast lane*!" Sable sang at the top of her voice as she bent low into a turn. The green and brown scenery of the passing road blurred as the wind whipped past her visor, distorting everything but the road ahead.

It was a warm summer day in Scotland, which meant that it was around seventy degrees. A watery sun broke through the gray clouds in the sky. Life was good! The birds were singing, the road was open, men were falling from the sky...

Falling from the sky?

Sable slammed on her brakes, tightening her grip as her monster bike slid to the side with a loud growl of the engine and the grating of the tires as they left a black trail on the paved road. As soon as the bike screeched to a halt, she dropped her stand and was running toward the fallen body.

"Oh my God!" she nearly screamed. "They're throwing bodies around like litter!" Then she took a second to think about who *they* could be before she sprang into action.

She raced to the body. She could see by the build that it was one hell of a big woman, or a nearly naked man who had just been tossed... from somewhere!

Paying no attention to the jeans that were getting covered in muddy grass stains -- her best jeans, it just so happened, she fell to her knees beside the man -- she decided after a closer look -- and tried to revive him.

"Hey, mister!" She patted his cheeks, trying to wake him up. "Mister? Are you alive?"

It was a stupid question, but her brain was not exactly functioning at its peak. For one thing, she had never seen a body pop out of thin air. For another, she didn't know if she was touching a corpse.

"*Ewwww!*" she gasped as that thought crossed her mind. She fell back, scrambled to her feet, and then stepped back a few more paces for good measure.

"Okay, Sable," she whispered to herself, giving herself a little pep talk. "He might be alive, girl. You have to go and see."

"Mister," she called again, stepping to him again and bending over, her steel gray and black leather biker jacket parting to reveal the thin T-shirt she wore underneath. "*Miiiissssterrrr.*"

She took another cautious step closer. "Mister?"

"Nello!" he gasped suddenly as his eyes snapped open.

"*Eeekkk!*" Sable shouted as she jumped back, involuntarily on her part, but his sudden move *had* frightened her... a little.

"Nello?" he gasped again, then groaned as he tried to raise a shaking hand to his forehead. Never had he felt such an ache. His head was pounding, he felt cold to freezing, and there was a tiny woman screaming at him.

Where was he? Had he died after all and this was the next dimension? He turned his head toward the woman, and blinked at her startled expression.

"Your eyes," Sable cried, her eyes going wide. "You have lavender eyes!"

She had never seen a human being with that color of eyes before in her life! They had to be contacts.

But then that mass of tangled silk he had for hair drew her attention, too. It nearly covered him like a blanket. Who was he? He had to be a foreigner; well, more of a foreigner than she was.

"Mister," she began again, suddenly wondering if she'd made a mistake in stopping to help him. "Maybe I should go and get some help."

"*Nier. Neoow*?" he asked, as he struggled to rise.

"No!" Sable called out quickly as she saw the color leach from his face. "Don't move! You might have broken something." With her hands, she gestured that he should lay still.

He looked at her oddly for a moment, then with a small groan dropped his head back to the grass. Wherever he was, the people here were smaller than the tiniest person from the Magic Realm.

The small woman had short red hair and wide brown eyes. He assumed that it was a female because of the two small breasts pushing out against the front of her funny tunic. That and her very feminine sounding voice.

But no matter how hard he tried, he could not understand a word she said.

"Oh, gosh, you *are* hurt!" Sable sighed as she watched him weakly drop his head back to the grass, uncaring that he was covered in leaves and dirt.

Leaves! He must have been up in the trees! That explained his falling.

"What were you doing in the trees?" she asked as she took another cautious step closer to the wounded man. She had to do something to help him.

She noted that he was wearing some type of leather strips that may have once been pants, and that his boots were torn and frayed. But it was those boots that caught her attention.

"Are you a biker?" she asked, wondering if she had found a wounded but kindred soul.

There had been a big festival near Glasgow this past weekend, and there had been tales of rowdies. Attracted by the lure of fancy, custom-made bikes and the riches those bike owners were sure to possess, the local rowdies were beating up lone travelers and stealing their bikes for parts.

"Is that what happened to you?" she asked, concern and regret filling her heart. "Were you coshed over the head and left in that… tree?" Well, she had heard of worse ways to stash a body.

And big as he was, someone would have had to brain him with a steel beam to get him out of commission long enough for anyone to steal his motorcycle. His chest, she noted as his dark hair parted, was extremely wide, extremely dark, and extremely bare. Did they take his clothes too?

"*Inipo opt Nello,*" he said as he again turned to her, Where is Nello? Couldn't she speak normally? The only thing coming from her mouth was childish gibberish!

"*Inipo opt Nello?*" he asked again, as he cocked his head to the side and examined her.

At his gesture, Sable exploded in laughter. "You definitely aren't from around here, and I have never heard Gaelic spoken like that. You must be from the festival. Stay here, and I'll go get some help."

"*Inipo apee yo kota?*" he asked. Where are you going?

"Stay here." She motioned with her hands, lifting hands up, palms spread and gesturing to the ground. "Stay here."

His cocked head reminded her of a curious child. She smiled and nodded her head reassuringly. "Stay here. Here!" She repeated the gesture slowly and his eyes lit up in understanding.

"Stay here," he repeated, slurring the words a bit.

Maybe he was Italian? But no, that dark skin said he had some African in him. Maybe he was both.

"Right!" She smiled at him, making the gesture again. "Here!"

Torn examined the woman, his senses reached out to envelop her, to examine her inner self. He found no hatred there, no taint of evil, no darkness, only a desire to help.

"Stay here," he repeated as he tried to roll over onto his knees to rise to his feet. Stay Here was not comfortable and was quite damp. His body began to shake with chills. Where had Nello sent him?

Ah, he suddenly remembered. Nello, in trying to save his life, had altered her father's magic on the collar. Instead of taking him far away in death, it just took him far away.

But how far away was far away? Did he have to remain on Stay Here? Would he ever see his beloved home again?

He tried to rise, but groaned softly with the movement. Changing into the Reaver always drained him and often left him as weak as a newborn babe. But never had he felt this painful body ache before.

"No!" the female was crying out now. "Stay here!"

"Stay Here, Stay Here!" he grumbled as he felt the cold penetrate the remaining leather from his tattered garments. *There goes his ceremonial suit*, he thought in disgust. Now he would have to hunt more range beasts to make more. "Stay Here," he gestured to the ground.

"You don't understand," she muttered, finally understanding what was happening.

"How can I make you understand?" Sable spoke in her frustration, looking up into the sky for answers.

But the big guy had struggled to his feet, and Sable took another step back, not out of fear, but out of awe. That man had looked big while lying prone on the ground, but standing, he looked gigantic! He had to be seven mother-loving feet tall!

"You are one tall drink of water!" she said with awe as she watched him raise his hands to his head and try to pull some of those curls off of his face.

"Tall drink of water?" he said, rolling the R's around his tongue.

"No! I mean… never mind." She sighed, rubbing her forehead with her fist.

"Never Mind?" he added wrinkling his brow. Her words made no sense! How was he to exist here if he couldn't understand the natives?

"No, no!" She shook her head.

"No," he said repeating the gesture.

Well, shaking your head no was kind of a universal expression. "Sable," she finally decided, pointing to her chest. "My name is Sable."

"Sable," he repeated, trilling the "L" in her name.

"Yes, Sable!" she said excitedly. "My name is Sable."

"Sable," he repeated. Must mean female, he decided. And she must have figured out that he was male, from the pointed looks at his groin that she was trying to disguise.

"Yes, Sable. And you?" she pointed to his chest, trying to stop her eyes from dancing below his stomach. The man appeared to be hung like the proverbial horse! How could she *not* take a peek or two?

He looked down, and then it dawned on him what she was trying to do! Sable didn't mean female! It was her name.

"Your name?" she said again, pointing to his chest.

Standing to his full inadequate height, he replied, "Torn sa Terror za Nello."

"Pardon me?" she said, her forehead crinkling in confusion. "Run that by me again?"

She pointed at his chest and tapped her ear.

He considered for a moment, them repeated his name. Maybe she had problems with her ears.

"Torn sa Terror za Nello," he repeated again.

"What?" she asked, looking more confused than ever. He must be from one of those eastern or northern desert tribes in Africa. "Again," she said, pointing to his chest then to her ears.

"Torn?" he offered, hoping that she wasn't simple. He needed someone to tell him where he was, and it looked like she was it. And it just wouldn't do to be led around by the insane. It would get him in more trouble than he currently found himself.

"Torn!" she said, smiling at him.

"Sable," he replied pointing to her.

"He understands!" She wanted to scream and laugh, but settled on a loud whoop.

Instantly, he dropped into a fighter's stance and began looking around the area. With one strong arm, he pulled the obviously afraid and screaming woman behind him, stepping defensively in front of her. Was there some wild animal about to attack, some fierce tribe of thieves?

He looked through the scattered trees and short grasses, searching for a clue. His hand went instantly to his waist belt, reaching for his sword, but it was not there.

Hand-to-hand then, he decided as he closed his eyes to concentrate on pulling in all of his power. But then he heard her laughter.

Sable was nearly doubled over, shivering in amusement as she watched Torn drop into a fighter's stance. What had he thought, that they were going to be attacked by something? Did her whoop of joy scare him that badly?

"*Nizo Ferntia*?" No enemies? he asked in his lyrical language as he realized that the woman was in no danger. He relaxed his stance, raising again to his full height, and pulling the hair from around his face, tucking the long strands behind his ears.

"I have no idea what you just said, but... oh my God!"

Again, Torn turned to look behind him, wondering what she had seen now? Her face had blanched pale and her eyes grew wide. Fear, shock... what was troubling her?

"Your ears!" she all but shrieked, pointing to the side of his head.

Torn noted her gesture, and felt a part of him began to deflate. He had realized that he was actually beginning to enjoy this female, but now she was obviously shocked and repulsed by his mixed heritage. So much for starting over. It seemed that he would be subjected to the same prejudices and fears that he faced at his home.

Sable suddenly regretted her hasty outburst as she watched the light dim in his eyes. But hell! The man had pointed ears! She was talking elongated Mr. Spock ears.

"Torn," she said as she reached out for his hands

as she watched him visibly withdraw from her. Had she hurt his feelings? Was he ashamed or embarrassed by his ears? "Torn."

Her gentle touch on his arm shocked him. No one had ever touched him! Not his father, not his mother. His joining partner had obviously touched him to seal his doom, but this woman showed no fear of him. She reached out and touched him. *She* touched him! Never had any contact felt so… warm.

"Sable?" he began again, noting how unbelievably small she was. A man, even one of small stature like himself, could easily hurt her. But it was luminous brown eyes that spoke to him most. They were filled with compassion and self-pain. She had not meant to hurt him, he realized.

With this revelation came joy. And uncontrollably, his lips spread into a full smile of happiness.

"Oh my God, you have fangs!"

Sable stared at his mouth, noting the two sharp incisors too long to be considered teeth.

He had real fangs! Real mother-loving fangs! Purple eyes, fangs… Her mind struggled to understand. Falling out of thin air and landing on the ground, bigger than life. Her mind reached and attached to the only thing that she understood. That tangle of hair and muscle that stood before her could be only one thing.

"Faeroe!" she fairly shouted. "You are of the fey folk!" You're *real*!" Sable squealed as she backed away from him slowly, her hand covering her mouth in amazement. "You're real! You exist!"

"Sable?" he asked confused, watching as she backed away from him. Funny, but he got no sense of fear from her, only amazement and a bit of awe. It was a look that he was not used to and frankly made him a bit uncomfortable.

One moment he thought that he was making headway with the pretty, small creature, then she did something so completely unexpected that she made his head hurt. It was confusing to say the least.

Giving in to the desire to gather his thoughts, he sat on the cool damp green grass that seemed to be everywhere.

"Oh no! What did I do?" she suddenly cried as she saw the big, powerful, fey man sink to his bottom. Did she have to believe in him to make him stay? Did her disbelief harm him, like in the Disney Movie?

"I believe in you," she chanted as she closed her eyes and lifted her head to her heavens. "I believe in you! Please don't be ill! If I made you ill… I'll never forgive myself! I believe, I believe!"

"Sable?" he asked, puzzled as he watched her perform some strange sort of ritual. Was she from the Realm of Magic after all?

"Stay here?" He asked, glancing up at her with hazy, pain-filled eyes as he rubbed his temples in an attempt to alleviate the pounding.

Her eyes snapped open and, again, she took in his stance, the pain in his eyes, and she felt her heart break.

"Oh, I hurt you!" she cried out as she reached down and took his hands. "Torn? Are you in pain?"

The only thing he understood out of that whole episode was his name, and that was not promising at all. He wished he could communicate with her to find out where he was, where his mother had sent him.

Then he noticed the weight around his neck. That damned collar.

With tentative fingers, he reached up and felt for

the metal restriction, cursing silently as he still felt his mother's magic running through it.

"*Ouzi ghima lantif eiza whien ba zot*!" he hissed in a rare fit of temper, but he was losing patience with this whole situation. You could have at least given me a translator!

"What?" Sable asked, reading only despair in his voice. She had hurt him, and it was up to her to make it right. *How did one make it right with the fey*? she asked herself as she observed the giant seated in front of her.

"Torn," she called as she came to a swift decision. "Torn! Can you stand? Stand?" She pantomimed rising to her feet by bending at her knees and moving to her full height. "Stand."

"Stand," he repeated, forgetting the band around his neck as he watched her movements. "Stand." That was simple enough. Maybe she was trying to get him to move somewhere.

He slowly rose to his feet, watching her for her next command. "Come," she said, motioning forward with her hands.

"Come," he repeated, mimicking her motions.

"No," she shook her head, using that universal gesture. "Come with Sable." She backed away, making the same movements.

"Come with Sable," he repeated, taking a step, following her.

This speaking game was growing wearisome, but if she took him away from this cold, wet grass, he would happily follow. Besides, she seemed to be over her shock at his Magic Realm blood.

It took some people months to get used to his appearance. Too bad he was so short and unattractive. She was a rather pretty creature, and he could only hope to garner her interest.

But then he censored his thought.

Hadn't a red-haired woman caused all of his grief, even though this one hated her hair so much she cropped it from her head? He was through with women. He would spend the rest of his time alone if he had to deal with another one. At least there was no chance of him falling in love with this tiny creature, but maybe they could cultivate a friendship. She was, after all, short like him, and therefore an object to be ridiculed.

"Yes!" Sable crowed, as the giant Torn took a step forward, then another. He was following her! Now was her chance to get him onto the back of her bike and... Oh, *hell* no! That wouldn't work at all! She needed a car, a truck, a tank to get him over the narrow, paved roads to her house, because his big butt would not fit on the back of her bike.

"Well, I wanted to take in the nice weather," she sighed as she looked longingly at her bike. The sky began to darken as soon as her eyes made contact with its wide-open expanse.

"Oh great!" she grumbled. "Just what I needed, a little more summer rain!" She shook her head as she tried to analyze the situation.

As the clouds covered the sun, Torn's head snapped up and he began to search the sky for signs of danger. Were there dragons about? Was some mystic casting a malevolent spell that blocked out the sun? Was that why it was so cold in this place? Was Sable in danger?

"Sable?" he asked as he scanned the grassy hills that surrounded them. Before she could answer, the clouds burst, drenching them with cool droplets of rain.

"*Zornery!*" he cried as his head swung around,

seeking the mystic who would lay such a dastardly trap! Sorcery! Who had ever heard of water falling from the sky? It was inhuman and messy. Did the wizard think to drown them all, one drop at a time?

"Torn?" Sable asked. He, again, looked ready for action, but this time not because of anything that she did. What had set him off? "Rain?" she asked as she noticed his disparaging looks in the sky.

Well, of course rain! He lived under the hills, under the earth. He wouldn't know rain.

"Torn," she called, then a bit louder to get his attention. "Torn!"

His purple eyes snapped to her face, the long locks now wet and plastering themselves to his face.

God, he was beautiful! The rain only accented the perfect shape of his head. His tongue flicked out to ease the wetness on his full, succulent lips, before his eyes settled on hers.

"It's only rain," she explained, suddenly affected by his face and body. Wet leather did cling like a second skin.

"It's only rain," he repeated, again looking around for the enemy.

Well, if Sable didn't seem concerned, it must not be a mortal enemy, just a bothersome one to cause the sky to spit at them. *It's only rain.* Now that he had a name, where was the villain? He closed his eyes and sent his soul seeking, searching for the source of the malevolent and annoying magic.

"Torn," Sable called again as she saw him close his eyes in intense concentration. Wasn't he doing some kind of Faeroe glamour thing? "Torn!"

This time she walked over and touched his arm.

His whole body shuddered and his eyes snapped open as he felt her touch against the skin of his arm.

Heat! Human contact was so warm! He had forgotten that. Even this cool water from the sky couldn't sap the fire of her touch. His gaze dropped to her small hand against the wide expanse of his forearm, before following it back to her shoulder and finally her eyes.

"Rain," she said pointing to the sky. "It is raining, Torn." She made a fluttery gesture with her fingers as she raised and lowered her arm. "Rain."

"Rain," he repeated. This stuff falling from the sky was rain. She wasn't concerned, and he felt no magic, so he relaxed his stance. But he still didn't like it!

"Stay here," he began, then shook his head. "*Neyt*, Sable. *Neyt* stay here!" That was simple enough.

"You don't like the rain? Well, buddy, did *you* pick the wrong place to appear!"

She shook her head, flinging water around as she made another decision and gripped his arm.

"I'm not waiting around to catch my death, Torn. You're about to get your first lesson in bike riding with an obvious head injury. The trick is to follow my moves completely, especially on turns, no matter how many Sables you see!"

Sable pulled the unresisting Torn behind her as she walked over to her bike. Then she pointed.

"Harley!" she said as she turned her eyes to his face. "Mine! While you stay here, if you want one of your own, go and conjure one for yourself!"

"Harley!" he repeated, blinking rapidly in the rain as he pointed to the strange horse thing she'd gestured to. Well, it kind of looked like a horse, but it was metallic. And it had wheels.

"Right!" She said decisively as she reached down and pulled her bike upright from its parked lean. It was no easy task, for the bike outweighed her easily.

"Harley!" she puffed. "My Harley! My baby! The only thing in this world I love more than sculpting. My Harley!"

"My Harley!" Torn repeated, still looking a bit confused.

So the thing was a My Harley. So what was a My Harley and what did it do?

He watched, amazed, as she picked up a small helm and popped it onto her head. "Safety first!" she said.

"Safety first," he repeated, pointing to the helmet. What a stupid name for headgear.

Then he watched as she threw her leg over My Harley to straddle it. So it was some type of mechanical horse! This was fascinating. What would it do now?

Smiling at how easy this was, Sable placed her foot on the clutch and jumped. The beautiful growl of her bike stirred the air and shook the earth. This was the sound of perfection, baby! This was why she'd been born. There was nothing better than riding on a Harley, except for maybe completing a sculpture, or really good sex -- really, really good sex.

"Torn?" she called, but he was staring, fascinated by the beast. "My Harley?" he repeated his mind pulling together facts.

One, she was riding that thing with no fear. It wasn't dangerous for her. Two, it hadn't attacked him. Therefore, she could control it; it was just a metal machine. Three, it had wheels. Did that mean it was made to drive upon the land, like some great wagon?

"My Harley, Torn. Sable's Harley."

"Sable's Harley," he repeated, getting the idea rather quickly. His mother's people, he had heard, had been experimenting with mechanical means of transportation for years, but they usually used conveyances of wood. This was fascinating and intriguing.

And it was Sable's. Would she let him experiment with it? Machines always fascinated him.

"Right." Sable nodded. This was easy. "Now climb on!"

"Climb... on?" he repeated, cocking his head to the side, his eyes glued to her face.

"On!" she called over the roar of the idling engine. "Torn, on!" She patted the space behind her.

"On?" Torn sounded a bit skeptical, but it was a big bike! A Harley Road Master, easily big enough to carry his weight.

"On!" she repeated, patting the seat enticingly. "Go away from the rain."

He looked up into the sky, flinging sodden hair behind his shoulders, before looking down at her again. What did she want now?

"Torn!" she wailed. "Come on! It's cold out here! Get on the bike!"

She was getting rather disturbed, he decided as he watched her bounce on the seat of Sable's My Harley. Then it hit him. Extra seat, small extra seat. She wanted him behind her and he wanted that too -- if he could fit, that is.

Tentatively, he raised one booted foot over the rear of the bike. "Yes!" Sable cried, nodding excitedly. "Yes, Torn!"

Straddling the bike, he gingerly began to sit, but he jumped right back up just as quickly.

"For the love of God, what's wrong now?" she wailed. She wanted to go home, have a cup of coffee, and dry off! What was wrong with him?

"It vibrates," Torn growled in his language, not expecting her to understand. "It quivers against my manparts and I do not like that feeling! It… itches!"

"Torn," Sable said as she let the incomprehensible stream of words roll past her. "Sable," he returned, a defiant look on his face.

"Get on the damn bike!" she roared, causing his mouth to drop open in surprise.

Her face, what he could see of it over the Safety First, was turning a mottled shade of red. This was amazing. He leaned in closer for a better look, shifting his weight and bending at the knees a bit.

"Thank you!" Sable crowed as she kicked the clutch and shot the bike forward.

A loud exhalation escaped from Torn's throat as the bike moved forward, hitting his bottom and slamming him most uncomfortably on the vibrating seat. His arms automatically went around her shoulders, stabilizing his body, and he lifted his feet out to the sides, not knowing where to put them.

His eyes widened in fright, then calmed a bit as he felt the rhythm of the bike flow through him. It was kind of like riding a horse. He could feel the bumps in the darkly paved road and the grumble of the My Harley as it picked up speed.

Sable was a firm and controlled rider as she slowly began to speed up the bike. He observed her actions and began to follow suit, though keeping his legs out at his sides.

This was kind of fun, actually.

"Ten freaking miles per hour!" Sable grumbled as the bike crawled forward. She was miles away from home in the rain and moving at ten miles per hour! There had to be a better way to go than this. He hadn't even put his legs in their proper place yet. This was maddening.

"Faster!" Torn called as she wondered why she

was moving so slowly. But then he realized that his legs began to tire. He couldn't let them drag the ground, but where to put them? Behind hers was the natural decision.

Sable squeaked, and the bike wobbled a bit as she felt his body shift and his legs slide in behind hers. He shifted his arms so that they rested around her waist, pulling her tightly to him, close to the heated V of his thighs.

Mercy, he felt so damn good!

"Sable?" he asked, noting her momentary loss of control, and wondering at it.

Sable shuddered at the low, intimate tone in his voice, feeling enveloped by his big body.

"Home," she managed to get out shakily. "Time to go home. Hold on."

She gunned the engine, pouring on the power and making the bike fly as she rounded the next corner. The sooner she got this Faeroe home, the sooner she could find out why he was here and why she was the one to find him. Then hopefully she could send him back where he belonged! He was too… unsettling for her nerves.

"This is almost as good as flying!" Torn cried, ignoring the wet slap of rain as it splashed against his cheeks and the gobs of mud that flew up to coat his cold body. If this was one of the delights of Sable's world, he would enjoy staying here for a time. And Sable herself… He quashed that thought. She was just a guide. Even if her body did feel soft and smelled like spring flowers. He was through with women. Especially women with red hair.

Chapter Three

"Three hours!" Sable snarled as she rode her bike into the garage she'd had built just for her most prized possession. "Three damn hours to go fifteen miles in the rain!"

"My Harley, Sable!" Torn replied, a clear droplet of water suspended on his nose.

"Yeah, yeah! I know! My Harley!"

She swallowed a sneeze and stifled a groan as she tried to unbend her frozen fingers from around the handlebars. With a groan, she pulled off the helmet and ran her fingers through her hair. The leather may have kept her upper body dry, but it did nothing for lower protection. Her jeans were a big, heavy, soppy, wet mess!

"All right, Torn. Off!"

"Off?" He smiled at her, those sharp little fangs showing.

"Off my Harley!"

"My Harley!" he said as he patted the tank of the machine, wincing as the remaining heat sizzled his wet fingers. "Ouch."

"Off!" she cried as she slowly pulled her body from the sodden bike.

"Off!" Torn replied in the tone of someone who had just had a major epiphany. Then he followed Sable's example and hauled his bottom from the bike. He took one step away, then shook himself like a wet dog, flinging water around the room.

"Hey!" Sable called out and raised her hands to protect her face from the sudden onslaught of water. "I had enough rain, thank you very much."

She narrowed her eyes and glared at him, but he looked so adorable standing there, long strands of hair hanging into his wet face, that teasing grin of accomplishment on his face that she instantly forgave him. "More fool, I." She snorted as she made her way to the garage entrance to her house.

"Fool?" Torn asked as he watched Sable walk away.

He had heard a lot of strange new words on the journey here, but he couldn't fathom their meaning. For instance, what was a son of a bitch? With a shrug, he turned to follow her.

"Stop right there!" she called, holding up her hand, palm outward. Amazed, he paused. You would have to be an idiot not to know what she meant.

"You will not drip rain all over my rugs! Wait until I bring you a towel!"

Rain, he understood. He was soaked with the stuff. Now, to figure out the context of the rest of her words.

Okay, rain was falling from his clothing -- well, what was left of his clothing. She had floor coverings that looked thirsty enough to absorb every drop and remain ready for more. But she was a woman, thus he had to think illogically. Would rain cause those bright colors on her floor coverings to run? Probably. Solution, remove all clothing.

Sable walked back into her kitchen entrance to see Torn, her fairy, rising up to his full height, his tattered pants in his hands, his worn boots lying next to him.

"You're naked!" she whispered in awe as tempting golden bits of him kept showing through his long length of hair.

"Naked?" he asked, looking for the context of her words again.

"Naked, naked, naked!" she nearly screamed,

pointing to his thick swinging... oh my God, no shrinkage there!

"Naked?" he asked, looking down at his flaccid manhood. This was naked? To be sure, he grasped himself in his hand and presented his cock to her. "Naked?"

"Oh Lord!" Sable groaned, her face heating with embarrassed delight. Chagrined interest? Curiosity? Her hand flew to cover her face, but she couldn't resist parting her fingers and peeking. Boy, he was built fine, uncut, and thick, even flaccid.

Stop it, you whore, she admonished herself as she tried to pull her tattered composure together. No lusting after the fairy, and be careful of what you say.

"Cover yourself!" she squeaked as she took a tentative step, arms thrust forward, and offered him a towel. Actually, a pink and yellow beach towel, the only thing she could find that was big enough to cover him. "Here."

"Here," he replied, taking the towel and rubbing its texture into his free hand. Then his hand lifted as he examined the nubby texture of it, not bothering to cover his naked body. It felt soft and rough at the same time, the perfect thing to dry off, he decided as he looked toward Sable. "Here."

"No, towel." Sable sighed, then pulled it from his hand.

His eyes widened in surprise as she began to briskly dry his hair, paying no attention to her own wet clothing.

She was touching him! Willingly touching him and wasn't laughing or making any comments about his mixed heritage! This was amazing! Didn't she find him a dangerous and repugnant mixture?

"Now we have to cover you," she said as she

wrapped the damp towel around his waist, hiding all of those tempting parts so that her mind would stop wondering what he would feel like between her legs. Mercy! Her face went several shades of red as she tried not to notice what she was covering up.

"*Neyt* naked?" he asked as he looked down to where she had hidden his manparts behind the brightly colored toweling. He kind of figured that he had made some faux pas by the interesting colors her face had turned and that she had hidden her eyes. That she was willing to overlook his social awkwardness meant a lot to him. He might have just found a friend after all.

"Naked is naked!" She sighed, then gave up in defeat. Knowledge would come. Now she needed a Faeroe-English/English-Faeroe dictionary, and all would be well.

Grasping his hand, she guided him from the kitchen into the large living room, which was comfortably carpeted in a plush green rug.

"Now, Torn," she began as she led him to her rundown but comfortable couch. "You sit here while I figure out who to call for help."

Then it dawned on her. Of course! Picking up the phone, she quickly punched in the numbers to her best friends in the world. Jack and Jill.

"Help!" she screeched at the first person who'd picked up the phone.

"Sable?" Jack's gruff voice poured over the phone, soothing her with its masterful yet calm tones. "Is that you? Is everything okay?"

"Jack, you have to help me!" she cried, sending a trembling smile in Torn's direction, noting his perplexed look as she spoke over the phone.

"What's wrong, love?" he asked, his American

accent sounding a bit worried as he questioned her. Sable never called for help unless it was something big.

"I have a naked man in my living room! I need clothes for him, and you two are the only ones that might come close."

"Naked man?" he asked.

"Naked?" Torn questioned, gesturing to his crotch. "*NO!*" she yelped.

"There is no naked man?" Jack asked, sounding more confused by the second.

"Naked man?" another masculine voice, but this with a deep Scottish brogue, piped in. "Where? And I wasn't invited."

"Yes, there is a naked man." She frowned and gestured at Torn to move his hand away from where he was about to unleash his, uh, magnificence for her again. "And I need you to bring some clothes for him, please. You are *not* going to believe this."

"Sable, love, why is there a naked man in your house?" Jack asked.

"Sable has a naked man?" the voice in the back cried out in delight. "This is too delicious. What's he doing? Was he any good?"

"I sort of found him," she hedged. "And I'll answer your questions, but please, I need clothes for him. He can't walk around here naked. It's too much!"

"What's too much, love?" Jack asked, suddenly all big dangerous man. "Are you in any trouble?"

"Too much?" The second voice laughed.

"Darling, don't you know that it can never be enough? Even if it hits a foot, there are still nine useable inches and the rest is a handhold!"

"No, nothing like that, Jack, and tell Jill I hear him in the background." She sighed again. "I just need a little help and I'll explain as soon as you get here.

And you are the only man I know who is about his size."

"A big bruiser, then," he said. "I'll be right over, love. And I expect a decent explanation for this one."

"Thanks, Jack," she breathed, feeling in control again, at least for the moment. "I really owe you one."

"You owe me nothing, love. Just keep pushing out those sculptures and I'll forgive you just about anything."

She laughed as she hung up the phone on Jill's ridiculous questions and accusations. Jill could always make her laugh, no matter what.

"Now, for you, Torn." she said as she turned to face her very own Faeroe.

He looked up at the sound of his name. He had been contemplating the magic this Sable possessed. A magic that he could not fathom. He felt no traces of it in the air, and yet she had been talking into a rounded rock thing and again when the voice answered.

He probed as best as he could, but could detect no evil intent. Was she truly from a magic realm, a different realm than his own, but still magical? Would his powers even work here?

"I think we need to get some basics down, Torn. So that you won't make the same mistakes you made with me. Jack and Jill are okay guys, but very protective. So let's say we begin with… body parts. Yes. That should be easy enough."

Torn nodded as if he understood every word she said, but in truth he only recognized his name. Constantly being at a disadvantage was beginning to bother him. Maybe he had a spell that could fix this language problem, but he doubted it would work, and he wouldn't risk it until he knew what type of magic she possessed.

But she was pointing to something now, something on her face. Her nose. "*Kopa*," he responded, giving her the word.

"Nose," she returned, looking at him hopefully.

So it was to be another language lesson. Okay, this he could deal with. "Nose," he responded, his answer rewarded with a brilliant smile.

"He understands!" she crowed, then pointed to her lips, saying the word slowly. "Lips," he repeated, flicking his tongue over his fangs a bit. "Lips."

"Very good," she said breathlessly as she looked into his intent purple eyes. Purple was her favorite color. Why did her Faeroe have to have purple eyes? "Eyes," she said, pointing to hers.

"Eyes," he repeated, for the first time noticing how her eyes seemed to glow with an inner beauty. *What beautiful orbs*, he thought. "Eyes."

"Ears," she said, noticing again the point to his. They were rather attractive, she thought. And they fit his purple eyes perfectly.

"Ears," he repeated, fighting against a blush.

Her ears had no telltale points, but she had to possess some magic. His ears were a dead giveaway and he used to hate everything about them because they declared to the world that he was a mixed breed. But she seemed rather fascinated by them and in no way repulsed.

"Hair," she said, tugging at a short lock of her own.

"Hair," he quickly returned, easily committing the word to memory.

"Chest," she said, tapping his chest with gentle fingers that were not caressing, no matter what her brain commanded of her. Even if his flesh was soft to the touch, and yet so well-muscled and broad. *Oh, hard, berry-colored nipples*, she thought. Would they get harder if her fingers slipped and…

"Chest," he returned, placing his palm against her right breast, then shaking his head. "*Neyt* chest!"

His was definitely different than hers, he decided. And there had to be a different name for them.

"Br-breast," she managed, sucking in a deep breath as the heat from his body caused her nipples stiffen.

"Breast?" he asked, feeling her reaction. "Breast."

He felt a stirring in his cock and curiously looked down as sudden warmth began to rush through his back and thighs as his hand, still cupping her breast, felt her reaction.

"Uh, Torn?" she squeaked.

He quickly brought his gaze up to hers, wondering if she noticed his swelling in his… who knew what they called it here!

"Off!" she gasped, pointing to his hand. "Off."

With a grin, he removed his hand and grasped the hem of her tunic. She said off. Off he understood.

"No!" Sable gasped as she took a step back, her face flushing in embarrassment, because for a second she would have let him bare her to his gaze. "Hands off."

Nodding, he dropped his hand to his lap, wanting to know what she would call a hardening prick.

"*Neyt* naked?" he asked, pointing to his crotch.

"No," she returned, recognizing his word for no. "Penis."

Oh lordy, she thought. A fat piece of man meat that was swelling and tenting out the towel. He looked rather… substantial.

"Penis," he breathed still looking down.

Then suddenly, there was a knock at the door, causing them both to jump.

In a flash, she raced to open the front door as fast as her feet could carry her. It had to be Jack and Jill. *Please*, she silently prayed, *let it be Jack and Jill.*

Peeking through the peephole, she smiled, relieved to see her saviors, and just in the nick of time, too! Before she did something stupid, like dropping to her knees and measuring his length with her throat!

Smiling a manic smile, she ushered the two men in from the rain.

"Jack, Jill!" she called out, receiving a hug from the big, tall, black American as he swooped down on her.

"Let her down, Jack, so that she can bloody well share the wealth!" the second man called, pulling her out of the first man's arms and placing a smacking kiss upon her cheek.

"Jillian!" She laughed and returned the kiss in kind. "You are as cute as ever!"

She took in his long, silver-streaked, black hair and his robust form as he breezed in wearing his customary leather.

"What about me?" Jack asked in his deep bass voice.

Sable pulled away from Jill to examine Jack from head to toe. As usual, the tall, muscular giant was dressed in his almost too tight, blue denim jeans and his long brown duster.

His bald head gleamed in the light from the room accenting the strength hidden beneath his toffee-colored skin.

"Gorgeous, simply gorgeous." She smiled up at him, recognizing him not only as a fellow biker, a gallery owner who sold her pieces for thousands upon thousands, but also as one of the best friends she had ever had.

"And for your friend?" he asked, looking over her shoulder.

Sable turned to see Torn standing there, not exactly aggressive, but protective.

Torn had noticed the affectionate greeting shared between the two men and his Sable, but he stood by, just in case. These days, it didn't pay to be too careful. *Anyone could turn on you at a moment's notice*, he thought darkly. He was living proof of that.

"Torn," Sable called as she gestured to him. "Come."

He took two cautious steps forward, automatically scanning them for evil intent.

"Jack, Jillian, I would like to introduce you to Torn." She nodded in his direction.

As Torn stepped forward, the towel slipped, puddling into a soft heap at his feet.

He looked down as the two men gasped, and Sable covered her eyes in abject misery. Nothing could get worse than this.

"Penis," Torn said, looking down at his semi-erect manhood that rested slightly against his thigh.

"Oh, yes it is!" Jill gasped, rubbing his fists into his eyes as he observed the longhaired stranger's proportions. "And it can't be real."

"Who is this guy, Sable?" Jack asked, looking concerned when Torn made no move to cover himself, and Jill kept gawking.

"Ah, he doesn't speak any English." Then to Torn, "Towel, please."

Shrugging, he bent at the waist and snagged the errant piece of material, slowly wrapping it around his waist as Sable had done.

These men were interesting, Torn thought as he kept a careful eye on them while he secured the towel.

The tall, dark-skinned man was about his size if a bit smaller and looked a bit defensive, but the dark-haired, pale-skinned one just stared.

His breeding must show, Torn thought as he automatically halted the hand that lifted toward his ears. But he could discern no disgust from the men, just a strong curiosity and a touch of wariness.

"Sable?" Jack asked, glowering at his charge and friend of many years.

"Well, he's my Faeroe." She sighed, knowing Jack would want to commit her.

"Fairy?" Jack asked, an incredulous expression on his face.

"As if we weren't enough fairy in her life," Jill said with a laugh, "she had to go and import more of us."

* * *

Torn tilted his head as he observed the two men. The darker skinned one was his height, but the other man with the dark hair was so short, he was almost the same height as Sable. Was there blood from the Magic Realms coursing through his veins as well?

"He's a real fairy, Jill!" Sable insisted as she gestured to Torn. "As in warrior from under the hill. Just look at those eyes! And wait until you see his ears!"

"If they look as good as the rest of the package," Jill said with a wicked laugh, "I'm petitioning for a threesome!"

"Jillian!" Sable wailed, blushing at his words, because she knew what the rest of the package looked like. "Behave!"

"At least until we can get to the bottom of this," Jack agreed. He closely inspected the near-naked man who stood in Sable's living room watching them with curiosity. "Well, he's one big mother, I'll give you that."

"The clothes, Jack," Sable pleaded. "He can't go around naked."

"Naked?" Torn asked. He was seriously beginning to doubt that he would ever understand the meaning of the word naked, but he didn't think it meant his manhood.

He sighed in true regret that his leathers were so utterly and completely destroyed. He would like to have some sort of covering while speaking with these two men.

While nudity was totally normal in the Magic Realms and inside one's own castle, when meeting strangers it was always considered good taste to wear clothing. While he might be short of stature, he wasn't... short in other areas.

Some men felt particularly jealous and insignificant in that area, especially since "the half-breed" was built longer and thicker. He didn't want to start out making enemies of Sable's friends.

"*No*! uh, Neyt!" Sable cried, shaking her head rapidly. "Keep that towel on, Torn."

Torn nodded. He actually almost understood that. Keep the towel and no manhood displays.

Sable sighed in relief and turned pleading eyes to Jack. "Please tell me you found something that can fit him?"

"I brought sweats," Jack said, a half-smile breaking out on his face. "I just do not share my undies, so he'll have to go and get his own, but the sweats should fit him. He's a bit taller than me, but we are about equal in the shoulders."

"And what lovely shoulders they are," Jillian murmured, grinning up at Jack. "And I was referring to yours, so don't get your drawers in a bunch."

Sable dropped her head a bit as she tried to hide a chuckle.

Of the two men, Jillian was notoriously jealous of any man or woman who stared too long at his partner. She once had to stop him from dumping a sundae on the head of a woman who wouldn't take no for an answer as she leered at Jack. He settled for slapping the most passionate kiss ever on Jack's unsuspecting lips before everyone at the ice cream parlor. It had shocked and scared the woman away, and gave Sable insight into how possessive and crazy in love Jill really was with Jack.

And Jack? He took it all in stride, calmly reassuring the man that he loved him, that he wanted him, and only him. Sable had great respect for them both, for Jill's ability to stand up for what he believed, and Jack's calming and reassuring manner. They grounded each other.

"Well, here are the clothes," Jack said, handing a large leather satchel to Sable.

"Pretty fancy bag," Sable admired as she took the bag from him.

"Paper bags would have clashed." He chuckled before turning again to face Torn. "Fairy, huh?"

Torn blinked slowly at Jack, his purple eyes lightening to a pale shade of lavender.

"I have never seen contacts do that," Jill breathed as he took a step forward. "What about the ears?"

"Ears?" Torn asked as a blush filled his face.

"Oh, this is getting good," Jillian said, a sly look on his face. "What do his ears look like?"

With a sigh, Torn tilted his head to the side and brushed his long, curly locks to the side. He might as well get it over with. These men would find out that he was a half- breed, and then he would have to find some way of ignoring the un-translated taunts and laughter he was sure to follow. He felt too vulnerable, too alone in this funny place where water fell from the sky and women rode around on wheeled metal steeds. He just hoped that he could maintain a calm dignity while defending himself and could control the urge to change.

"They're pointy!" Jill exclaimed as he took a step closer to Torn.

Torn, noting his movement, took a step back, bracing himself for an attack.

"Why is he doing that?" Jill asked as he watched Torn's eyes turn a murky, angry purple color.

"Torn?" Sable asked as she reached out and touched his arm.

Torn jerked as if struck at her touch, but instantly calmed when he saw who it was.

"Torn," Jill said calmly, noting how tense Jack had become. "Come here, please." Torn read the man and found no hostility there at all. Just a growing curiosity, but he had to be closer to be sure, maybe even touching him. Men were so hard to read.

He took that step closer to Jill, and was not surprised when the man reached out and gripped his wrist. Now was his chance. As Jill's hand tightened, Torn sent out a searching spear of energy from his body into the air around the dark-haired man.

Sable gasped as a bright purple light flashed out and enclosed around Jill and Torn, snaked around their bodies, starting at their feet, and quickly circling around to their heads. Torn's hair flew wildly around them and Jill's straight hair stood on end.

"What the hell?" Jack cried out as he took a step forward, intent on separating Jill from the glowing man.

Yet when he touched the glowing energy surrounding them, he froze in place for a second and then was thrown back into the front door.

"Jack!" Sable screamed as she looked from the fallen man to the glowing pair. Who needed her help the most?

Before she could move to jump on Torn's back, the only thing she could think of to stop him, Jill began to laugh.

Jack pulled himself to his feet and watched, amazed, as Jillian began to laugh so hard, tears ran down his face.

The glow began to ease, and in a blink, it was gone as if it had never been.

Jill stepped closer to Torn and reached up to push his hair to the side. He exposed Torn's pointy ear, and Torn just stood there, calm and unmoving.

"Hey, this guy really is a Faeroe," he said as he carefully examined Torn's ear, reaching up to run a gentle finger over the pointed tip.

"Are you okay, Jill?" Jack asked lowly as he cautiously moved closer to his friend and lover. "Are you hurt?"

Sable stood in her place, stunned. It had all happened so fast, yet here was Torn allowing Jill to touch his ears and Jill was grinning like a loon.

"I'm fine, I feel fine!" he said cheerfully as he stepped back from Torn and smiled at Jack.

"Then what happened?" he demanded, one eye still on Torn as he spoke to Jill.

"He kind of checked me out, I guess." Jill

grinned. "And you know what? Suddenly I feel as if the weight of the world has been lifted off of my shoulders."

With a smile, he stepped back, and looked into Torn's solemn eyes. There was a wealth of understanding there that made Jill almost cry with joy.

"Checked you out?" Jack asked, remaining braced to attack. Jack had had extensive training in the martial arts and it showed in his graceful movements. He'd been taken by surprise by whatever had tossed him across the room and wouldn't make that same mistake twice.

"Come on, big guy." Jill urged. "Shake hands with him. I swear that nothing bad will happen and you will really love it."

Torn stood and watched the interplay between the two men. He wished with all his heart he could understand what they were saying, but their body language gave enough of their thoughts away so that he had a vague clue what was going on.

The taller, dark-skinned man was concerned about his friend. Usually, Torn would not have been so graphic in the physical reading, but he was tired, confused, and uneasy. That little show of power was designed to put some distance between the two before they could hurt him with their accusing eyes and stinging words when they found out about his heritage.

But in checking over the dark-haired man, he had found something extraordinary. Emotions the like of which he'd never felt before swamped over him, and before he could help it, the urge to cleanse this man's soul of pain and suffering overwhelmed him.

Almost without a warning, his powers had leapt free, encircling the two of them, taking a painful scar away from this man, and transferring it to Torn instead, freeing a trapped portion of that man's soul.

Being a misfit and misunderstood was universal, he decided. The impotent rage and fear this man carried was almost as strong as his own.

He understood being an outcast, being hated, or even worse, ignored, because of what you are. This man had to have had similar experiences in his background for those soul-deep scars. It was almost a pleasure to give freedom to the gentle soul. It had been battered and torn so many times that if the scarring continued, its very existence would have been threatened.

So eagerly, Torn took this man's pain unto himself, now realizing that he had added to his own burdens, but not caring at all.

Now he wanted to scream, to rage at this unfair world that so abused people. He wanted to rant and rave and destroy things on both of their behalf! But by purging the taste of injustice, he could not deal another injustice.

If he destroyed Sable's trust in him by harming her home, her realm, what pain would that cause her? So instead, he willingly let the man touch his strange ears, let him touch his person, and he stood firm and let him do it.

Now all he could do is smile weakly at him and add his misery to the collection of pain he'd gathered in his heart over the years.

"What did you do to Torn?" Sable asked suddenly.

All through the two men's exchange, she had kept her eye on Torn, watching for any changes in his person, but all she saw was a profound sadness that seemed to have grown larger than before he'd touched

Jill.

"What?" Jill asked as he turned back to Torn, finally noticing the sadness and despair on his face. "I have no idea, Sable." Then "Torn?"

The big man turned purple eyes to Jill, and he smiled a little, but it was a pitiful effort.

"Torn?" he tried again.

"Torn," he repeated, pointing to himself, then to Jill.

He should at least know the name of the man whose pain he now carried. "Jill," he said slowly, catching on quickly.

"Jill," he said. "*Oct tom a nie.*" I feel your pain.

Jill blinked, then nodded as if he understood what was said. Torn then pointed at Jack. Although he could read no evil and felt a lot of pain, he also felt an overwhelming love that seemed to be directed at this man.

"What?" Jack asked, still looking a bit uncomfortable.

"He wants to know your name," Sable supplied.

"Jack," he said quietly. "And no Jack and Jill jokes, please." He eased his stance as if he too could feel the pain pouring off the purple-eyed man.

Surprising all in the room, Torn bowed gracefully, showing his respect. From what he'd read off Jill, this man had done a lot to start Jill's healing process. He admired that, the desire to help others with their deepest anguish.

"Uh, thanks, I think," Jack said as he gave Torn a shallow dip, trading respect with this creature, though he didn't know why.

"Jack," Torn repeated with a small, genuine grin, then he turned to Sable. "*Neyt* naked?" he asked, pointing to the towel.

"What?" she asked, confusion written plainly on her face.

"I think he doesn't want to be naked anymore," Jill interjected helpfully. "Pity."

"Oh!" Sable a blush stained her cheeks. "He means clothes."

Taking his hand, she tried to pull him toward the back room, but Jill stopped her. "I think I should be the one to do it, Sable-cakes."

"Should I be jealous?" Jack asked, half-serious.

"No," Jill said quietly. "But I think he needs someone who understands to help him." For once there was no teasing quality to his voice. "And I want to help him. I have no idea what he did, but he took something dark away from me. I would like to return the favor."

Silently, Jack nodded and Sable turned over the bag and her Faeroe to his capable hands.

When he left, Jack wrapped one enormous arm around her shoulders and guided her to the couch.

"All right, small stuff. You have some explaining to do."

* * *

"Sweatpants," Jill instructed as he pulled the garment in question from his bag.

As soon as he tugged the docile Torn into the bedroom, he immediately opened the bag and began pulling out clothing.

He wanted Torn dressed and ready for the explanations he knew Jack would insist on. Jack, his savior, his knight in shining leather riding a charger made of steel, would not rest until he had a reasonable account of what had taken place, and that was something that even Jill wasn't sure of.

"Pants," Torn repeated as he looked at the soft-looking garment. He could figure out its use easily. He took the pants from Jill and dropped the towel.

"Too bad I'm committed." Jill sighed as he watched Torn expose his endowments again. "You look like you could deliver quite an exceptional experience."

But he said nothing further as Torn looked at him quizzically.

"Never mind, my friend." Jill added. "I may be a size freak, but that is a little bit too much for me."

"Pants?" Torn asked as he held up the garment, and Jill nodded in agreement. "Pants, and please don them so that I may regain my sensibilities."

Torn shook his head at the words sounding like so much gibberish, and began to dress. His first thought was that it was very soft and very warm. This was so much more comfortable than his dress leathers or his stiff work clothes. But he would feel even more comfortable leaving this house with the good, solid protection of his leathers.

He wondered if he could get more here. They didn't seem to have a problem fitting the man called Jack in leathers, so maybe Sable would be good enough to show him where he could acquire a good herd of skinning animals to make new clothing for himself. He wondered if Jack or Jill made the leather they wore. The tiny stitching was almost invisible to the naked eye and yet they seemed well-made.

But first, he had to purchase a herd. It would probably take a herd to cover him, as it no doubt had taken that many to clothe Jack. The man was short but he was wide.

He eased the pants over his hips and discovered that the form-fitting material spread warmth throughout his lower body, even though his cock was a little confined and resting along his left thigh.

He bent at the waist and examined how the soft material outlined almost every inch of his masculinity, then he blushed red.

Although some flaunted their endowments, Torn had never been comfortable doing so. He had always tried to conceal what these clothes so obviously and blatantly revealed. He wondered if either of the men would be bothered by such a display and take it as an affront to their manhood.

He wanted no envy brawls started as the two tried to prove that they were the better men through violence because their cocks were not as large as the half-breed's.

But Jill just shook his head. "Yeah, nice to look at, but dangerous to acquire," he said as he reached into the bag for a shirt -- hopefully a long shirt. "But we need to cover that up before you give Jack and Sable a heart attack. I know my ticker is pounding to beat the band. I thought nothing could shock me anymore!"

Not understanding a word, Torn stood up and eagerly reached for the shirt Jill held out to him. It seemed to be made of some material that was as soft as the pants, but thinner and less fuzzy on the inside, although that fuzz felt good against the skin of his thighs.

"T-shirt," Jillian added as he watched Torn examine the garment. "It goes over your head."

"Head," Torn replied, and pulled the shirt over his head. Sleeve first.

"No, let me help." Jill smiled as he reached for the shirt Torn was trying his best to pull down -- never mind that the hole was too little to let his head pass through.

* * *

"He really is a Faeroe, Jack!" Sable said as she looked up into her friend's dark eyes. Even sitting, Jack was much larger than her, but she found it rather comforting.

"He is something, but I just don't buy into the Faeroe bit, Sable." Jack sighed as he ran his hands over his head in frustration.

He had abandoned his leather coat, and the black turtleneck he wore strained to contain the large muscles that flowed under his skin. He looked down at Sable, arms crossed over his chest, his brown eyes worried, as he stared at his friend and favorite sculptor.

"Then what do you suppose he is?"

"I have no idea!" He threw his arms up and leaned back into the cushions of her couch. "But I don't think he's human."

"How else would you explain the ears, and the sudden appearance, the fact that he doesn't speak a word of English, or that purple light show that has Jillian feeling all warm and gooey?"

"Hormones?"

"Not even Jillian in all of his glory can produce that many hormones to make his very own laser-light show in my living room! That man is a Faeroe, Jack, as sure as my name is Sable."

"But Faeroes are tiny creatures," Jack argued, still having trouble coming to grips with he'd seen. "They have wings and grant wishes."

"You've been watching Disney too long," Sable countered. "All you have to do is look around, Jack. We are in the heart of magic country. Scotland is known for magic rings and other magical devices and Druids. And in Celtic legend, Faeroes are large warriors sent to stop evil and help the weak. Look at

Finn McCool."

"Even if this farfetched story is true, Sable, what evil is surrounding you so that you need your very own personal Finn McCool? Are your sculptures suddenly going to come to life and terrorize the populace?"

That brought Sable up short. Why would she be sent a Faeroe?

"Maybe, he is here to... I don't know, Jack. But he is here, and we have to see to him until we know why."

"We?" He lifted one black eyebrow at her, and his eyes darkened in disbelief. "Well, I have to see to him then."

Before she could answer, there was a thump and a holler from the bedroom. Abandoning their conversation, both Sable and Jack jumped to their feet and raced, tripping over each other, to the bedroom.

"Jill!" Jack called as he and Sable played slap and tickle with the doorknob, each trying their best and fumbling over each other's fingers to turn the darn thing. "What is going on?"

Forced open by the combined weight of Jack and Sable, the door exploded inward, slamming against the wall with a thump. Jack and Sable almost hit the floor in a tangle of long arms and legs as they stumbled inward to see...

...Jill and Torn lying on the floor, or rather, Jill lying on top of Torn on the floor, both of them tangled in a stretched-out T-shirt.

Torn's head was missing, probably stuck in a sleeve, one arm under the writhing mass of masculinity, the other trying to hold Jill off the floor.

Jill, on the other hand, was half-straddling Torn's writhing body, one arm inside the shirt, trying to untangle himself from the cotton, the other trying to pull ropes of Torn's hair out of his face with the other. His head was twisted at an odd angle as he tried to scream soothing words to Torn through his laughter.

"Need help?" Sable finally managed, fighting to hold in her own amusement. She never thought she would see the day when Jill was relaxed enough to sit on someone to get them dressed properly, although he had threatened her with that same fate many times.

"Help? I think he's cheating on me!" Jack added, his deep voice full of amusement as he observed this phenomenon.

"Very funny." Jill chuckled, then winced as Torn again tried to shove him off of his chest. "A little help would be in order right about now!"

"But you look so comfortable," Jack teased as he made his way over to the writhing pair. "You look almost happy."

"Jack!" Jill called, turning red in the face. "I don't think that he can breathe."

"Get him off!" Sable called as she stood wringing her hands helplessly. Could someone die from inhaling a T-shirt?

With one mighty heave, Jack lifted Jill off Torn, pulling his face free from the Faeroe's clinging hair and his arm free of the shirt.

Torn sighed in relief as Sable quickly moved in and tugged the shirt off his face. As she pulled the shirt aside, a pair of exasperated purple eyes met hers, and blinked slowly.

"T-shirt," he offered before struggling to sit up.

"Oh Torn." Sable sighed as she pushed his hair out of his face.

Torn froze at the contact. Still, she was touching him like no one had before. He found that the more this female touched him, the more he enjoyed it. That she was touching him and not being forced to do was almost unbelievable to him.

Her touch was comforting as she pushed the hair off his face, her fingers calloused, yet soft and feminine. It tingled where her fingers brushed against his lips, the side of his face. It tingled deep in his stomach and along his shoulders, and in his lower back, such a delicious tingle.

And when her eyes looked deeply into his, he felt a flash of heat right down to his toes.

His cock jumped and swelled a bit, beginning to tent his pants before he could pull his reaction under control.

He blushed as he looked around to see if any of the men caught his breach of manners, or if Sable had felt his growing desire.

They all stared back at him, Jack in bemusement, Jill in amusement, and Sable in sheer amazement.

He felt damn good between her thighs.

"I don't think he likes you that way, Jill," Jack finally managed to say, his eyes going from Torn to Sable, who was still trying to mother the large man despite the flush filling her face because she was trying to fight her own reactions to the man.

Jill just exploded into laughter.

"What?" Sable asked as she turned from the endearingly innocent face of her Faeroe to view the two men.

"Never mind, doll." Jill snickered. "It's something that you wouldn't understand."

Sable shrugged and reached for the shirt and efficiently popped the white cotton garment over his head and tugged his hair free.

The armholes were self-explanatory, so in

seconds he had the shirt on and was standing, admiring the new ensemble.

"*Crietched don geta!*" he said. Leather looks better.

But he would not insult his hosts by pointing out that the garments left little to the imagination.

"I think he likes it!" Jill laughed as he saw Torn bend sideways and crane his neck around to see what he looked like from the back.

"I think Sable likes it more," Jack added, peering at his friend.

And Sable stared in open-mouthed disbelief. Torn was one hot Faeroe, no matter how he was dressed -- or undressed for that matter. But in his clothes, he looked more human, more manly, and less otherworldly. Even though the eyes and ears were a dead giveaway, Torn still looked... tasty.

"Uh, Torn, you look fine," she squeaked, and Torn just stared at her, his eyes glowing softly as he read conflicting emotions in her eyes.

But he remained silent, taking in all that her body told him, and puzzling over it. Was she beginning to desire him as well? She couldn't understand a word he said, he thought sadly as he stared at her body, still covered by layers of clothing. He wondered what she would look like nude.

Too bad he would never know. Sable was not for him because he didn't want a woman -- *any* woman, and especially one with red hair.

No matter what his body tried to tell him, he didn't need another woman in his life. He didn't need a lover who would betray him or try to kill him. He was better off on his own, relationship-wise.

What he needed was a friend, and that's what Sable was. But then, why was his body telling him otherwise?

Not knowing what else to do with the confusion that settled in his soul, he smiled, then sighed as she returned the gesture. When had her smiles begin to feel so nice, to mean so much? Like a pair of idiots, they stood there and smiled at each other. They never even noticed Jill's look of contented joy or Jack's worried gaze.

Chapter Four

"How could he do this to me?" Zultha raged as she paced in the confines of her hiding place, rodents scampering out of her way in the dim light of the fire.

Dancing shadows cavorted along the walls as she crossed her arms over her chest and muttered to herself.

"After all that I did for Torn, he would betray me this way!"

She had yelled, paced, and stormed in the small stone cavern until her throat had hurt, but her anger remained, eating at her soul.

"I will find him and make him pay," she muttered as she stopped to sit at a large boulder. "He brought me to this low place, and I will make him pay!"

In the past days, she had hidden from Terror's guards and the hunters from the Magic Realm. Brought here by her father's supporters, her family had angered the Master of the Magic, and he wanted all parties involved to pay him a little visit.

He wanted someone to blame, she thought, because he'd fallen for her father's plan. And because his daughter had turned on him once again after suddenly appearing from the dead, he wanted to unleash his anger on her family's blood.

But how was she supposed to know that Torn, with his strange ways and odd looks, was the Reaver? It was a solid plan, a good plan, but Torn had ruined it for her.

He had never shown any hint of the mystical properties that the Reaver possessed in the past, and he was just supposed to be a pawn in the game. She had underestimated him. And he had killed her father's men, and brought the wrath of the Master of Magic down upon their heads. Even the talisman the Master had made for her had refused to work against Torn in Reaver form.

She reasoned, therefore, that it was Torn's fault. She needed someone of her own to blame, and he was it. This was all Torn's fault! If he had died like he was supposed to, none of this would have happened. If not for that violet-eyed mistake, her parents would not be trapped in the Magic Realm, all of their holdings taken away, and she would not have to hide herself away in this wretched cave.

This was all *his* fault, and her latest information from the few loyal ones left in her father's entourage told word of Torn being alive. Lost, but alive.

So, now it was her job to find him… and make him pay. He would die slowly at her hands, drained of all his magic and lifeblood. But first, she had to find him. It would be a challenge, but Zultha loved a challenge.

"I'll get that half-breed bastard," she growled as she again rose to her feet and resumed pacing. "I'll get him, if it costs me my life. I have nothing else to lose and everything to gain by bringing him down."

Then she stared into the darkness around her, growing even more angered.

"You will pay for what you have done to me and my family, Torn!" she bellowed, scaring the rodents into hiding once more. "You will pay with your pain and suffering. You will die!"

* * *

Torn sat at the table, eyeing the assortment of food before him. He wanted to scratch his head in confusion, but that would have been bad manners.

"Are you sure that they don't eat meat?" Jack

asked, eyeing Torn's impressive frame and the collection of vegetables on the table. A body that large needed a lot of protein to maintain its tone and condition. He should know. He had lifted weights for ages and always had to use protein supplements to help build and keep his muscle mass.

"I read it someplace," she countered. "They don't eat the flesh of any animal and live on dew, milk, and honey."

Jack looked down at his thick ham sandwich and almost felt guilty about the poor bugger having to eat grass. But the looks Torn was casting at his sandwich made him wonder if Sable's reading was accurate.

"Feed that man," Jillian declared as he tore into his own sandwich -- ham and turkey on rye with mustard, just the way he liked it.

Jack shook his head as he looked at his lover. He'd always had a problem getting the man to eat, but now he was devouring everything in sight, as if he could not get enough.

"I don't know," Sable said, looking at the almost miserable expression of Torn's face.

She had tried to dismiss their earlier attraction, but now she knew that it was something that could not be dismissed. Was it Faeroe glamour? Was she bespelled by him? She had to look into this. After all of the years she dated and made love to men, never had the feelings become so intense and soul-grabbing so quickly.

Finally, Torn gave in to his urge to scratch his head. He heard the words going around, and understood a few. So he surmised that they were trying to get him to eat this animal fodder that they placed before him. He recognized a few similar vegetables, but for the others he was at a loss. It looked more like a special diet for his horse than a meal for a man.

Now, what Jill and Jack were eating looked filling and delicious. It *smelled* delicious anyway. But what was the key to getting some of it?

Finally, he pointed to Jack's sandwich and looked up at Sable.

"I think the meat is disturbing him," she said, looking worriedly at Jack's plate and the last of the sandwich Jill was cramming down his throat.

"Feed the man!" Jill added again as he picked up a beer and chugged back a few swallows. "He needs meat and potatoes, woman! *Real* food!"

"*Salad*, Torn!" Sable said, pointing to the rather large bowl in front of him and ignoring Jill. "It's good for you."

Torn considered this for a moment, before shaking his head no.

"*Neyt*!" he replied, and pointed to the sandwich, hoping to get his point across. There was real food to be had, and he wanted some of it.

"See? The meat is bothering him!" Sable decided and glared at Jack. "Eat it or I'll toss it!"

Jack sighed, and bent to pick up the plate, but the plaintive look in Torn's eyes made the man want to laugh or feel sorry for him.

"Jack," Torn finally said, an anxious look on his face. "*Neyt* salad!" Frustration was evident in his every word and move.

Jill exploded into laughter at this telling gesture. Torn was no idiot, and he knew what he wanted. And what he wanted was that sandwich, and maybe a little Sable on the side.

"I don't think he wants the salad," Jack said as he handed the man the plate.

"Thank you," Torn enunciated carefully, remembering the word and guessing at its meaning.

"See?" Jill crowed. "The man is starving and you give him rabbit food. Bad on you, lass," he chided Sable, who flushed a deep red.

Never had she let a guest starve before, but that is what she had been doing to Torn. It embarrassed her to no end.

"The books said no meat," she groused, glaring at Jill.

"And when did you learn that you couldn't trust everything that you read?" Jack retorted, turning her ire to him and away from Jill.

"I learned that a long time ago, *Dad*," she said, then rolled her eyes as she watched Torn tear into the sandwich like a starving dog with a meaty bone.

"I guess I'll make another one for him and for you, Jack," she added when she realized that the man had given up his lunch.

"I'll have the salad."

Men! Hah!

After everyone was fed to her satisfaction and her kitchen righted under Torn's interested gaze, they all retired to the living room to plan the next course of action.

Jack, as always, went right to the meat of the matter. "Why is he here?" No one had an answer.

"Okay," he said, after a moment of silence, "why did you find him?"

"I have no idea." Sable sighed at that. "And it bothers me. What bad is going to happen in my life because he decided to turn up? From what I understand, fairy magic is always a double-edged sword."

She thought back to the feelings he caused in her

body and instantly thought of Faeroe glamour again.

"No gifts without a payment, is it?" Jill said, looking unconcerned as he lounged in a chair near Torn, who sat in a stiff-backed chair, head swinging from person to person like a fan in the stands at a tennis tournament.

"He hasn't demanded anything from me and I feel as if every blot on my mind had been… cleaned up a bit, I guess," Jill continued. It's a wondrous thing. I haven't felt this well in ages."

Jack looked carefully at his friend and lover and had to nod in agreement. When he'd first met Jillian, the man was so depressed he seemed to be on the verge of suicide. Yet he was strangely attracted to the prematurely silvering man, and had always been here for him, offering a shoulder to lean on and a pair of arms to embrace. But never in the years that they were in a committed relationship had he ever been able to make the man feel this good without sex. He was almost ecstatic, loving life, and it showed on his face.

"I see no harm in Torn," Jack added then got back to his earlier point. "He can't be a fairy. I still can't believe it."

"Then what is he?" Sable asked hotly. "An alien from a different dimension?"

Torn tried his best to follow this conversation and had to fight to hold back the resentment he felt because he couldn't understand a word that they were saying. It made him feel like a child. He also thought it was rude to speak about a person as if he wasn't there, because he was sure that he was the topic of conversation as his name had been mentioned several times.

Annoyed, he let a small tendril of his power seep out into the room; just enough to read more than the body language that he was interpreting.

If he was reading them all correctly, Jill was happily defending him, Sable was confused, and Jack was worried.

He already knew that Jill and Sable offered him no harm, so he directed the tendril to the large, dark-skinned man. He gasped as his energy suddenly shot out of control again. The bright purple/white bolt hit Jack in the center of his chest, just as he opened his mouth to say something, and trapped him and Torn in a magical tunnel of power.

Torn opened his mouth on a silent scream as the power exploded against his will and leapt toward Jack.

Jack lurched as if shocked, then his body arched out of the chair as the cleansing began.

Hate! He felt hatred surrounding this man, the hatred of others. He felt that he'd been forced to do things he'd hated to save others. That much they had in common. He felt the warmth and love for the man, Jill, and the loving concern for Sable. He also felt the scars from years of abuse at the hands of his... parents? No! His father!

He could empathize.

But what he was feeling now was insane! He felt as if he were being torn in two as Jack's dark past flooded his mind.

The pain!

He grabbed his head and slid to the floor, curling into a fetal position as all the dark emotions, fears, angers, and hatred slammed into him.

Tears flooded his eyes as he read the torment Jack hid so well underneath his calm mask. He felt and suddenly saw the names that he was called, the fear that he lived with. Then his body arched and shook as he felt each of the physical blows delivered by someone he had loved and trusted. He felt the mistrust grow, and how the man had shut himself off from the world. How he ignored the taunting of others because of his race and… Jillian?

He felt the overwhelming love that the man had contained deep within himself, how he gave his all to his friends and family. Even more than that, he considered Sable and Jillian his only family.

Torn latched onto the love, using it to pull him from the deep pit of despair that he'd entered into, flying with Jack's inner pain and anguish. Slowly, he pulled himself upward, concentrating on the light and good, freeing himself from the pain as his body absorbed the darkness into his already tortured soul.

Jill and Sable sat stunned as the energy bolt shot from Torn and entered Jack. They both tensed as a purple/white bolt of light surrounded them both. Not knowing what to do, Sable nervously jumped to her feet, walking first toward Jack, then Torn.

"It's okay," Jill said as he returned to his seat. He too had leapt to his feet as the energy bolt shot past him, but now, recognizing the feel of the power, he relaxed and took his seat.

Sable chewed her bottom lip, wondering what she had brought into her home, among her friends. All kinds of alien horror movies began to swirl through her mind. Was he actually an alien, bent on world conquest, changing people one person at a time?

She looked over and Jill, who raised one mocking eyebrow, and tossed that notion aside. There could only be one Jill, and he was sitting on her couch. But what was happening in that tunnel?

Torn lay in fetal position on her floor, a look of pure torment on his face. As for Jack, his pain-filled look was lessening.

As she watched, his body began to slowly slide back into its chair, his face softening more than she had ever seen it before.

The tunnel of light began to fade, and just as abruptly as it lashed out, it dissipated. "Jack!" Sable called as she rushed over to his side. "Jack, speak to me!"

"Sable?" he asked, slowly blinking his eyes as if he had just come out of a trance. "Sable, have I ever told you how much I love you?"

Sable's laughter was half sobs as she reached out one shaking hand to caress Jack's smiling face.

"I always knew, Jack!" She laughed and sobbed at the same time. "That's why you brought me to this, cold rainy country with you when you left the U.S. I always knew!"

"But I never said it," he replied as he struggled to sit up properly and adjust his clothing. Their next words were cut off by Jill's sudden call.

"Guys, I think we have a problem!"

Sable turned to where Torn lay, but he wasn't moving.

"Torn!" she called as she raced to Jill's side and dropped to her knees.

Torn lay as still as death, his breathing shallow and labored. His dark golden skin was now pale and appeared almost as thin as paper. His mouth was slack and tremors shook his large frame.

"What's happening to him?" Jack asked as he struggled to his feet and lurched across the room toward the strange man who had... altered? No, cleansed away some of his darkest pains and fears.

But no one had an answer. Torn lay trembling and cold to the touch, his very essence seemed drained away.

"Torn," Sable whispered as tears filled her eyes again. "Don't die. What have I done?"

* * *

Terror sucked in a deep breath as he felt his life force being pulled and twisted. He tried to rise up from his bed, but the pressure was too intense for him to handle. With a groan, he collapsed back beside his mate Nello, panting heavily, his face mottled red.

"Terror?" Nello called out, fear making its way into her delicate voice. "What is wrong, my love?"

Reaching out, she placed her hands over his rapidly beating heart, feeling his life muscle strain and pound. Sweat beaded up on his naked body as his eyes grew wide in comprehension.

"Torn!" he gasped. "My son is in danger!"

* * *

Nello raced through to the dimensional port, desperate to reach the Magic Realm and her father. She sucked in her breath as she entered the room where the portal was kept stabilized. She felt the pressure, felt her ears *pop*, and breathed in the rapidly swirling air.

Her hair whipped about her face, covering her anxious eyes, whipping the blanket, all that she wore, around her bare legs. She gripped the blanket tighter and pulled fistfuls of her hair out of her face. She felt the temperature drop, but paid it no heed. She had important work to do, life-saving work! She needed all of her wits about her, her concentration pure.

"Father!" she called, knowing that her father would hear her no matter where he was. "Father, I am coming home for a time. I need your help!"

"What help of mine do you need, daughter?" the cutting voice questioned. "What do you need of me? Everything that you are and everything that you will become is there, in the mortal plane. What use will I ever be to you again?"

"Father!" she called, shocked. "You would treat me this way? Your only daughter?"

"I have no daughter!" he called back.

"I *am* your daughter, you stubborn old fool! And you owe me! Do you hear me, old man? You owe me!"

She screamed as she felt precious time slipping through her fingers. Now, only her father could help her and *he'd* decided to play childish games.

"I owe you?" Anger rumbled in that voice and reverberated around the small room, making the stone wall shake and tremor.

"Yes, you owe me!" she yelled back, asserting herself, proving that she was his daughter. "First you deprive me of my husband and son for far too many years. Then you curse my child, *your only grandson*, because of who I mated, based on half-truths and falsehoods. Then you almost kill my family because of lies that some power-mad people told. You owe me more that you can ever repay, Father!" she sneered.

"Trifles," the voice returned. "Trifles compared to what you left me with!"

"I left you with yourself!" she replied angrily. "I left you with time to think about all of the bad you have done in the guise of protecting me, protecting the realm, and protecting your own selfish heart!"

"Nello," the voice growled. "You go too far!"

"How far is far enough, Father?" she retorted. "How much? Depriving a woman of her honest and true mate, her life, her child? And if you do not help me now, I will lose him permanently!"

"I am punishing the mortals who told those lies and manipulated me," he groused. "What more can I do?"

"You can help me find Torn!"

There was a beat of silence and Nello grew fearful that her father would refuse his help.

"Father?" she asked, her eyes frantically trying to pierce the swirling orb of color that made up the center of this room. "Father?"

"Why should I?" he finally asked. "He is nothing but a nuisance anyway."

"He is my son and your grandson and heir!" Her eyes narrowed in rage. "He is a part of me, the best parts of me. And to see him die is to see a part of me die, never to be reborn!"

"Nello," he soothed. "You can have other children, children of this realm. Why waste your time on the cursed one?"

"It's best you remember who cursed him!" she snarled back. "Never mind, Father. I can see I have wasted precious time trying to convince you to do what is right and just. The sad thing is that you are a worse monster than you could ever paint my Terror to be! You are a lonely, foolish, bitter old man, and may you rot in that realm that you love so well!"

"What do you need?" the voice called out urgently, trying to halt her leaving.

"I would not respond to you if my need wasn't so dire and my time quickly passing."

"I know of your disdain for me, daughter," the voice said on a sigh. "Tell me what you need and I will grant your wish."

"I need to know where Torn is and I need to know how to reach him."

She would not say thank you. He had so many debts to repay that saying the words would just add more to what he owed.

"Very well," he acceded, and then there was a bright burst of light as the glowing, swirling orb in the center of the room began to change. It pulsed as if taking on a light of its own, growing, changing, and solidifying.

"Touch this and it will take you where you need to go," the solemn voice said. "Anywhere at all." There was an almost wistful quality to the voice now, and it trailed off.

"And those who caused this mess?"

"The pit of agony, Nello," he said. "Recompense is being taken, no mercy shown."

"The least you could do," she said quietly, not giving in an inch.

"Yes," he replied as she turned to leave the room.

She never noticed the tall woman hidden just in the entrance of the room, the almost painfully thin body that scurried out of view and made for the exit of the keep.

The mistress needs to know, the woman thought as she raced onward. *This will please her mightily*!

* * *

"Put him on the bed!" Sable croaked as she nervously danced from one foot to the other, her eyes filled with tears and her voice catching. "And be careful!"

"Take a deep breath, lass," Jill said as he and Jack both struggled to get Torn's inert weight onto the bed. "We can handle the lad."

Torn had not moved since the power field evaporated, not even to open his eyes. Jack looked down at the face of the man who had leapt into his being and stripped the scars from his soul. Now he knew what Jill meant by saying that he had been cleansed. Never had he felt so light, buoyant, and yes, so free.

All of those old memories that constantly ate at

him, giving him nightmares, chasing him from place to place, were but a distant thought now, not even worthy of consideration. As he eased his half of the man onto the bed, he wanted to reach down and shake him awake, so that he could thank him.

"I knew he was allergic to meat," Sable wailed as she watched the two men position Torn to their satisfaction. "Faeroes don't eat meat!"

"Nonsense," Jill denied. "If the good Lord didn't want us to eat meat, then animals wouldn't taste and smell so good and come in convenient plastic wrapping."

"Jill!" Sable cried, not understanding his need to joke. "This is serious! Something's wrong with Torn!"

"Probably all tuckered out, lass," he replied as he stepped around the bed to envelop Sable in his strong arms. "He probably needs a rest, is all."

"But he looks so helpless." She sniffled, wiping the tears from her face with both hands. "I've never seen him look this way."

"You've only known him for a few hours," Jack said.

"But it feels like forever," she retorted, narrowing her eyes in the big guy's direction.

Jack held up his hands in mock surrender, deciding it was better to let that line of conversation die.

"What's wrong with him?" she asked again, pulling free of Jill to sit at Torn's side. Almost lovingly, she ran her hands over his face, easing his creased brow, hoping against hope that her touch could ease the tremors racing through his body.

"Sable?" Jack called as he settled his hands on her shoulders.

"Why do I feel as if a piece of me is dying, Jack?"

she asked. "Why does it hurt so much and I barely know him? Hell, I can't even understand him, but I feel as if my future is slipping away."

"Maybe you were just meant to be?" Jack asked as he ran a hand through her tousled hair.

"Or maybe it's Faeroe glamour," she said dubiously. "Faeroes have the ability to enslave the human heart."

"Torn wouldn't..." Jill began a heated defense, but Sable cut him off.

"Maybe it's unintentional, Jill. Maybe it happens because they need a guide to help them on their quest. But I know that I have never felt like this about any other man I've met, and that includes some I've screwed into my mattress!"

"Don't sell yourself short, love!" Jill laughed as he joined them on the bed. "You just hadn't met the right man yet."

"And I still refuse to believe that that man is a Faeroe," Jack commented.

"But you felt what he did! You saw!" Sable argued.

"Yes, I did, and if he wakes up, I'll thank him most graciously, but until he tells me otherwise, I refuse to believe that he is from some magical plane where seven foot immortals rule!"

Sable bit back her comment, knowing that she was wasting her breath with Jack. But she knew what he was. She felt it in her heart. She now knew that she had one. He had given her that, and that was truly a miracle.

As she looked down at the pale trembling man, she was certain she had a heart. It was now breaking.

* * *

Torn swam in a sea of darkness and confusion.

Where was he? He felt lightheaded and cold, the room spun and twisted, and he felt cast adrift. He would have been completely at ease in this world of darkness, of seclusion, but for the painful lump in his chest, burning at the core of him.

Forcing himself to concentrate, he moaned and tried to make himself find his bearings, find a center, find a place of balance. But the room spun too wildly; the fall was too steep.

He groaned as he spiraled out of control, only to be brought to some semblance of stillness as the pain suddenly exploded.

"Why?" he screamed out as he tumbled to a sudden jarring halt.

"Why not?" came the reply in a voice that he knew all too well.

"You!" he hissed as he opened his eyes to find himself floating neatly in a small round room. Between him and the owner of that accursed voice stood a deep abyss, far deeper and blacker than the one he had just journeyed through.

"You and me!" the voice corrected as its body stepped into the dim light of the room, just at the lip of the abyss.

There, in all of his dark glory, stood the Reaver. Tall and imposing, with a massive wingspan and silky black feathers, the Reaver looked like some dark angel of destruction come to reap a terrible price for the small happiness Torn had embraced since coming to this plane. The deep purple eyes glinted as they examined his other self; his talons clicked against each other as the near midnight skin easily showcased muscles he controlled with such ease. He stood naked, in all of his glory, as he examined the husk of the man he inhabited.

"What more do you want?" Torn growled as he floated near his nemesis, and nearer that dark abyss that was more frightening than his sudden and unplanned freefall.

Ignoring the question, the Reaver pointed to the abyss. "Do you know what that is?" he asked, his three-toned voice whispering around the room, filling it with a sense of power.

"Again, I ask, what do you want? Is it not enough that you control my very existence?"

"The pit?" the Reaver asked again. "Do you know what it is?"

"Damn the pit!" Torn screamed, identical eyes flashing at the beast that dwelled within. "Damn the pit and damn you!"

"It is our soul," the Reaver replied, ignoring Torn's outburst.

"It can't be!" Torn gasped, finally listening to what was being said.

"It is," he was assured. "The darkness has nearly consumed us."

"But I can take on a limitless supply of evil without turning! The only danger to me is myself!"

"Exactly," the voice agreed as the Reaver flexed his wings then folded them neatly against his back. "*You* are the one hurting *us*!"

"Me?" Torn asked, looking incredulously at the beast, the monster. "I caused none of this! This is the hatred and the evil that I absorb to ease the suffering of others! That is from the people who are beyond retribution, and I needs must destroy! That is what being who I am causes! This abyss should not be near to overflowing! My core is pure!"

"*Our* core is tainted," the Reaver argued. "*Our* core is weak. *We cannot continue* this way for much longer. *We* cannot turn evil by what we have taken into ourselves, but *we* can cease to be."

"Impossible!" Torn hotly denied, floating across the abyss to get into the monster's face.

"*Our* inner core is flawed, weak, diminishing. You have caused this, and soon, *we* shall perish."

"No!" Torn snarled, glaring at the creature that he could so easily become.

"Yes," he countered. "Would *I* lie to *myself*?"

"Why?" Torn finally asked.

"*We* have no agreement, no accord," the Reaver explained. "*We* have no love in our core."

"I love many things!" he replied hotly, but considered the Reaver's words.

"How do *we* have love, love for another, when we *cannot* love… *ourselves*?"

Torn froze, as he stared at the suddenly sad violet eyes. "How can I love what I am, what I have become?" he finally asked, his voice ragged and torn. "How can I love what has caused me no end of grief?"

"Maybe when *we* have that answer," the Reaver replied, "maybe *we* can love *ourselves*."

Torn looked down at the pit, watched as the darkness grew.

"How?" he finally asked.

"Reave thyself?" the multi-toned voice suggested as the Reaver followed suit and looked deep into the abyss.

"Impossible!" Torn snorted. "And you and I both know it."

"Then find someone to show us the way."

Torn looked into the face of his monster, the beast that he two-fisted with daily, and all at once noticed that it was sad. "How?" he asked again.

"Acceptance?" the Reaver asked, the voice

sounding so very tired.

"From who?"

"The body grows weak," the Reaver said, neatly avoiding answering the question.

"The pain?" Torn asked.

"Inconsequential. Yet the body grows weak. *We* must awaken."

"How?" he asked again.

"Find someone to show us the way."

Then the Reaver was gone, lost in the darkness, and the round room disappeared, leaving him to float weightless once again, cut adrift in a sea of darkness. He groaned as he suddenly found himself again spiraling out of control, falling deeper and deeper into a fathomless night, twirling dizzily at a high speed. He moaned partly in fear, and partly in surprise as he lost all sense of direction. He needed to fall, but fall up! Was that possible? Where was up? How could he make it stop? Who would show him the way? Did he care? Then he heard her, like a shaft of pure white light in his ocean of despair.

He heard *her*.

"Torn, please don't die!"

* * *

It had been two days since Torn had lapsed into this uneasy coma. No one knew what to do.

Jack and Jill had remained at Sable's side, helping her tend the weakened man, turning his shivering body, keeping the blankets piled on to raise his temperature, but to no avail.

He was slipping away from her.

"It's not your fault," Jill said as he gave her shoulder a squeeze, tucking her head under his chin. "Nothing you did would have caused this."

"But I fed him meat," she wailed, all that she

could think of to say.

"Uh, be that as it may, I doubt a little pig would lay the man this low," Jill said, struggling to restrain a laugh.

"What makes you so joyful?" she nearly snarled at the man, trying to pull away from him. "And let me go before I pop you one!"

"You beating on my man?" Jack asked, walking into the room and staring at them in mock disapproval after taking a quick look at Torn.

Still no change.

"Only because he's asking for it." She sniffed.

"Yeah, he's a bit into pain, but as long as he is on the receiving end, I generally give him what he wants."

Both Jill and Sable turned to look at the taciturn -- well, usually taciturn -- man. "What?" he asked.

"You made a joke!" Jill breathed. "In all of my days of walking with you, *mon*, you've never made a joke! I'll be gobsmacked!"

Jack shrugged off the commentary, but blushed a little as his eyes met Sable's. "I feel… good," he admitted, looking ruefully at the bed and the man who had seemed to work a miracle.

Sable shook her head. This had been a week for miracles. Maybe she would find one more.

"Torn," she said again, taking his hand as Jill rose from the bed to stand beside his partner. "Please don't die. I think I may need you."

For days she'd lived with this fear, with this great sense of loss. She knew in her heart that if she didn't reach him soon, there would be nothing left to reach. What caused this, she didn't know, but how she wished she did.

She was a scrapper, as Jill would say, a fighter. But in this case, she didn't know who or what she was fighting. If she knew, she could have handled it better, made plans, designed a strategy. But all she had was the almost lifeless body of the man who could have meant so much to her.

That loss, the loss of future possibilities, made her heart ache and her soul burn with regret. He had been in her life such a short time, yet she wanted... no, she needed more.

But then, just as suddenly as he'd collapsed, his eyes flew open, his violet gaze confused and dazed.

"Torn!" she called, and ignored the sharp gasp that came from behind her.

All of her attention was focused on the man, the Faeroe that had suddenly become such a part of her.

"Sable?" he asked, blinking rapidly to clear his eyes. *"Johen compt opt wlaee."* Instinctively the words sprang from his lips. He really didn't know where that had come from, but they felt so right to say.

He gazed at her, her eyes red and swollen, her lips trembling, her precious tears running down her face, for him. She had called him back. It was her voice, sweet as a honey treat, yet strong as the Reaver, that had given him an anchor, a tether line to grasp onto, to pull himself out of the deep pit in which he had fallen.

Her eyes stared in amazed joy as he focused in on her, noticing her red hair, but for once finding the color comforting.

He blinked weakly again, and repeated the words. This time, struggling to understand why they felt so right, but knowing that it was what he had to say. *"Johen compt opt wlaee."* Show me the way.

* * *

"Where is he?"

Zultha's low voice hissed at the servant who brought her the news.

Torn had been found, and even better, the Lady Nello was traveling to join her son, or at least she assumed as much.

"That, I do not know, Lady," the cowering woman stuttered. "She spoke with her father, then she created the vortex. It leads to her son."

"Yes, she would rush to the half-breed's side," Zultha murmured as she paced the confines of her hidey-hole.

"Lady, she appears to be distressed," the servant added, hoping to ease the Lady's temper. She had thought that news of Torn's location would cheer up her mistress, but instead it made her sink deeper into… madness?

Zultha smiled, her hair a tangled mess around her head, her clothes travel-stained and worn. She no longer resembled the grand lady about to marry into the most powerful family in the land. She looked like an unkempt urchin ready to beg for scraps… or kill for them.

"Distressed?" She raised one red eyebrow and peered at the trembling woman. "Why?"

"I do not know, Lady," the woman added, calming a bit when Zultha made no further attempt to climb the walls.

"You do not know?" She laughed a bit, her eyes twinkling merrily as she viewed the woman kneeling at her feet. "You do not know?"

She turned and walked a few steps away.

The servant felt a smile tugging at her lips, but was hard-pressed to say exactly why.

"You do not know?" Zultha tossed her head back in amusement.

"No, Lady." The woman sighed. The danger had passed. The lady's laughter had ever been infectious and now was no different. So what if her parents were locked away and suffering and she was banished to this dreary cavern: The lady could always make those around her laugh.

"Incompetence!" Zultha suddenly screamed, swirling around in a cloud of tattered, stained cloth to confront the suddenly cowering woman. "Ignorance! Stupidity! Why am I surrounded by bunglers, idiots, and fools?"

The servant, almost as if she feared being knocked back down, slowly rose to her feet and took a step back, trembling at the insane fury that twisted her lady's face. She stumbled and ended up back on the floor anyway.

"You will take your skinny hide back to that castle, and I don't care if you must screw the whole garrison. You will bring me back the information that I require, or the *torture* that I shall put you through will make the Magic Realm's ruler seem like a *tame kitten*!"

She crouched low and stalked the white-faced woman, who was slowly crawling backwards crablike, across the floor, away from this deranged lunatic.

"Are my words not heard, you worthless sack of skin and hair? Find out where he is! Find out who he is with! Find out if he is still alive, *so that I may kill him*!"

Her breath panted heavily in her chest as she loomed over the frightened woman, spittle flying from her mouth to land on the trembling servant's face.

"Bring me what I require about Torn, or I swear by all the knowledge that my family holds dear, you will not survive to see another sunset! You have two days!"

"T-t-two days?" The woman stumbled to her feet as she skirted further backwards, dignity long tossed aside in favor of salvation.

"Two days, starting now," Zultha growled as she turned again and stomped over to a large boulder, her new throne in her kingdom of madness and tears.

She glanced out of the corner of her eye as the servant backed out of the chamber, even now showing her the respect she deserved as a princess.

"I am ever a good ruler," she muttered as she ran her hands through her matted hair, wincing as tangles twirled around her fingers. "But I do need better help."

Chuckling under her breath, she lay back against the wall, eyes closed and lips parted in a smile.

"First," she whispered to herself, "I'll need a new traveling gown, one encrusted with jewels. Then maybe a steed to take me there in style. And I need a new hairstyle. I wonder which style works best for skinning men alive? Or beheading... No! I have it! I will cut off his wings and decorate the back of my new cloak. Demon feathers will be all the rage!"

* * *

"What do we know about this place?" Nello asked as she watched her husband rise from his bed, staggering a bit, but on his feet.

"I know that my son is there and it's time I brought him home."

"Terror, you can hardly stand!" Nello gritted out between clenched teeth. "You are in no condition to lead this party into the great unknown! I will go instead."

"I am in this condition, mate, because my son is in this condition or far worse! He needs me, and damn it, I will be there for him. I may be a bit late, but better than nothing!"

"Who are you trying to prove that to?" Nello asked finally, ready to pull her hair out in frustration. "Torn loves you, no matter what. He understands your standoffishness and loves you just the same!"

"My son needed me, Nello, and I was too wrapped up in my own guilt to see to him properly. Now he is lost, alone, and hurting. Do you know how I know this, Nello?"

"No," she said quietly, reading a mixture of frustration and self-anger on his face.

"I know because it feels as if my heart is being torn from my chest! I know because I can feel part of me wilting away, dying, Nello! I know because I am a part of him, and he of me. No matter what. We are not two halves of the same coin, Nello, but damn it, if I am the core, he is the imprint. And I can feel his imprint fading away from me. I will be there to help him, no matter what!"

"Will you die for him, Terror?" Nello asked, her purple eyes flashing curiously at him. "Because you just may!"

"A son is supposed to outlive his father," he groused, turning his back to Nello, focusing. The pain was lessening a bit, but still felt critical.

"Then I shall tell the guards to prepare extra provisions."

"One guard, Nello."

"But Terror! You are the ruler! If anything should happen to you --"

"Then the rulership will revert to you. But nothing will, Nello! Nothing until I see for myself that my child is safe. One guard is sufficient. We have no idea what type of people we will meet. They may be spooked by our warriors and seek to do us harm."

"It is nature to destroy what we cannot have or understand," Nello said sadly, remembering Zultha and her parents.

"And I will not see my son savaged more

because of me."

"Terror!" Nello protested, but he cut her off with a wave.

Turning to face his mate, Terror had only finality and determination on his face. His mind was set, his course clear.

"I will go to fetch my son, to protect my son. And may the Creator help any who harms him or stands in my way."

This was the legendary warrior standing before her, the man whose exploits needed no embellishment. The man with no equal and no rival. This was Terror, the man whose name made the denizens of evil and injustice quake with fear. This was a father, a father protecting his only child. This was a man.

"Yes, Terror," Nello agreed. Nothing would stop him, and she would rather be an aide to him than a hindrance.

"And I want Overton to accompany us."

Again, "Yes, Terror."

"Woman, I love you," he said suddenly, walking over to his wife and running the back of one hand caressingly down her face. "I never stopped, and I always will."

"Yes, Terror." Nello grinned. "And I love you as well."

"Good. I know it, but it's good to hear."

* * *

By the door, a servant cowered, listening, but finding nothing worth bringing to her mistress. *Maybe better luck with the guards,* she thought as she scurried away from the door. But she had to hurry; her time was running out.

Chapter Five

"Why, Sam I am?" Torn asked, his deep rumbling voice showed confusion as he stared at Sable. "Why not, I am Sam? What green eggs and ham?"

In the three days since he had awakened, Sable had done her best to teach him this backwards, confusing language. And it wasn't as easy as it looked.

He still could not pronounce all of the words correctly; instead of a monotone he was used to, the words were pronounced with emphasis on either the beginning or the ending. And of the men, Jill spoke even stranger, his words lilting and songlike.

He sighed deeply, but gamely squared his shoulders and faced his teacher. If she wanted him to speak this language, then he would learn. Besides, he needed to communicate while in his new home... for as long as it was safe for him to be there.

"Because it is." Sable brushed her hair off her forehead.

In the three days since he had awakened, she had begun to doubt her sanity. After mumbling in some strange language, he had fallen asleep again and dozed for a few hours, long enough for Jack and Jill to be reassured and to make a trip home. They both had business to attend to, but Jack made sure to drop off a few more articles of clothing, along with a stipulation: If Sable didn't want two permanent roommates, she would keep Torn in the house until they could figure out what was to be done.

Jack still refused to believe the fairy thing, but what other possible explanation could she have for the sudden feelings that she felt around him? It had to be Faeroe glamour.

"Horny," Jill told her when she again explained

her belief that he was a Faeroe. "Pure horniness. He is a well-built hunk of man." He chortled at the dark look on Jack's face but laughingly continued. "Not as perfect as Jack, but still nice in his own long-haired, purple-eyed way. He makes you feel lust, lass. So jump on him, ride him to a lather, and we can all get on about the business of finding out what is going on with him."

Jill still kept any opinions on Torn's origins to himself, but just said that the man was one of the good guys and needed to be protected.

Now as Sable looked at the overgrown baby, Jill decided Torn needed the protection. From her!

"Dr. Seuss wrote these books to help children with language… and things like that. And you are learning the language, so he must be right!"

First, Torn wanted to get up and explore, but he was too weak to do more than stumble around breaking things. Second, he wanted to eat meat.

He kept trying to sneak off to the cold food holder called a "fridge" when she wasn't looking, but she always caught him.

Refrigerators apparently haven't made their way into the land beneath the hill just yet, Jill decided after the second accident. Torn either ripped the door open, knocking around the glass jars in the door, or slammed it as if the big bad wolf was peeking his head in, trying to take a nip out of him.

Every time he got caught, Sable had to take the meat away. She would not have the crime of corrupting a vegetarian fairy on her hands. It was fresh fruit and vegetables for Torn.

Then he persisted on learning how to speak as if he were driven by something she couldn't understand. Just earlier, he burst in on her while she was sitting on the toilet, *Green Eggs and Ham* in hand, and demanded a new lesson.

Sable kept the stack of children's books in her house for the pleasure the simple verses and uncluttered illustrations brought to her. But they were also a useful learning tool. Problem was, Torn learned too well.

Already he had grasped the rudiments of speaking English; how to write the language was something else entirely. But then speaking it was more important than writing it well at this point; speaking and reading.

Now he sat in the bed where she forced him to stay and blinked at her with innocent violet eyes, waiting for her to answer his questions.

"Oh," he replied, one of her favorite words. "Torn, I am!"

"Oh dear." She shut the book as she felt a headache flair up behind her closed eyes. "That's enough for now, Torn. You need rest." *And I need a break*!

"*Neyt*... no rest. Learn! Torn, I am, want learn!"

"If you must." Sable sighed as she looked around to find something that would occupy his fertile and annoyingly quick mind.

Then she shook her head. There was no help for it

"Come on, Torn. Let's go to my studio."

The only way she could get some work done, pay some bills, buy fresh fruits and veggies, buy gas -- uh, petrol -- for her Harley, was to get to work.

She watched as he tossed back the blankets and rose to his feet.

As usual, he was wearing a pair of Jack's sweats; they almost looking like spandex on his muscular body.

Come to think of it, they looked that tight on Jack! Maybe it was one of Jill's favorite outfits, she thought with a smile. He was wearing a large T-shirt and straining the seams as he moved, but he was decently covered.

He quietly followed her. Sable was always teaching him something new, always teaching him, always the teacher. He paused as he remembered that it had been her voice that called him back from the brink of destruction as he plummeted through the abyss. *Her* voice, the one that could teach him how to save himself.

That thought in the back of his mind, he hurried to follow her, feeling stronger on his legs than ever before, even as he wondered why. With all of the grass that she was feeding him, it was a wonder that he recovered without real meat!

Running his hands through his tangled curls, he followed Sable as she marched out of the room and traveled down a hall that he had not been through before. She paused to open the door, then led him into paradise.

Paradise had tall sloping ceilings made of glass, letting in the watery light of another Scottish summer day. Around the walls were high shelves stacked with books and strange-looking metal tools.

There were no rugs on the floor, just the same slippery surface that made up the food room -- kitchen floor, he corrected himself.

There was also a couch and small table toward the back of the room, both sitting on a wonderfully colored rug. What drew his attention was the large table in the center of the room. On it sat a wide assortment of strange machines. The explorer in him had to find out their uses!

He hurried past Sable into the room and paused a scant foot away from her worktable. There was a wheel of some kind on one side, a tall seat beside it. On the table itself was a large covered piece of something, with various sharply pointed tools beside the mass. A tall seat in front of the table too had a back to it and was lightly padded. Jars of liquid were off to one side and a stack of cloths on the other.

"Welcome to my studio," Sable said quietly, watching Torn examine everything with curious eyes.

"Studio?" he asked, turning to face her on his socked feet.

"Studio," she affirmed. "The place where I work."

"Work?" he asked.

This was the tricky part, how to explain the meaning of the word when he would not understand a word of the explanation.

"What I do," she attempted to explain.

"Sable breathe, do?" he asked, placing his hand on his chest and inhaling deeply.

The way she explained the simple bodily function.

Other functions had been explained by the guys, and took the hands-on approach that they were more capable of giving. Well, that's what they told her, when the water bottle as substitution for the penis during urination idea was nixed, stomped on, and kicked to the curb.

Jack, because Jill was unceremoniously denied the pleasure of this trip, took Torn into the bathroom and showed him how to use the facilities. Blushing deeply, Torn exited the room with a formal understanding of toilets and bodily functions in this realm, which he was happy to see were not much different than at his home.

"Just like showing a child," Jack said to the disappointed and quite put-upon looking Jill. "Only he picked it up on the first try."

Jill harrumphed and moved to stand beside Sable -- where he was trusted to behave -- and declared, swearing that Jack had to make his dismissal up to him at a later date.

Jack and Jill had left with huge grins on their faces, and looking lighter and happier than Sable had ever seen them.

"Not quite," Sable said pulling, herself away from that, uh, interesting memory and facing Torn. "*Neyt*," she said, remembering his word for no. It almost sounded Russian or German.

"No?" he asked, raising one eyebrow and tilting his head to the side.

"I sculpt," she tried again, but noting the deeper confusion on his face.

Shrugging, she pulled the cloth off of her most recent work, and smiled as he took in a deep breath of air, awe written all over his face.

BLAM!

She screamed as his fist plunged down on the clay, destroying a week's worth of work!

"Torn!" she shrieked, as she lunged for his arm to stop the horror, the destruction, the total annihilation of her sculpture, but alas, she moved too late.

"*Nevina*!" he called out. Demon!

"Torn!" she wailed, wrapping her body in desperation around his plunging arm, trying to stop him.

But with one arm he swept her behind him and

kept on with the total annihilation, as if it was Carthage and nothing but total destruction would appease.

"No, Torn! Stop!" Sable wailed, almost in tears as she watched her masterpiece, her baby being destroyed.

"Sable." Torn gasped as he finally stopped beating the lump of funny flesh that the *nevina* was forming and backed her to safety.

Unleashing a tendril of energy, he probed the mass for any lingering signs of magical life.

Finding none, he turned to Sable, a wide smile on his face. He'd smote the evil *nevina* and had saved untold lives from the free-flowing bit of wild demon magic that sought to consume the flesh of those around it.

He never even saw the punch coming.

In an instant, Torn found himself lying flat on his back on the cold tile floor. Surprise written clearly on his face, he looked up at the furious red-haired woman.

Twice, he thought. *Twice, I have been felled by a red-haired female, and it has got to stop!*

"Sable?" he asked, a look of confusion and hurt on his face as he tried to blink the stars out of his eyes. For a little thing, she sure did pack a wallop!

"My work!" she screamed as his eye turned red and the tender skin surrounding it began to throb and puff up. "My work is destroyed, you... you, long-haired idiot! Why did you do that?"

She stood above him, arms akimbo, chest heaving with the force of her anger. Her eyes flashed down at him, daring him to move, least she plunge another fist into his to his other eye, decorating it like the first.

"*Nevina*?" he asked, nodding to the rubble that

was once a half-formed sculpture. "Bad?"

Another one of the words that he still struggled with.

"*No!*" she bellowed, tossing her head back and glaring at the not quite sun that tried to shine through the glass. "*Sculpture*! My *work*!"

Striding over to a bookshelf, she pulled down a small statue of a woman cradling a child.

"I make!" she said, pointing to the wreck of her masterpiece, then to the small sculpture in her hands.

"Sable make?" he asked, confused.

Sable was calling forth *nevina*? That just didn't seem possible. She had no ability to pull that type of dark magic. If she had, his senses would have picked up on it. He turned a small probe in the direction of the small woman in her arms and felt… nothing. It wasn't real.

"Sable   make!"   he   said   suddenly   as comprehension dawned. Then he turned to the table in horror.

"Sable make! Torn, I am… no make."

"Destroy!" she corrected. "Torn destroyed it!"

Then she felt the beginnings of guilt seep its way into her anger. He was still sitting on the floor, looking so horrified and embarrassed that she felt her anger begin to melt away.

"It's okay, Torn." She sighed as she replaced the statue and walked over to him.

He looked warily up at her, expecting nothing less than a full thrashing for destroying her work. If she had been making another person as skillfully as the small woman on the shelf, he deserved nothing less.

Pulling himself to his knees, he bowed his head and waited for the punishment to begin. He had not taken this stance before, not since he was a child with his tutor, but he remembered how to make his penance.

"Torn?" Sable asked as she watched him prostrate himself before her, tensing his muscles as if waiting for a blow. "Torn, get up!"

"*Neyt*. Torn, I am, make... bad. Sable... fix?" he questioned, ready to take his punishment.

"Torn. Get up." Sable urged, reaching down to grip his arm and tugging.

Now she really felt bad. Did he expect some sort of corporal punishment from an honest mistake? *Mistake my ass*, part of her mind wondered. He destroyed a week's worth of work!

Mistake, the other half, the glamourized part, argued. Because there was no way she would have forgiven even her own mother if she had willfully destroyed one of her pieces. It had to be Faeroe glamour, but he was sincere in his apology. Hell, he was offering her a pound of his flesh. Not the flesh she would have liked to pound, but he was offering. Maybe the glamour was not of his doing. Maybe he really was sent for her, her responsibility, the... answer to her prayers?

Watching him, she realized that she had never been happy with that particular piece. She had a show to put on soon, but she was dragging her feet when it came to the work itself. Maybe he was sent to be her inspiration, her muse!

The more she thought of it, the more the idea had merit. He was sent forth for her to sculpt. Hey, the theme was mythical creatures, and she had her very own breathing myth standing, uh, kneeling before her.

"Torn, I could kiss you!" she shouted as she dropped to her knees beside him and grabbed his face between her hands.

He cocked his head to the side, wondering when the punishment would start, when she clamped her lips to his and laid the most powerful, the most energetic, the most arousing kiss on his mouth.

"Sable?" he asked as she broke off the kiss, only to reach up again and pull his mouth back to hers.

This time she forcibly ran her tongue over his lips, ending all his protests. He shuddered and opened his mouth in shock at the sheer sensuality of the movement, and inadvertently invited her inside.

With relish, Sable took up his invitation and slid her tongue into the deep cavern of his mouth, marveling at the almost-minty sweet taste of him.

She felt her nipples harden as she pressed deeper into the kiss, nudging his tongue with hers until he responded, and began to tease back. Just as she was about to rub up against him like a cat in heat, she realized what she was doing and gently broke off the kiss. Not that she regretted it, but this was not the time, the place, nor the person. She broke off the kiss to grip him in an enthusiastic hug instead.

"Torn I am, bad?" He blinked at his Sable, wondering where that had come from, but not complaining in the least.

"You are so bad!" she laughed as she pictured him in several different poses! Standing, kneeling as he was now, lying naked on his back...

Too far, she decided as her cheeks began to heat up. "Bad meaning good!" She laughed nervously as she pulled away from his heat. His body was beginning to get to her again. Maybe she was horny, but that would be a byproduct of the glamour, right?

"Torn I am, good?" he asked as he blinked his one good eye at her. The other was continuing to puff and swell.

Again she felt a sharp pang of guilt as she urged him to his feet.

"Torn is so good!" she said softly as she led him out of her studio and into the kitchen for a steak for his eye. "So very good!"

Torn shrugged his shoulders and followed the now happy Sable. Maybe the punch was enough penance. It didn't hurt much, but it was annoying the way it swelled. But what was wrong with Sable?

First, she'd hit him, and then she kissed him. Was something wrong with her, or were all women here this hormonal? Maybe it had to be all women in general, he decided as he recalled his ex-mate-to-be.

He started to send out a tendril of magic to test her, but remembered what had happened with Jack and held back. Maybe his Sable was kind of mentally... off. Maybe his Sable was like most other women. Then he remembered My Harley and shook his head.

Maybe she had a flash of the thing that made other women the confusing creatures that they were, but maybe it was now squelched, excised, like a boil. Now maybe she would go back to being his teacher and friend, just like she always had been from the day he met her. But secretly, he sighed. If she went totally back to being a tutor and a guide, he sure would miss those kisses. They got his blood flowing!

* * *

"The recon party is ready," the soldier said to Terror as he paced at the edge of the room containing the magical orb.

"Then depart, and be careful!" he cautioned. "As soon as you have the basic information that we need, hurry home. I want to find my son."

The men nodded and stepped into the room.

With a brilliant yellow/white light, they were

gone.

At the same time, an anxious servant made her way into the caverns deep within the neutral territory. Her mistress would find this information useful. Then it would buy her a bit more time to find out what the scouts knew. That was at least worth her life, she decided as she scrambled into the dark tunnels. It had to be. Her very existence depended on it!

The recon team had been assembled personally by Terror. He would take no chances with his son or his men in this strange and possibly hostile place.

"You all have your orders?" he asked the three men of his personal guard selected for this mission.

"Yes, Terror," Mace, his right-hand man and most formidable warrior, said as he looked up at his mentor, pride and determination in his eyes. "We will scout the terrain, send back information on the natives, and get to know the environment in which Torn has been surviving."

"Very good," he said and clapped Mace on the shoulder, then turned and gave the same gesture of support and respect to the other two in the small party. "Return to me as soon as you have what we need, but do not stay more than three days. I don't want to lose you men, and if the atmosphere is hostile, get back here on the double. Is that understood?"

"Yes, sir!" the men answered in unison.

Terror stepped back from the unit of loyal men, a deep pang in his chest. Had he just sent his men off to die? Would they return with the information he needed? Would they locate his son? Could all of this been avoided if he had only seen beyond his own guilt, to be the father that Torn so desperately needed?

He didn't know. The questions bothered him, but the answers that he was drawing bothered him even more. This situation was his own damn fault. The new worry and guilt added to his burden, making him sigh deeply as he watched his brave men walk into the dimensional chamber in preparation to possibly give their lives for his faults.

"These are good men, Terror," Nello said as she came to his side, easily reading his distress. "They will survive and triumph because you trained them well."

"If I had trained my own son this well, he never would have been taken in by that cold, scheming fish, Zultha. Do you know he gained no pleasure from their bed, but pleased her? That he said the intimate act was not that important in a relationship! That he would settle in and learn to enjoy their coupling? I did that to my son, Nello. I gave him that insecurity. This is all my fault. If I had been a real father --"

"Enough, Terror," Nello said, taking his face in her hands and pulling his head level with hers, interrupting his self-deprecating tirade. "You did the best you could. You made mistakes, but you are only of the mortal realm, my love. No one in any of the realms are perfect, Terror."

"Nello," Terror began, but a cool finger on his lips silenced him.

He looked into the deep lavender eyes of his love and felt a few of his doubts drift away. How he loved her, almost as much as he loved their son. He never really took the time to tell him, but that would all change, he vowed.

"*I* love you, *he* loves you, and we understand. He will be fine, Terror, because Torn is *your* son. How could he not be?"

Her simple statement of trust made his heart light and restored a bit of his self-confidence. If she held so much belief in him, how could he not hold that belief himself? He nodded as he rose to his full height.

"Good," Nello said with a smile. "Now let us concentrate on more important matters, mate. What are we going to do about Torn when he gets home?"

"Love him, Nello," Terror said with conviction. "Just love him."

* * *

"Sit still!" Sable laughed as she positioned Torn on the high stool.

Like a naughty child, he squirmed on the seat, clearly uncomfortable with his new station in life. Male model was not a job of choice for him, as his fidgeting showed.

"My Harley?" he asked, looking out of the windows at the watery sunshine.

He wanted to be out and about! He felt great, totally refreshed, and eager to explore his new world. He looked over at Sable entreatingly, but she only shook her head and smiled at him.

"I," he managed, finally mastering that personal pronoun, "want to go outside." He blinked down at her, tired of sitting and waiting.

"Not now, Torn," Sable said absently. "I need to finish this sketch, then we can go and play."

Torn snorted. He had been sitting on a cold chair for the better part of an hour, and thought it was technically no longer cold, it was still hard as hell. He was wearing something called posing slips that Jack had brought over yesterday after a small conversation with Sable.

He seemed very happy, happier than usual as he brought the tiny shorts over.

"This is a great idea, Sable!" he intoned as Jill entered, bringing up the rear, a big smile on his face.

"Can I watch?" Jillian asked cheekily, making

Jack roll his eyes and Sable explode into laughter.

Torn had merely cocked his head to the side, anxious to get the joke. But after having Jack and Jill stuff and prod his body into the tiny trunks, he was still no closer to amusement than he had been when they first entered the door.

The slips were uncomfortable and tight. They squeezed his manhood and left little to the imagination. Where the soft sweatpants and T-shirt were comfortable and relaxing, this new garment was tight and confining.

Then he had to face the indignity of being posed on this stool like a vain Eirda, the tiny winged folk who spent all day staring at their reflections in ponds, and forced to hold as still as a statue. This was *not* his idea of fun! He stared balefully at Sable and then at the sunshine, noting that the rain would probably start again, hiding the sun from view.

"Done yet?" Jill asked as he stuck his head into the room. "It's been hours, lass. Are you not going to give the kid a break?"

"What is it with you people?" Sable asked as she blew a hair out of her face in frustration. "I'm trying to work. Doesn't anyone respect the artist?"

"How about respecting the model?" Jill said as he pointed to the slim chrome watch on his wrist. "You have been torturing the boy for a good seven hours now. Time to cut him loose, Sable."

"Seven hours?" Sable almost shrieked as her eyes flew to a clock set up in the corner, then back to a bored but still fresh-looking Torn. "I didn't know so much time had passed. Sorry, Torn."

Torn blinked at his name, understanding a bit of the conversation. He nodded his head, causing long spirals to fly in his eyes, giving him an almost boyish charm for one so large and naked.

"My Harley?" he asked hopefully.

He still remembered the rush of air in his face, tearing through his hair. It was almost as fun as flying. He wanted more of that feeling, more of the rush coursing through his whole body, more of the flying feeling, without the wings. He didn't want to expose his demon to his new friends, and he *did* considered the trio as friends. He knew the two men more intimately than they did each other. But with his Sable, his mentor, he shied away from using his powers.

He didn't want to be disappointed if he delved too deeply and found something dark and dangerous.

"Oh! Our laddie wants to ride! Well, saddle him up, Sable. Time's a'wastin'. And the boys should be at the club."

"Oh, brother," Sable grumbled, picturing an innocent and tame Torn in the riotous, gay biker bar where Jack and Jill hung out. It would be like leading a lamb to slaughter. She couldn't let him go there. Of course, she was a regular there, but she could handle herself. Torn was just so innocent and sweet. Did he even know how to defend himself?

"Come on, love," Jill urged. "We even brought in some spare stovepipe stirrups for Torn. He will love the fit. They're black, to match his hair and set off his eyes."

"You are not pimping him, Jill," Sable growled as she tossed her pad onto the table and stretched her fingers.

She had not noticed how stiff and cramped they were before, but she had good nine sketches of Torn from all angles. That should be enough to start the sculptures. She hoped.

"Would I do a thing like that?"

"Yes," Jack said as he entered into the verbal fray, while walking over to the pad to see the day's progress. "Not bad, Sable."

"I would not." Jill had a wide innocent look on his face as he gazed at his huge, dark-skinned partner. "I just want to show him off and have a wee bit of fun. That's all!"

Torn's eyes flew from person to person, knowing that the topic was him and annoyed that he couldn't follow the whole conversation. But one of the best ways to learn was to be totally immersed in the subject matter, and the back and forth between the three of them was improving his understanding of the language.

"We have to protect him, Jill. Maybe now is not the time to take him for a jolly good rout with the boys."

"Sable, I'm shocked that you think we wouldn't protect him," Jill said as he stepped into the room and stopped beside Torn. "Why, he is like me own son."

"Stop it, Jill." Sable snorted, trying to hold in the laugh as the well-built Scots blinked innocently at her and managed to convey sincerity in his every move.

"One beer, Sable. Then we will return your Faeroe to you in good health!"

"Jack!" Sable turning to the man in question. "Will you do something about him?"

"Well," he said slowly, his deep voice considering. "I kind of agree with him, Sable. Torn needs to get out and experience what it is he is here to experience. It's not fair of us to keep him here. I agree that he's been sent to you for a reason, but until we find out that reason, he needs to be able to find the trouble on his own."

"His reason is to be my model," Sable argued.

"Too easy," Jack decided. "If he is here for a higher purpose, then it has to be more than being a piece of eye candy for you to mold clay after."

Sable glowered at her friend and resisted the urge to punch him. She hated it when he was right.

"Besides," Jill piped in, "all work and no play makes Torn a very dull boy. We must prevent this tragedy from happening."

"Fine." Sable gave in with ill grace. "But I'm going with you!"

"Why? Scared we might switch him, Sable love?" Jill laughed, tweaking Sable's humor and lightening up her expression.

"Seeing that his only reaction came from me, I think that I'm quite safe on that account."

Jack roared with laughter at the funny look that popped up on Jill's face. He hated to be one-upped.

"Anyway," Jack said when he toned his laughter down to a low roar, "I brought him some clothes for the trip. I assume that we will be taking the Harley?"

At the word Harley, Torn's eyes widened and a huge smile split his lips.

"I go play," he said, turning toward Jack and smiling hugely at the large man.

"*We* go play," Sable insisted as she headed for the door. "Jack, will you help Torn? Please make sure that Jill doesn't dress him up like a male prostitute."

"You mean like me?" Jill asked, preening in his tight brown chaps and matching jacket. He looked like every fashion designer's dream of a Hell's Angel, tough yet stunningly attractive.

"You are one in a million, Jill," Sable said, laughing as she left the room. "But don't make him look too hot. I don't want to have to fight for my Faeroe," she called back.

"Um, better not refer to him as 'your Faeroe,' dear," Jill replied back as he left the room to retrieve the gear he'd selected for Torn. "Then we really may have a fight on our hands."

* * *

"I'm in trouble," Sable breathed as she got a good look at Torn.

He was almost seven feet of pure sin and temptation. The black leather biker chaps molded to the thick muscles of his long legs, emphasizing his strength.

The revealing cut of the leather showed his tight rounded backside to its best advantage in the form-fitting black jeans.

A white T-shirt covered by an open black and yellow work shirt drew out the colors of his eyes, making them glow with energy and life. Over his shoulder, he carried a long black leather duster that only could belong to Jack.

On his feet were a pair of black leather boots, the small heel lending him additional height as well as throwing his pelvis and the bulge, so prominently there between his legs, forward and into plain sight.

His hair flowed long and loose from a tight tail at his nape, and around his neck, the brass torque gleamed brightly.

He was a walking god, the dominant male, and the master that could make any slave crawl to his feet. But the innocent smile and the humor in his eyes told her that it was her Torn, the same quiet Faeroe who had come to rescue her.

"I'm going to kill you, Jill!" Sable called out. But inside, as her internal organs clenched and a sudden wet heat made her blush, she said, "I'm in deep trouble!"

* * *

"Remember what I told you?" Jillian said as they walked into the dimly lit bar.

"No, thank you, I am taken," Torn repeated as he eagerly scanned the room. A large, long table set against a wall ran the length of the place. Behind this stood a man, almost large enough to be one of his father's warriors. For a moment, he felt a pang of loneliness and homesickness, but that quickly passed as he noticed that all of the men here were shorter than he, Jack, and the tall man behind the bar. Were they all half-breeds of some kind? Was he banished to a place where everyone was a half-breed, like himself? This could be… fun!

"Never again," Sable snarled as she stalked into the bar behind Jill and Torn. "Next time, he rides with you!"

If it hadn't been for Torn's demands to go faster and the delicious feel of his leather-clad legs framing her body, she just might have enjoyed the trip to town. But no! Torn had leaned over her shoulder and asked with a plaintive whine in his voice, "Faster?" More interested in speed than in the body operating the bike.

And if that wasn't bad enough, the man generated heat like a furnace. She could still feel his penetrating body heat tingling along her back and sides. It had to be the Faeroe glamour again. It just had to be. Riding with a man on back had never affected her this way. Not even "bareback riding."

This Faeroe stuff was driving her insane. But not as insane as the situation that drew her attention when she stalked into the bar before Jack. All of the men were staring, and they were staring straight at Torn. And a few of them were licking their chops.

A sudden fury galvanized her and forced her feet

to move forward. Linking her arm around Torn's waist, she narrowed her eyes and glared at the men, even a few of them she knew, until some of them turned away.

"Aren't we a bit possessive?" Jill stage-whispered to Sable, making Jack stifle his laughter as he moved them further inside K & S, one of their favorite biker bar hangouts.

"Somebody has to look out for him," Sable stage-whispered back as Jack motioned to a table nearby.

Torn moved forward then stopped as something crunched under his feet. It was some type of shaved wood on the floor, that and the shells of some kind of food a few of the men were consuming with relish, then tossing the empty hulls over their shoulders.

Very strange.

These men had to be warriors, he decided as he moved in the direction that Jack was herding them all. They were all so big and dressed in leather. He almost felt as if he was in his father's garrison in the warriors' quarters, relaxing after a hard day in the practice fields.

But those days were so very long ago, he mused with a happy little grin. And of course, he had been just a small child, not old enough to know of the taint of his mixed blood, or old enough to realize that the men had befriended him out of pity. His happy grin began to melt as his eyes took on a sad cast. This place brought so many memories, not all of them pleasant.

"Sit here, Torn." Jill pointed to a chair that was against the back wall, but facing the room. "You can protect your… assets better." He chuckled at his own wit.

"That was bad, Jill," Jack moaned as he took a seat next to Torn. Jack never sat with his back facing the room.

Sable sat across from Torn at the small round table, while Jill sat next to her. She didn't like having her back to the room, but knew that Jack would protect them if something unpleasant happened. But she doubted that anything would. She knew the bar, knew some of the people, but she just didn't like taking chances.

Besides, with her facing Torn, she could see him if he was suddenly overtaken by fear. She thought she could read his expressions pretty well by now, and knew she would watch for any signs of him becoming uncomfortable, then hustle him out of there, pronto.

"What will it be, big guy?" a deep voice asked, and they all looked up to see a man, roughly the size of the bartender, which put him around seven feet tall, hovering over their table.

"Jase!" Jack exclaimed as he stood to shake the tall, red-haired man's hand. "It's been a while."

"And whose fault is that?" the man asked back, his mouth splitting into a grin showing gaps where several teeth were missing.

"Well, you know how it is." Jack smiled. "Running a business, keeping the partner happy, trying to keep my head above water."

"I hear ya," the man answered back, his thick Scottish brogue sounding musical to the ears. "Times is tough for us all. And who's the laddie there beside you?"

"This is Torn," Jill said, rolling his eyes at Jase. "And you can at least say hi to an old friend."

Jase's face exploded into color, as he shuffled his feet, an almost funny gesture for a man his size.

"I saw ya, Jillian," the man said, a small bit of shame coloring his voice. "And you too, Sable." He gave her a polite nod. "I was just curious about your new friend and all."

"Torn," Jillian said, turning to face the too-wide-eyed, innocent, curious stare of his "friend," "this is Jase. We used to ride together, before he and his brother bought this bar."

"I· am taken," Torn said, smiling happily up at the man. He could follow a bit of the conversation and he found him to be rather nice. He resisted the urge to send out a tendril of power, seeing that his control was so shaky now, but he tilted his head to the side and smiled.

"Damn," Jase said, and pouted a bit. "Just my luck. All of the good ones are taken or straight."

Jill, Sable, and Jack exploded into laugher, leaving a still smiling Torn to look confused and bemused.

"So who's he with?" Jase asked, still eyeing the cut of Torn's jacket. "And I know that you two married queens aren't into threesomes."

"He's with me," Sable said, a smile in her voice as she watched the man check out her man.

"I knew it!" Jase said with a good-natured laugh. "It was just too good to be true. All of that hair and the man is straight. My heart is broken."

"I really feel for you." Jill snorted as he rolled his eyes at the sadly pouting Jase.

"Since I'm not getting any phone numbers, what can I get you to drink?"

"Sex on the beach!" Jill piped in and laughed as the tall man groaned.

"You are breaking my heart, boyo. And that's the truth," Jase wrote down the order.

"I could have a Screaming Horny Monkey, but I thought that would be pushing it," Jill said, with an absurdly serene face.

"A beer, please," Jack said, breaking into the conversation before it escalated into a battle of wits. "And one for Torn."

"A beer?" Sable hissed. "I don't know, Jack. Remember the sandwich."

"It wasn't the sandwich," Jill protested. "I keep telling you if God did not mean for us to eat meat, he wouldn't have made it taste so good!"

"A beer should be fine, Sable," Jack reassured her. "He's a big man. He can handle it."

"Well --"

"Let a man be a man," Jase interrupted. "And besides, what could happen?"

As it turned out, he nearly got them all killed.

Chapter Six

Torn examined the tall frosted glass they put in front of him. "Beer?" he asked, having understood much of their conversation.

"Not just beer, Lad. *Guinness*! The stuff that's good for you. This stuff beats the hell out of milk," Jase said with a grin as he reverently placed a similar mug in front of Sable and Jack, a tall red mixed drink in front of Jill.

"It's okay, Torn," Sable said as she looked at him reassuringly. "Try it. It may be an acquired taste."

"What's wrong with him that you guys are ordering for him and whatnot?" Jase asked, his brow furrowing a bit.

"Nothing," Jill easily answered. "He's from out of town. He can barely speak English."

"Oh! A foreign devil then." Jase laughed and Sable groaned. "Well then, drink up, lad."

Drink and *up* were two words that Torn understood quite well. *Drink* because he had earlier discovered a wondrous delight called orange juice, and *up* because it was the new word he used to describe his body.

Around Sable, it was almost always up. The ride over here nearly killed him. He could still feel the outline of her body pressed against his chest and inner thighs.

From the moment they took off down the rough roads, he kept being bumped closer and closer to her. And the vibrations of the machine made her tight flesh quiver inside of the leather pants she wore like a second skin.

His only hope of not embarrassing himself and her was to lean over and urge her to drive faster. But that only brought his chest in closer contact with the taut flesh of her back and her feminine heat he could feel, even through the barrier of their clothing.

He had to sit back and remind himself that she was his teacher and friend, not a bed conquest. As if he would ever try that again!

He looked up at her just in time to see her lick a bit of white foam off her upper lip as she lowered her mug of beer to the table. Then she smiled at him. Torn groaned and reached for his mug, suddenly very thirsty.

With one last look at her, he slammed the drink down, not tasting it one bit, but needing the cold liquid to cool his blood. The empty mug hit the table and he looked up at the surprised faces of the men around him.

"Wherever he comes from," Jase said reverently, "they sure taught him how to knock it back. Want another, lad?"

"Another?" Torn asked as he blinked at the empty mug, unable to believe it was gone when he still had this fire in his veins. "Yes! And Torn, I am!"

"Got ya." Jase laughed and left to get another.

"Is he supposed to be drinking like that?" Sable asked as she looked from the empty mug to her Faeroe. "Do you think that it's safe?"

"Well, Finn McCool was always getting drunk," Jill said as he also stared at the empty mug. Guinness was a hard drink, a strong drink, and Torn had pounded it back as if it were water.

"He's not Finn McCool," Sable said, examining Torn for any adverse reaction.

"And he's not a Faeroe either," Jack added as he sipped his own liquid libation.

"Is too a Faeroe!" Sable hissed, narrowing her

eyes at Jack.

"Then I'm a really lucky man," Jase added as he plunked the next mug in the table in front of Torn. "But I'm not getting a beep on the radar, and it never fails me."

"Never mind." Sable picked up her mug and took a long pull.

"Believe me, I won't!" Jase said as he turned away to see to his other customers. "But if you want me to test him just in case…"

He laughed as he walked away.

"Beer," Torn said again, this time taking a sip of the brew, tasting it, hoping that moving his concentration to his drinking endeavors would cool his ardor.

"The best beer," Jack said as he lifted his glass to Torn.

"Another," Torn said as he lifted the mug and drained it, then got a glimpse of Sable licking a fleck of foam from her upper lip, her pink tongue quick and tempting as she left her upper lip glistening.

Concentrating on the taste wasn't helping. "I think --" Sable began, but was cut off.

"If he wants his spirits, let the man have his spirits." Jill laughed, picturing a sloshed Torn on the bike ride home. Good thing he rode with Jack. They might have to call a taxi for Sable and Torn and ride Sable's bike back home.

"If he dies on me, you are dead meat, Jillian," Sable growled.

"It's hops and barley, woman. They're vegetables!"

She glared just glared at him.

"Ignore her!" Jill took Torn by the hand and pulled him to his feet. "Time to dance."

"Dance?" Torn asked as he began to blink rapidly. Funny, but suddenly the heat in his blood had nothing to do with lusting after his teacher. Suddenly, it was just plain *hot*!

He pulled off the long leather coat Jack had lent him and neatly folded it over the chair before following Jill to a cleared area in the room.

"What is he doing?" Sable hissed as she began to rise to her feet.

"He's having a bit of fun, Sable," Jack said as he placed his hand on her arm, halting her movement. "The worse that will come out of this is that Torn may have a hangover tomorrow. But he is a big boy and Jill will look out for him. He's a lot tougher than he looks."

"If you think so…"

Sable wasn't really convinced, but then maybe she was holding on too tightly to him. Maybe it wasn't fair to try and keep him under lock and key. But almost losing him the way she had -- well, that was enough to scare anybody.

But he looked so healthy now, and he had rhythm, she laughed to herself, watching him gyrate on the floor to some music Jill had started with a few coins in the jukebox.

I'm too Sexy! Jack laughed as he watched Jill and Torn romp on the dance floor to that old Right Said Fred song. "He *would* pick that song."

"It fits," Sable admitted and blushed as Jack shot her a piercing look. "Well, he *is* too sexy. Look at his shoulders, Jack. The man is seriously built. And that butt…"

She laughed as Jack smirked at her.

"I thought you didn't notice things like that."

"I'm a woman, Jack. And all of those hard muscles and that golden skin. Golden shoulders without a mark or a scar."

Sable sighed as more and more of his damn near perfect body was exposed to her eyes.

"And check out the definition in the delt... Oh my God, Jack. He's stripping!"

By the time Sable forced her way through the considerable barrier of leather-clad men, the music had changed again. Now, Groove Armada's *I See You, Baby!* was blasting, and Torn was definitely *shaking that ass.*

"Torn!" she screamed as he tossed his second shirt to a grinning Jillian and began to gyrate in earnest. Sable's eyes just about popped from her head as he ripped the thong holding back his long curls and tossed his hair to the beat of the music.

The crowd went wild as his whole body played an erotic game of peekaboo with his hair. His arms held in front of his face, his hands fisted, Torn was oblivious to it all, lost in the beat of the music.

This is like the warriors' quarters, Torn thought as he moved his body to the rhythm of this strange music. He couldn't follow the words, but the intent of the music was clear. It was designed for one thing and one thing only -- to make you move your body.

At the warriors' quarters, it was considered a game of skill to see who could keep the beat and invent the most outlandish movements. Torn had never been the best at this game, but he wasn't the worst, either. So as the music continued to pound from some unknown source, he decided to prove his masculinity by outmaneuvering every other man in the place. And maybe impress Sable at the same time, although he still had no idea why impressing her was so important.

Maybe it was the drink, he decided, this beer. It was tasty, although nothing like Zolk's Blood, the potent, fiery red drink made from fermented *zolk* plants. But this beer possessed a weak charm of its own.

Why was it suddenly so hot in here? Why was the room beginning to spin? Torn shrugged off those worries as the beat of the music changed and he tossed his clothing to Jillian. He would have been content to toss them anywhere, but they were not his clothing. They belonged to Jack.

Big Jack, strong Jack, Jack who kissed Jill, he thought as his mind began to swirl. Jack and Jill went up a hill. Isn't that what he'd read was in the learning books? Maybe this beer wasn't weak at all! But the rhythm moved him again, and again he was lost.

"Torn?" Sable asked. "Torn!" she said a bit louder. "Torn! You put your clothes back on!"

Torn's eyes popped open as he thought that he heard Sable's voice. By now, he couldn't see her; she was lost in the sea of men that had surrounded him. Did they want to practice the skill of dance also? No, he decided. They just wanted to watch a new warrior and perhaps pick up a few new moves. He hoped he could teach them something. A lot of them looked like they needed to do some sort of exercise more often, with all the bulging drink bellies he observed.

"Torn!" Sable called again, then decided to put an end to this herself.

Now, Torn was doing some kind of martial arts' maneuver kind of thing. He bent his knees, bent forward then jumped, twisting his body in midair and landing on his feet, all to the beat of the music. Hair flying madly as he moved, he was a picture of grace and skill.

He even had a smile on his face as he completed a full Russian split, legs completely out to his sides and torso resting on the ground, then pulled himself back up again.

"Jean-Claude Van Damme, eat your heart out," someone bellowed.

"Go, baby! Move it, stud!" another man called out, and Sable's patience snapped. Forcing her way through the throng of excited men, she stormed over to a laughing Jillian and snatched the shirts from his hand.

"Hey, Sable!" he called loudly to be heard over the bass of the music and the roar of the men.

"Don't you hey me!" Sable snarled. "I leave you alone for a minute with Torn and now he thinks he's a Chippendale!"

"He is hot," Jill protested, a huge smile on his face.

"I'll hot you," Sable threatened as she turned her back on the laughing man to stop Torn before he decided that he was still hot and removed his pants.

"Torn!" she screamed as he began to gyrate his hips, while rolling his shoulders in an unwholesome manner. "Stop it!"

Torn paused mid-hip roll and looked over toward his teacher's voice. "Sable!" he called, moving to stand at his full height and reached for her.

"Torn, put your clothes back on!" she called, and her words were met with a barrage of boos and hisses.

"Leave him alone," some man called out while another exclaimed. "Just like a woman to ruin a man's good time."

Still another called out, "Ditch the bitch and make the switch! I'll help you out, stud!"

Sable face flushed with furious color as she pulled back against Torn's grip.

"No dancing, Torn! Get dressed!" she said under her breath, trying to prevent a confrontation.

"If she won't dance," one intrepid soul called out, "I will!"

His comment caused loud guffaws among the men, and she blushed even redder, if that were possible.

"Dance?" Torn asked, gyrating his hips at her and tossing his hair back to get a better view of her face.

"Dance." She nodded, then pushed the shirts at him, hoping against hope he would get the message so that they could get him dressed and out of there before something bad happened. She suddenly had a funny feeling...

"*Neyt*! Too hot!" he said shaking his head, but pulling her harder. "Sable dance." Sable dug her heels in and shook her head frantically.

Feeling her discomfort, Torn released her, but still decided to impress her with his moves.

As the music changed again to Lenny Kravitz's version of "American Woman", Torn's eyes began to glint with challenge. He would show Sable his skill with body movements, and then he could kiss her.

Kiss her? Yes, kiss her, he decided as suddenly as if the taste of her lips was sweeter than any orange that he had tasted here.

A wicked smile pulled at the corners of his lips as his eyes narrowed in sudden desire.

The men, noticing a different feel to the air, hooted and called out encouragement, knowing that something big was about to happen.

Taking three steps back from her, Torn suddenly threw back his head and chest, and thrust his whole crotch in her direction.

It was a blatantly sexual move and the crowd loved it. The tension in the room increased suddenly, and a few men found themselves growing hot as well, not to mention a shocked Sable.

Coming out of the powerful arch, Torn threw himself forward on his knees and slid a few inches to stop in front of her.

Somebody screamed a wild hoot of excitement, as Torn began to wind his body to the beat of the music.

Shoveling both hands through his hair, he shoved it back off his face as he rose high on his knees before her, lightly brushing her with his heaving chest.

Sable was entranced and mystified as she watched the innocent, calm, and demure Faeroe who lived in her house, turn into this sexual dynamo. He packed each move with more testosterone than a triple shot of the most potent aphrodisiac man had ever devised, or even thought of.

He oozed sex and the forbidden erotic arts. His every gyration screamed of the pleasure one could find in his bed, and she was not the only one affected. Torn gripped her hips in his hot hands as he rose to his feet, slowly dragging his hands up until his thumbs rested just beneath her breasts. Her breathing caught and her eyes widened at the feel of fire spreading along her body from contact with his heat.

But Torn was not quite done. Pushing back from her, he gripped her hand and placed it low on the ripped eight-pack of a stomach he possessed, rolling his abs as he held her hand to his body, letting her feel his strength. Sable gasped and someone screamed, "Owwwww!" before he released her hand and suddenly dropped to one knee.

In a series of quick moves, he ducked an invisible attack, turned and threw up his hands as if warding off a blow, threw himself backwards, his legs flying out in front, then behind him as he executed a neat backflip, landing on bent knees. Then just as quickly, he lay back on the gritty floor, oblivious to the scratchy wood that coated its surface, and pulling his legs up, threw himself to his feet and rose to his full height.

Loud clapping and hooting accompanied his move as he executed it with ease and skill. Tossing his hair in Sable's direction, he threw out an arm, hand extended in invitation as his chest, coated in a light sheen of sweat, heaved with his breaths. Dumbfounded, Sable stood there, his shirts clutched in her hand, not knowing what to do.

"Take his hand!" Jillian hissed, suddenly appearing behind her.

"If she won't, I will!" another man called out as the room grew silent except for the heavy beat and Lenny's voice listing all of the reasons that he should walk away.

Without even realizing it, the whole room had become entangled in this courtship of sorts. They were now holding their breaths in anticipation, waiting anxiously to see the outcome of this tableau.

"Sable? You don't have to if you don't want to," Jack said. He'd appeared behind Jill and laid a hand on his partner's shoulder. He too was drawn into this drama being played out on the dance floor of a biker bar, somewhere in the middle of Scotland, and he waited to see what his friend would do next.

Hands trembling, Sable reached out slowly, tentatively, wanting to touch this man and share in the wonder of him. Her eyes grew wide and her nostrils flared as she inhaled his essence. The clothing dropped unnoticed to the floor as her feet took those first steps toward her destiny.

Torn stood motionless, arm extended, his heart

still beating heavily in his chest. Would she accept his invitation? Would she touch him again, like she had before he drained his energy? Would she take him as he was?

Their fingers touched, just a light, brushing contact, and an almost visible heat flared between the two. The room, as a whole, drew in their collective breaths as those fingers slid together, mingling, becoming one.

Then the front door slammed open.

"Well, looks like we have ourselves a problem, boys," a loud voice sneered. "I want to party, and the place is filled with wankers!"

"Garth!" Jase bellowed as he stepped forward. "I thought I told you never to come back here."

"I didn't come alone this time, Jase, old buddy," the man replied meanly, his British accent sounding odd in a room filled with Scotsmen. "This time, I brought me pals."

Three warrior-sized men entered the bar, all carrying small but effective weapons, sending a ripple of unease through the crowd.

Suddenly, all of Torn's senses went on red alert, the creature inside him began to gnash its teeth and fight for an opening.

These men smelled like evil, smelled cold and dank. They smelled like prey to the Reaver. The only question was to either cleanse their souls, to take their evil into his abyss, or to reave their souls.

"Torn?" Sable asked, but he had already pulled away from her. He pushed his way through the crowd, almost on autopilot as he made his way to the front of the group of suddenly tense men to stand beside Jase.

"What's this?" the intruder asked in sarcastic tones. "You got yourself a pet, Jase?" His cronies laughed. But they fell silent as Garth's next words rang out loud and clear.

"Which one to kill first?"

"Torn," Sable whispered as she tried to work her way to the front of the crowd.

"Leave him alone," Jillian urged. She had not even noticed the Scotsman make his way to her side. On her other side stood Jack, looking menacing as ever.

"Is there a problem?" he asked Jase as he looked at the bar owner.

Jase's brother calmly made his way from behind the bar to stand near his brother and Torn.

"Mason." Jack acknowledged Jase's silent brother with a single nod.

"I think you blokes had better leave," Jase said, not backing down from the man and his two friends who had invaded his bar. "I want no trouble with you, Garth."

His voice was deadly cold, and all who heard him knew that the playful Jase meant every word.

"Who's your new girlfriend?" Garth sneered, recovering himself a bit and glaring at Torn.

"I wish!" Jase said loudly. "Or better, *you* wish. You were always a size queen, Garth!"

"You calling me a poofter?" Garth roared, his face turning bright red at the insult. "Why you --"

"You didn't complain last year, friend," Jase interrupted, smirking as Garth's two buddies lost some of their outrage and glared at their ringleader.

"That's a bloody lie!" Garth raged, his anger spurring him on despite the fact that he was outnumbered by the men in the bar.

"Breakups can sometimes be *so* nasty!" Jase said loudly an aside to anyone who would listen, which basically was the whole bar.

"I thought you said that he owed you something." one of Garth's friends said, backing away from his fearless leader.

Seeing his backup abandoning him drove Garth to actions any normal, sane man would have avoided.

With a wordless roar, he barreled toward Jase, pipe raised above his head. Even if he got the snot beat out of him, he would at least mess up the pretty smile on Jase's face first.

His action, although expected, was so swift everyone was caught off guard. Everyone, that is, except for Torn. One of the hallmarks of his father's training was to always be ready for the unexpected. Garth's sudden lunge toward Jase's unprotected body was something Torn had hoped wouldn't happen but expected nevertheless.

Jase stepped back reflexively, the pipe momentarily stealing his ability to move. The bar-goers all drew in a gasp, sure they would see blood fly. But the pipe never connected with Jase's shocked face. Instead, it slammed into Torn's open palm, who'd thrown out his left arm just as the metal was about to make contact. It hit his hand with a meaty *thump*, causing him to wince in pain.

Garth had swung the pipe with his considerable weight behind the blow. It would have broken Jase's nose, or worse, with the force of the blow. But it stopped dead in the bare-chested man's palm, his hand not moving an inch.

"You hit me," Torn said as his eyes began to glitter and glow.

"What the fuck?" the man uttered as his body began to shake with fear.

"You hit me," Torn said again. "I do not like you."

"My God!" Jase said, the color draining from his face as he saw how close he'd been to several painful days in a hospital, if not a morgue. "You saved my life! Garth tried to kill me."

Then his face turned a mottled shade of red as he realized what he'd just said. "Garth tried to kill me. You bloody bugger. I'll have your head for this!"

With a roar, Jase launched himself at the still shaken Garth, determined to put an end to his miserable life. But Garth's two buddies were not about to see their friend get pounded into a bloody pulp. With chains swinging and bats raised, they went after Jase, who was trying his best to get around Torn to reach Garth.

"Damn it!" a voice yelled as Mason leapt into the fray, protecting his brother. Jack dove at the third man, bringing him to the ground, as Jillian grabbed Sable by the arm and pulled her to safety behind the bar.

"Torn!" she screamed, trying to fight her way through the rowdy bunch of bikers to reach his side. "Torn! Jillian, let me go! I have to help Torn!"

"Help him by staying out of the bloody way!" Jill hollered back as he pushed her head below the bar just as a large beer mug flew past her head.

"Torn!" Sable screamed again, then rounded on Jill. "*This is all your fault!*"

But Jill couldn't answer; he was busy pummeling the unfortunate who'd decided to make the fight a free-for-all and hopped over the bar to get the ones he saw as weak.

Jill's fist had neatly connected the man's jaw when Sable began to rail at him.

"What harm can happen in the pub, you said," she screeched, ignoring the man who'd collapsed to the other side of the bar with a helpful shove from Jill, only to be replaced by another eager contestant. "He'll be safe, you said!"

She picked up a full bottle of Canadian Mist -- she never liked the stuff anyway -- - and broke it over the head of a man who was trying to get around her to get to Jill's back. "This is all your fault!"

"Fight now, get hormonal later," Jill shouted as he ducked a wild swing and delivered a solid punch to brawler's stomach. The winded man was then promptly tossed over the bar as Jill prepared for the next combatant.

"Hormonal?" Sable screeched as she picked up a half empty mug of Busch beer and poured it in the face of some unfortunate who got too close to her then smashed the bottle over his head.

"Hormonal!" Jill repeated as he dodged a flying mug of Guinness. He bowed his head for a moment at the tragedy of the spilled brew before yanking Sable out of the way as a body came crashing over the bar. "Anything that bleeds for days on end and doesn't die is just too damn weird to be anything but hormonal!"

He heaved the loopy man back to the other side of the bar and leaned back to take a breather.

All around them, the fighting rose to melee proportions. Men yelled and cursed, threw punches, and knocked heads together. It was a scene out of the old western saloon brawls, but worse. It was almost a good old-fashioned Scottish Riot.

Soon the fight would spill out into the street, and the Bobbies would be called in.

"Jillian! I have to do something about Torn. He could be getting hurt!"

But at that moment, Torn was delivering a roundhouse kick to some man's chest, then spinning on the balls of his feet to come around and throw a punch at another man's face.

Roaring in outrage, he lifted one man bodily over his head and tossed him into a pile gathering around Jack and Jase.

Mason had taken someone's bat and was lining up his head for a swing, while Garth struggled to his feet to make a rush for the front door.

Torn saw him leaving, and using the back of a stumbling man, launched himself across the room; his brass torque glowing like the swinging pub lights as he dove at Garth. He landed on the man's back and took him to the peanut shell-encrusted floor.

Garth twisted around as best as he could and started swinging. He hadn't wanted this to escalate into a riot; he'd only wanted to pay Jase back for making him gay. He never knew that the man was gay until Jase told him over a few beers. And that led to that night when he...

Feeling betrayed, he'd vowed to pay the man back for making him waste his time with a queer, although secretly Garth felt an attraction for the large man. That fear of his own sexuality had egged him on to prove that he was the better man, that he was superior, that he was most definitely *not* gay.

He hadn't expected payback to get so out of control. Now he only wanted to get out of there as fast as possible, before something else went wrong. But now, there was the shirtless pansy on his back!

"You hit me!" Torn said again as he rose to his feet, bringing Garth along with him, lifting him to his toes by the front of his jacket, then off of the ground as he forced him to meet his eyes.

"I didn't mean to!" he stammered. "I meant to hit Jase!"

"Why?" Torn asked, shaking the man. These

people were hard to understand and erupted into violence so easily. He wanted to understand before the kill.

"Because he kissed me!"

Garth's answer didn't feel right. Taking a chance, he opened the hold on his powers a bit, and felt a tendril leap out of control and wrap around the struggling man.

"My GOD!" Garth screamed as he felt the power pulsing through him.

But everyone was too busy brawling to pay attention to what was going on at the front door. No one noticed the faint glow that surrounded two men in the excitement and violence that swirled around them.

Torn stared into Garth's eyes and found the truth.

"You kissed him!" Torn said calmly. "*You* kissed *him*! You think him... pretty."

"That's a lie!" Garth screamed, struggling against his hold.

Holding back the tendril with some effort, Torn broke contact with the man and stared at him.

"Tell the truth," he said. There was something good left in this man's soul, but he felt no need to cleanse him. If Jase wanted him dead for his insults, then he would kill the man outright, but Torn felt there was something worth salvaging.

"It's a goddammed lie!" Garth yelled as he struggled to break free of Torn's hold. Torn shook his head at the falsehoods that kept pouring out of the man's mouth. He felt an overwhelming sense of fear coming from him and wondered why.

Jack kissed Jill and didn't lie about it. Sable, his teacher, had never lied. Jase hadn't lied about being attracted to him. Why would this man lie about being attracted to Jase?

"I not lie!" Torn said calmly, the eyes of truth staring into his soul. He felt his power began to pour through the man, easing the fears and allowing him to see with unfettered vision what he was doing to innocents.

"Let me go!" Garth pleaded, seeing his own soul and not liking truth. "Please, man! Leave me with my dignity!"

While Torn was trying to piece together the meaning of the word dignity, there was a shout from behind him.

"Let him go, freak!" the man called, and Torn reacted just in time to duck under the chain that was headed in his direction.

Dropping Garth, he turned to face the man wielding the chain.

"Let it go, Robbie!" Garth yelled as he hit the floor on his backside and saw who was attacking the man. The same man who was trying to force him to see the truth he already knew. "Just leave off!"

"Bugger off!" Robbie shouted back, the battle heat flaming in his eyes. He swung the chain again, only this time, Torn threw his arm up to deflect the blow, then sucked in his breath as the hard chain wrapped punishingly around his forearm, bruising the bone with the force of its blow. "That bastard's unnatural!"

Robbie had seen the glow shoot around his friend, and now he wanted this devil gone and away from this place. He was a demon. No mortal man could fight like that!

Gripping a portion of the links in his fist, Torn gave the chain a heave, ripping it from the man's hands, leaving him defenseless.

"Leave off!" Garth yelled again, climbing to his feet and rushing by Torn. "This was a mistake. Let it go!"

But Robbie ignored him. With a roar, he plowed into Torn, knocking him through the doors and into the street.

"No!" Garth yelled, racing after them. He didn't want anyone to get hurt, and Robbie was a bit of a lunatic when it came to fighting.

Seeing Torn get knocked out of the door, Jill and Sable raced from around the bar, dodging struggling bodies, to follow.

Seeing his partner and his friend rush out, Jack knocked out his opponent with a quick jab to the face, and charged out after them.

It happened just as Torn shook off the crazed man, knocking him into the alley beside the pub and following him in. Garth, Jill, Sable and Jack quickly followed them, only to hear the man shout, "I have a pistol!"

"Gun!" Sable called out, racing toward a confused Torn.

"Pistol?" Torn asked as the man backed further into the alley.

"Robbie, no!" Garth screamed, racing forward.

"Torn!" Jack bellowed. "Get away!"

But confused, Torn took another step toward the man. "Pistol?" he asked, head cocked to the side.

"Get away!" the man screamed. "I saw what you did to Garth! Get away from me!" Torn blinked twice, then a sound like concentrated thunder shook the alley with echoing vibrations.

Torn reached down, touched his hand to a sharp, burning pain in his chest, then raised it to his eyes. His breath caught and his eyes watered, but there was too much pain for actual movement. He let it wash over his body.

Blood, he thought, before the next searing wave of pain hit, almost bringing him to his knees.

"*Torn*!" Sable shrieked, racing forward, ignoring the man with the gun, followed by Jill and Jack, who was trying their best to stop her.

"Robbie!" Garth yelled. "What have you done, man?"

But the pain cost Torn the last of his control. The torque around his neck glowed, and a low wind circled around the alley. His eyes radiated an eerie red as his hair floated around his body.

A low growl began to flow from his throat as the smell of sulfur filled the alley.

No, Torn screamed inside as he felt his body began to shift and change. *Please no*! But it was too late.

The creature inside him stirred, awakened by its counterpart's pain and need. It flexed its muscles and prepared to force the transformation, now that Torn was too weak to hold him back. Inside, it rejoiced. The Reaver was reborn, and it was breaking free!

* * *

Mace gasped as he and his two men dropped out of thin air and into the midst of a battle.

Men cursed in a strange language while soldiers dressed in gray uniforms blew whistles and wielded clubs. Blood ran in the street as fists collided with bodies, and bodies hit the ground with great regularity. Strange glasses of nut-brown brew were being drunk by some weary combatants as they observed the remaining fighters, while still others cheered for their favorite warrior.

The men were basically coarse, loud, and arrogant.

The only thing separating them from the warriors that they trained with was the fact that they were all so terribly short.

"Bloody hell!" one man stammered as he looked up and saw the three giants getting to their feet. "What beanstalk did you fall from? I think I'm in love!"

Jase, fresh from the battle and making his exit before the coppers could catch him, bumped into three king-size wet dreams! They were all dressed in tight black leather pants and vests of the same shade. All three carried hefty packs on their backs.

"Blooooddeeee heel?" the one who looked to be in charge said, face scrunching up in confusion.

"I take it you blokes aren't from around here?" he asked, just as a shot rang out in the night from the direction of the alley running alongside the bar.

"What now?" he asked as he turned and raced in that direction, the cops hot on his tail, and curiously enough, the three tall men.

* * *

"Torn!" Sable screamed again as the tall man fell to his knees among the dirt and filth of the alley. "Let me go!" she railed at Jack and Jill. "Let me go to him, damn it!"

She struggled and fought like a madwoman as Robbie shrank back against a wall and Garth stared in shock at the situation before him.

The glow from the torque lit up the alley as Torn folded over in pain. His eyes began to pulse, matching the torque's glow, while a low groaning sound filled the air.

"What is happening?" Garth stammered as he took a step back and almost into Jack and Jill, who were doing their best to subdue Sable. "What in the name of all that's holy is happening?"

Torn bent low, fighting against all odds to keep this transformation from occurring, but it was impossible at this point. His corporeal body was too weak, draining fast, and his will to fight it seemed to be leaving with his blood.

He slammed one hand down among the muck that surrounded him and steadied himself for the change.

No, his mind wailed as he felt his friends and his teacher, his beloved teacher, behind him, witnessing the abnormality that he was. There would be no more smiles or gestures of friendship from these dear, sweet people. From now on he would only see revulsion and disgust.

He braced himself to let go of all that he had learned and had come to love.

"We are one, brother," the Reaver seemed to whisper, breaking into his thoughts. "There is no you or I. Here there is only we."

Then the transformation began, fast as lightning and as fierce as a magical rampage. Lights flashed around his body as his hair flowed freely on some unseen wind. His eyes flamed bright, purple fire, and a deep growl started in his throat. The force of his body changing thrust him backwards on his knees, arching his chest painfully as his arms flew out to his sides.

Angel's wings, black as sin, exploded from his back to spread out around his arms as his skin darkened in color. His eyes, glowing a bright, fierce purple changed to red as his claws exploded from his fingertips. His body began to grow until even on his knees, his growth was amazing and noticeable.

There was a sound of ripping flesh as his thigh muscles expanded, tripling in size, sending murky water splattering around him as they grew to monstrous proportions. His whole body became one large mass of intimidating muscle as laughter rumbled from his chest.

Those glowing red orbs pinned Robbie to the wall; the man's fear at the sight overrode his flight-or-fight instincts. He could do nothing but whimper in shock as the gun trembled useless in his hands.

"*Betocit* Reaver!" the Torn-beast rumbled, and Robbie opened his mouth to scream, but no sounds emerged from his body. Awaken, Reaver!

"Holy Mother of God!" Jillian muttered as he stared wide-eyed at the beast standing in front of him.

"Torn?" Sable asked, her voice shaking and cracking as so many emotions flooded her body. Strangely enough, fear wasn't one of them.

Jack remained speechless. There were no words for what he was feeling.

"What is it?" Garth asked, eyes wide as he stared at the creature his friend had released.

"Help me!" Robbie babbled as the creature turned glowing red eyes to him and rose in one seamless motion to his feet.

He was over eight feet tall! The remnants of his leather pants lay around him like so many castoff peanut shells, only a few remaining scraps left to cover his masculinity.

"Help me!" Robbie cried again as his bladder suddenly released, flooding the front of his pants.

"*Holstos Reaver*!" the creature hissed and thrust out his hand.

Robbie screamed as the light encased him. But instead of a comforting white glow, this light was as red as blood and felt like the hand of death. Suddenly, all the things that he had done in his past floated before his eyes.

He saw the time he'd slapped his mother in a fit of rage because she wouldn't leave his drunken abusive father, and in the doing became just like his old man. He saw the bar fights he'd started, the innocents he'd preyed upon, the money he'd stolen. Then he saw the first person he'd shanked, and how powerful he'd felt at the life draining out of that man, his warm lifeblood flooding over his hand, the dying gurgles his victim had made. He saw how the killing became easier, how he'd lost respect for life, his or anyone else's. He saw that he'd had come to this bar with that idiot Garth with the intentions of killing some fags, that he would go home and wank off with the thought of the excitement, the god-like power he felt, destroying people. He wasn't homophobic or racist; he was an equal opportunity killer, and he'd needed to get his fill of blood that night. He had no remorse.

But now, guilt and shame ate at him, tugged at his very core. He saw what he had become, and not the glorified image he managed to maintain to cover the ugliness that dwelled beneath his very shallow surface. Now he saw himself for what he really was, a predator -- no, a scavenger. A predator killed for a reason; he just preyed on the weaker for the sport of it, for the artificial rush of power, and he knew he wouldn't stop. And now, he faced a creature that was far greater than himself.

He saw a reflection of himself in this creature with skin as dark as the evil he'd absorbed, and he trembled.

The red light began to fade as an eerie silence filled the alley. Everyone remained mute, staring in horror at Robbie, who whimpered and fell to his knees.

No one dared to move, dared to blink, dared to

breathe. The creature dominated the alley and all waited to see what he would do next.

Large wings snapped, the sound of flowing silk, as he thrust them outwards before extending them to their highest span. He raised one hand, lifted one finger, and pointed at Robbie.

"*Tock laif et Reeve-ah*!" Your soul is reaved!

"What the fuck?"

Everyone turned as Jase, followed by three huge men, rounded the corner, the police not too far behind.

"Torn!" Mace called out, eyes wide in amazement as he once again saw the Reaver of Souls up close.

"*Za volt*!" the Reaver called as a single feather, black as death, snapped at Robbie, striking him in the chest, before the Reaver took to the skies. The mark.

Torn launched himself into the night, quickly blending into the blackness, leaving nine stunned people behind. Before he lost himself into the cloaking darkness, he looked back and glimpsed Sable's face. It was pale and shocked, her eyes wide in disbelief as she watched the creature that he had become, saw the beast that resided within him.

In that instant, he knew he could never return to her, to subject her life to the darkness that lay beneath the surface of his skin.

What his father's warriors were doing here, he hadn't a clue, but if they could help him get back home, he would welcome even their intervention.

It was easy to trace those of the Magic Realm, he thought to himself as he flung himself ever higher toward the velvet, midnight-blue sky. The stars shone brightly around him as he flew toward the moon, trying to forget the pale, haunted face that his teacher now possessed because of him.

He looked upward at the diamond-bright stars and never once noticed his tears added to the shining brightness dotting the heavens.

Chapter Seven

"Who *are* you people?" Sable asked, voice hollow with shock, eyes wide, as she turned to face Jase and the three newcomers. "You called out his name."

"What the fuck was that?" Garth half-laughed half-cried as he looked at the feather sticking out of Robbie's chest. "Ah, Robbie, what have you unleashed, man?"

"What was that thing?" Jase asked, still breathing hard from his running and from what he had just witnessed.

"Who are you?" Sable said again, turning to Mace and the two warriors who accompanied him. "Where are you from? *Answer me!*" she yelled at the silent giants, dimly noting they stood at least seven feet tall, towering over Jack and Torn.

"I don't think they can understand you," Jack said quietly, touching her stiff shoulder, drawing her wild gaze.

"Somebody had better understand something!" she demanded hysterically, jerking free of his touch.

"Now, love…" Jillian began, but she whirled on him.

"A night of hanging with the boys, Jillian? Let the man breathe, Jillian? I let the man breathe and look what the fuck happened! Shit!" she screamed. "What is he? What is the man I love?"

She began to shake, to pace, unable to deal with what she had just seen, oblivious to the men standing around her.

"*Ib got Torn*," Mace said quietly, eyeing the woman who had screamed the name of their leader's son. It was Torn.

"What caused this change?" Del asked. He was

first behind Mace in command, and with his bright red hair and black eyes, he looked fierce and in control.

"It's this place," Joz said quietly. "Remember what we entered into?" the third warrior added.

Joz was the youngest of the three, but was almost taller than Mace and outweighed him by a good fifty pounds of muscle. His hair was a sable mix of curls that sometimes appeared red, then gold, then deepest brown. He was by far the largest of the group, but his eyes still held a youthful exuberance and a lust for life that told of his young years.

"But what would force the change?" Mace asked again, this time carefully scanning the group of primitive people standing in the darkened street. Then his gaze fell on Robbie, who still stared down at the quill in his chest, eyes filled with tears of self-recrimination. "Maybe I just answered my own question."

Taking three large steps, Mace reached out and plucked Robbie off of the ground as easily as one would lift a leaf or a feather.

"*Vold cad tu*?" What did you do?

"Please," Robbie babbled as his feet left the ground and his head lolled to the side. "Please kill me before I kill again!" he sobbed.

"Put him down, ya bloody wankers!" Garth tried for a roar, but his voice shook.

Mace turned to face the other man and watched as he shrank back. All bluster with no bite, he decided.

"Calm down, Sable." Jack said as he looked over at a stricken Jillian. "Jillian didn't do this."

"I know! I'm sorry." She stopped pacing and stood still, looking at Jill. "None of this is your fault. It's all mine! Me! I'm the one who brought him home, the one who gave him a place to stay and let him into my heart. This is all my fault."

"Well, he is your Faeroe, love," Jill said quietly as he stepped close to Sable, close enough to wrap her in his arms.

"He is not my anything," Sable said on a shuddering breath. "Did you see what he turned into? What he did to that bastard with the gun?"

"I saw," Jillian said as he placed his hand on her head and urged her to rest on his sturdy shoulder. "But I still believe that he is good. He only defended himself, love. Maybe that's how they do it, turning into walking griffins with black feathers and red eyes." He smiled a bit as he hugged her harder. "There is no evil in him."

"I guess you were right, Jack," Sable said, not answering Jill, but allowed him to take more of her weight. "I guess he's not a Faeroe after all. In fact, I don't know what he is!"

"He is yours," Jack said with a finality that brought her head up.

"Mine?"

"As Jillian is mine, and I am his."

But then two things interrupted them. The very tall, foreign-speaking man was holding onto a sobbing Robbie, and the cops rounded the corner.

"What's going on here?" one of the three officers demanded as he slapped his truncheon across his palm.

Thinking that the newcomers were not a threat, Mace dropped the marked man and turned to face the woman who'd called Torn's name.

"*Johd tock*?" Where is he?

When no one answered, Jase began to make his explanations to the nervous police. "Well, um, you see, uh, I heard a noise and um, these foreign visitors came to investigate… with me."

He wasn't sure what was going on, but neither Jack nor Jill seemed to be afraid of the three men, so he decided to wing it.

"Visitors?'' the cop asked, motioning to his partner to get a better look at the big men that seemed to overflow the alley.

Before another comment could be made, Robbie rushed the cops, dropping to his knees before them, and the second strange thing happened.

"Please take me away!" he sobbed. "I deserve to die, I deserve to pay!" The cops looked at the man and then started to turn away.

"Keep it out of the alley," the cop in charge growled, before turning to make his way back to the street. The brawl in the bar had been quelled and there was no reason to make more paperwork for themselves.

"But I shot him!" Robbie cried as he looked up plaintively at the officers. That froze them in their place as they turned again to look at the broken man.

"Robbie, no!" Garth sighed as Robbie began to spill his story.

"I came here to start trouble, and I brought my gun. But he ain't human, man, and he is after me!"

"Who?" the cop asked, thinking this was just another drunken fantasy of a depressed and frustrated citizen on the dole. But he continued to listen anyway. This story would be good for a few laughs back at the station.

"I shot him! Don't you understand? I shot him with that gun, man!" He pointed to the weapon still lying on the damp cobblestones. "I shot him and he turned into this… thing! He's going to come and get me for what I done!" he added tearfully. "And I deserve to die."

Ignoring talk of transforming men, the first officer bent to get a good look at the gun Robbie had dropped.

"It's real," he said to his partner. "And I think it's been fired."

* * *

Three hours later, they were all in lockup, getting their stories straight.

But the three foreign men were held until an interpreter could be found. It had been quite a trick getting them into the wagon, but twenty officers later and a lot of commotion, they only got into the transport because the tall, dark-haired one gave them a command, and they were on their way.

What the command had been, no one knew, but they were glad that they hadn't had to shoot them to get them into custody. Because of the language barrier, communication was impossible and they didn't want some foreign diplomat coming down on them for abuse of their citizens.

Alone in her cell, Sable waited and thought. Thought about Torn, what he was, what he had become, and came face-to-face with one immutable fact. While he wasn't a Faeroe and she could not be under glamour, she still loved him.

* * *

The night air was cool. Torn was amazed as he felt the airflow below and above his wings. He watched as treetops became purple-gray shapes and forms. Saw the ground as if it was cast in shadows, hidden from the world. He watched strange creatures leap into the darkness, becoming nothing more that glowing eyes staring at him in confusion. Yes, he was different, and different meant alone. Never more had he been aware of this than now.

You always have me, the Reaver purred in his mind.

"I have no one!" he shouted back, missing a beat with his wings and faltering in the sky.

Knowing that he had to land to puzzle through his dilemma, he picked a mountain that seemed devoid of all life and headed for it. Beating his wings rapidly backward against the air that carried him, he descended toward solid ground. His knees bent as he landed, and he quickly folded his wings to his back before slowly rising to his full height.

You are never alone, the Reaver whispered, and he felt his skin tingle.

"What do I have?" he shouted silently. "I am a creature that scares people, drives them away. I remember the look on Sable's face, and I know that I am lost!"

You are found! the Reaver insisted. *You will never be alone again! Don't you realize what you have*?

"I have *nothing*!" His words rang out loud and clear in the cool night air. "I have nothing," he repeated quietly as tears filled his eyes.

So you are going to feel sorry for yourself now? his alter ego sneered. *You are going to tuck tail and run*!

"Because of you, I *have* a tail!" he returned as depression descended on him like the gates to a castle.

Shoulders drooping, wings hanging listlessly, Torn spotted a large boulder and made his way over to it. With a sad little sigh, he sat and rested his elbows on his knees, giving him the perfect perch to rest his head upon, while he tried to hide from the world.

You have it all! the Reaver argued. *You have everything in the palm of your hands and you are letting it slip away.*

"You keep saying that," Torn muttered. "But you are mistaken. What woman would have me? What men would let me join them? I *scare* people! I frighten them witless, and it is my job, *our job*, to do that! I am meant to be alone, yet my foolish heart will force me to forget that."

You -- we -- only frighten those who deserve it.

"Did you not *see* Sable's face? Did you not see the men I fought beside? Tell me what you saw on their faces. Tell *me* what you saw."

Confusion.

"Fear!"

Disbelief.

"Betrayal!"

You betray yourself!

Those last words hurt. Torn stood up and began to walk. He knew he couldn't leave the voice behind, but he had to do something. He walked through the tall, cool grass, instinctively avoiding the marshy bogs, until he came to a small clear stream.

Never, he thought, had he ever seen such beauty.

The running water was surrounded by tall marsh grasses that swayed in the gentle night breeze. Unfamiliar insects that lit up dove and flew through the grasses like stars of the heaven. A strange chirping sound, rather relaxing, also emanated from the base of these grasses, he noted, as well as the water flowing over flat rock seeming to glow in the moonlight. A large tree rested near the banks of this stream, its branches dipping low as if taking a drink while its leaves provided a small canopy, inviting the weary to stop and rest.

If ever there was a weary man, it was Torn.

Man, the Reaver repeated his thoughts to him. *You are a man!*

"A man," Torn breathed, then snorted. "This is a man?" He walked to the water's edge and he peered into it to see his distorted visage.

Slanted red eyes, surrounded by a dark blob that defined description, glowed back at him.

"I am a beast," he said slowly, as he bent closer to the water. "A horrid beast created out of shame and malice to do the dark work no one else could."

You were created out of love, the Reaver insisted.

"Where was the love as I grew?" he retorted sharply, staring at his image in the water. "My own father could not stand to be around me."

His problem, not yours!

"And my mother, where was she with her Magic Realm power when I needed her?"

Loving you from afar!

"And Zultha? What about my beautiful almost-mate? She never knew what I was, saw me as a man, and still the bitch plotted to kill me!"

Bad luck?

"Bad luck?" Torn asked incredulously.

When looking back on the past paths with present eyes, one's vision is nearly perfect. Thus you learn where not to step in the future.

"And that means?"

You exercised poor judgment.

"Poor…" Torn roared with laughter at the understatement, but it served to knock him out of his blue funk for a while.

Zultha never looked at you the way Sable does.

"I am her student!" Torn paused. "She sees me as a child to be taught," he added almost wistfully.

Then you are blind, the Reaver retorted. *She looks at you with desire in her eyes.*

"Well, it is disgust now!" Torn shouted loudly,

slamming a fist into the image of himself in the water, sending cold droplets splashing on his body. "Now she will never want to see me again. She will hate me, what I am, what I have to do. It will kill me to see that hate in her eyes as she stares at me. And I can do nothing about it because I am a freak! I am an unnatural creature that will only cause her grief. I wish I had never met her! I wish I had never thought to believe for once I had a place to fit in. I wish I had never been born!"

Torn jumped to his feet, eyes wild and hair flying around him. He stared at the rippling water, saw his reflection, and slammed both hands through his hair. The pressure building in his chest had to be released; the pain in his heart needed an outlet.

"I am nothing!" he screamed as he threw his head back and roared his pain to the world. "I am nothing! I. Am. *Nothing*!"

Tears rolling down his face, he looked around as his options flew through his mind. Go back to Sable, watch as the kindness in her eyes turned to distrust and fear? Go to Jillian and Jack and watch as they turned their backs on him? Go back to the drinking place with the leather men and watch as they shrank from him in horror? Surely the liar and murderer would have spread his tales by now. All that he had achieved on this foreign and strange plane was now gone, destroyed because he'd had to protect!

But who was there to protect him?

He had no one, was no one, would never *have* anyone, and he was tired. Tired of being alone, tired of having nothing -- just plain tired.

Don't do it! the Reaver hissed as it read his thoughts.

"Nothing!" His chest rose and fell with his

rough, tearing breaths. "I have nothing; I am nothing!"

Turning, he ran, flying on the ground, feet pumping as he moved rapidly across the damp green earth.

"Nothing!" he roared as his feet carried him toward a sudden cliff, a large break in the lush earth. He had nothing left to live for. He had nothing on this plane of existence or on any other. He had more than proven that. No one could accept his differences. No one could accept him. He was alone, a waste of space, and unwanted. There was nothing left for him.

Folding his wings tightly to his body, he raced toward that cleft and prepared to leap.

* * *

Terror sat straight up in his bed, sweating as his eyes went wild. He opened his mouth and screamed so loud, his voice echoed around the whole of his castle.

"Nooo!"

* * *

"They have found him?" Zultha purred as she stared at her servant. "Quickly, tell me where!"

"I have no idea," the woman stuttered as she cowered at her mistress' feet. "But there was a disturbance this morning. Terror is planning on retrieving Lord Torn," she added quickly, hoping to save her life.

"Very interesting," Zultha said lowly as she ran a dirty hand through her equally dirty hair. "And when shall they make their move?"

Her eyes were wild in her dust-smeared face, but a keen intelligence glittered behind the insanity as she fastened her gaze onto her servant.

"As soon as Terror hears from his search party," the servant said weakly. Upon entering the room, she'd prostrated herself on the floor hoping to avoid inciting her mistress' wrath, but even that had failed to appease her mistress.

"When will he speak with them?" Zultha asked as she twirled one lock of red hair around her finger, as a child would, while an innocent smile played upon her lips.

But her servant was not fooled. Those innocent lips could spew forth such venom that a normal person would be reduced to tears.

"Later this morning, lady," she offered, feeling a cold fear sinking bone deep within her body.

"Then why are you here?"

The soft question was so gently asked that she knew that some horror awaited her.

"I-I thought to bring you news, Lady," she stammered, burying her face in the dirt while hoping a mortal blow would not fall.

"You diseased piece of human flesh," Zultha said gently as she reached low and grasped the trembling woman by her hair to raise her face. "You are, what, thirty-eight? You are not old enough to think."

Then with a mighty jerk, she ripped several locks of the now screaming woman's hair from her scalp.

"Go," Zultha purred as she ran the painfully stolen hair across her face, disregarding the spots of blood that left crimson trails across her white skin. "Go back and come to me when you have something important to tell. Do not fail me again."

Even this was said in an almost sickeningly sweet voice as she stepped over the cowering woman as if she were a spot of garbage in the road.

"Go now!" she ordered as the woman lay there, sobbing. "Off with you now! That's a good girl! Run along and do your duty."

Still on her knees, her hands clutching at her

throbbing scalp, the servant scrambled from her mistress' sight, before rising to her feet and taking to her heels.

Her moans of pain and fear were held until she was out of the secret caverns, then raising her head to the sky, she roared out her pain and anguish. Would this hell that was her life ever come to an end? Tears flowing freely down her dirt-streaked face, she raced back toward the castle. Back toward the man she was supposed to betray, but secretly wished would discover her and put an end to this miserable existence.

* * *

Sable sat alone in her small cell and thought about the Faeroe-not-a-Faeroe that she'd given her heart to. "I guess it wasn't glamour," she said to herself as she absently plucked the fuzz off a stiff gray blanket.

She was learning to like institution gray, she thought. She had better learn to love it. It was all the rage in the more popular mental asylums.

Sighing, she thought back to the creature that she had seen her Torn turn -- morph, rather -- into.

It was like that black beast had dwelled within his person all along, just waiting for a moment to be free. Was that the creature that had tested Jack and Jill, and found them acceptable?

Well, it was the same creature who tested the lunatic with the gun and had pierced his dark heart with a feather. She had never seen such a hardened criminal turn stoolie so quickly before in her whole life.

Yet, all it did to Jack and Jill was to ease them of their burdens, cleanse them, as Jack had said.

But where did that leave her?

Okay, she thought, as she rolled a fuzz ball into a tight knot of fiber and flicked it across the room, Torn could not be evil. Hadn't he spared the life of that miserable Garth who was so intent on causing problem for Jase? That proved he wasn't evil, she considered.

No, he hadn't even killed that scumbag who'd started rattling off names and places as fast as he could inhale air! Names and places who and where he had killed, maimed, and stolen, no less.

That was good work, she thought, but not a guarantee of an un-evil person. Well, then there was Torn himself.

She thought of how his eyes seemed to light up whenever she was around. She thought of the way he had looked at her while feeling comfortable doing a drunken striptease in a room full of gay, leather-clad bikers, as if they had not existed. And in truth, they had not existed for her either. From the moment his gaze connected with hers, the world had faded into the background and his precious innocent and oh-so-sexy face dominated the foreground.

Then there was the way he'd sighed while she abused her artist's privilege and made him sit in uncomfortable positions for hours on end. And the way he looked pleadingly up at her as if he needed her permission to experience life. Not to mention the way he made the average things that she was so used to seeing seem so… extraordinary. She had been rediscovering the world through his eyes and she had loved the feel of it.

But most telling was her heart. Her heart was weeping with the loss of him. She almost felt physical pain as he'd looked back at her stupefied face and taken off into the night.

Now her Torn was out there lost and alone, not knowing where to turn to for warmth, understanding, or help. He was so innocent, her Torn, so unused to the people here. He could be hurt and confused right now.

He could be in danger! What if the circus found him? Or even worse, the government? They would rip him apart to see what made him tick!

Disregarding the way he'd fought in the bar, taking out a good number of armed bikers, Sable lapsed into panic for his safety. Her Torn couldn't survive without her. She had to get out of this cell!

* * *

Torn opened his eyes, wanting to see the end coming. The cold Scottish air whipped past his face, tangling his hair, ruffling the feathers of the wings he refused to extend to save his life. His tears dried in the sharp breeze that no longer held him upright, his body shivering with desperation and fear.

He watched as the dark ground rushed faster and faster toward him, the earth extending its hard stone arms open in a welcoming embrace. Then he closed his eyes and waited for the loneliness, the confusion, the pain to end.

There are so many ways to face death. Some people see their lives flash before their eyes, others see nothing but escape. Some face their final solution stoically as if the life that rejected them had no right to real emotions.

And then there are those who change their minds.

A moment before Torn hit the hard stone, a split second before he "gave up the ghost", a millisecond before all the mysteries of death would be revealed to him, he discovered he couldn't do it.

"Coward!" he screamed inwardly. Opening his eyes, he sent out a blast of energy, a blast so concentrated it hit the ground, bounced back into his body, and propelled him back, away from that death-giving plunge. He flopped backward only to land on his ass several feet away from the cliff's edge.

Torn groaned as his butt slid across the pebbly damp surface of the ground until he came to rest up against the base of the cliff from which he'd plunged.

"Ouch," he muttered as he settled against the earth, waiting to catch his breath and readjust his thinking.

Fool, the Reaver hissed at him. *We cannot die! Our mission is still incomplete.*

With that, a transformation began to occur. Slowly, almost as slow as the dew collecting on the heather, Torn began to change.

Every aspect of the Reaver began to melt, to merge with his true form. The dark skin lightened slowly, turning purple, then blue, then gray before settling on the normal golden tint of his skin.

His eyes, red and fierce, gently faded into a deep violet, a color only seen in rainbows. His angel's wings, feathers as black as sin, receded, pulling back into his body and leaving no outward trace of their existence.

His body shrank into itself, bringing him back to his normal height that was still rather impressive to humans, but such an oddity in his realm.

Finally, with one, long full-body shudder, Torn shook free that outer energy, the aura of menace that surrounded the Reaver, and was once again just Torn, a man lost and alone in a strange world. Groaning under his breath, he struggled to sit up, ignoring the pulls and twinges of discomfort from his abused muscles and the sore spot where the bullet had struck and then healed over with his transformation. Brushing his tangled hair out of his face, he surveyed his surroundings.

"I am in the middle of nowhere," he commented as he painfully pulled himself to his feet, hoping his muscle aches would end soon. "I need to… to see her." He sighed as he dropped his head and let his tangled curls cover his face.

Then he recalled seeing Mace, his father's second-in-command, just after seeing the look of sheer terror on Sable's face.

He had to discover what they were doing here. Were they searching for him? A new urgency filled him.

"But first, I have to find her, I have to find my teacher," he mused. "I need her to… I just need her."

Gathering himself together, he turned toward the cliff and decided that getting down was a lot easier than getting back up. He shrugged and began to climb. He was his father's son, after all, and a warrior in his own right.

And one of the first things he'd been taught was to never give up.

* * *

Mace sat straight up in the metal cage in which these small creatures had imprisoned him and his men. He would never understand these things. They looked like people -- small people, but they acted like maniacs. Had Torn been subjected to this the entire time he had been lost to them? If so, then he pitied the poor man.

Upon arriving at the scene, they'd encountered a brawl of epic proportions. Well, maybe that was a gross exaggeration, but it had been a pretty good fight going on between those leather-clad warriors.

Then, after encountering the almost warrior-sized man, who'd spoken in some strange, garbled tongue, they'd come across Torn as the Reaver.

The shock of knowing that the gentle quiet Torn was the Reaver still reverberated through him and his men, but knowing that the creature served the greater good eased their fears. They'd easily found their quarry and their mission had been completed almost before it began.

The creature Torn held must have been severely tainted for the Reaver to mark him as the walking dead, but the shock on the faces of the men in that small walkway, especially the look of surprise on the small, red-haired female, obviously had affected Torn. He'd taken to wing before they could stop him and the strangely dressed men with the loud whistles and the small round sticks flooded the street. Well, actually it was only two, but they'd called to others of their ilk, and he and his men had wound up in this cage.

The three of them could have easily handled the small, loud people, but he decided it would be for the best if they all discovered as much about this place as they could before returning or contacting Terror. Alas, hat they'd found thus far wasn't too promising.

But maybe if they could find the girl…

* * *

"You are released," a female officer said to Sable as the clang of her keys announced her presence. A loud buzzer sounded and the door to her cell slid open. "You are free to go."

"Just like that?" Sable asked, sliding from the bed to her feet, a large pile of fuzz falling to the floor. If the woman noticed or even cared that she had mutilated local property, she gave no hint as she dispassionately waited by the door.

"Yes, just like that. The judge decided that you and your friends, the two poofters, were just in the wrong place at the wrong time."

"If you are referring to Jack and Jill, the correct term is homosexual," Sable bristled, but the woman shrugged absently.

"Whatever," she said in a bored voice.

"Whatever, indeed," Sable muttered as she stalked out of the cell and followed the officer another set of iron bars.

"The poofters -- excuse me, *homosexuals* -- and their friends have been released."

"Friends?" Sable asked, but the buzzer again sounded, drowning out her question.

She almost skipped to keep up with the woman as she was led to a desk and handed an envelope filled with the things she'd had on hand when she was picked up.

"It's all there," the female said impatiently as she watched Sable count the money in her wallet. "And your friends will meet you out front."

With that, she escorted Sable through a set of glass doors and into a large room filled with desks, ringing phones, and the stale smell of days-old coffee.

"You are free to go," she repeated, and turned to walk back toward her lair of cages, leaving Sable to make her way slowly through a maze of confusion to a bench set up in the front of the room. The waiting room, she supposed as she watched the hustle and bustle in the room.

Now, how could she find Torn? she wondered as she became lost in thought. She would get Jack and Jill, and then she would --

"I'm telling you, I don't know these men!" Jill's aggravated voice sounded throughout the room.

"I wish I did." Jase added as an officer escorted the six men to the front of the building.

"Yeah, yeah," an officer said as he pointed to the front doors. "And I'm Finn McCool! These men are the Finnians and we're here to right wrongs and create a utopia free of giants and a six-eyed monster. Just don't leave town, leather boyos!" he added as his comment drew a few chuckles from the officers around them. "We may need you for further questioning."

Sighing in defeat, Jill latched onto Jack's hand and pulled him toward the exit, Jase and the three strangers following closely.

"Jill!" Sable called, drawing his attention, and that of his leather-clad honor guard as all heads turned in her direction.

"Sable!" Jill exclaimed, pulling Jack along as he made his way to his favorite girl. "Are you all right, love? Did they do anything to you? You didn't meet up with the business end of a broomstick, did you? I was careful not to bend over and pick up the soap," he prattled as he released Jack to grip her shoulders and give her a thorough looking over. "I might have been tempted, but I had my baby with me."

"Jill!" Sable wailed as she tried to hold in her laughter.

"Are you fine?" he asked again, looking deeply into her eyes.

"I am," she decided after a brief pause, knowing he was asking after more than her mental and physical state. "I have to find him, Jill. I have to find Torn."

At her words, the three leather-clad giants, who had followed Jack, Jase and Jill, reacted.

"Torn?" the largest one said somewhat urgently. "*Tosa ke it to!*" Take me to him!

"Friend of yours?" she asked quietly as she stared up at the men in awe. How many herds of cows did it take to cover even one of those bodies?

"Torn," he insisted again as he took a step forward, looking anxious and concerned.

"Friends of his?" Jill pondered as Jack got between Sable and Jill and the men who came closer.

"They sound like Torn," Sable breathed, still staring at the three.

"Torn!" he repeated again, looking more worried than before.

"I think I just figured out how to find him," Sable said as she eased out of Jill's arms and walked around a cautious Jack.

"Torn?" she asked. The three started nodding, looking a bit relieved themselves.

"Okay!" Sable said as a huge smile broke across her lips. "You know Torn and probably can't understand a thing I'm saying. But you are going to help me find him. I want my man back," she said, and Jill began laughing. "I want him back and I'm not letting him go, no matter what he is!"

Chapter Eight

Terror paced in the hall, his gaze skittering past Nello and turning to the room that would give him all of the answers he needed yet held its secrets.

"What is taking them so long?" he growled as he ran his hands through his hair in frustration, pressing his palms to his face. "They know they should report in! Something is wrong!"

"You had a nightmare," Nello soothed as she watched her mate wear grooves in the stone floor. "Nothing more, nothing less."

"You, of all people," he said, pausing in front of his mate, "know better than to believe that. There are no such things as dreams, Nello."

Sighing, Nello lowered her head, her eyes tearing up as her mask of confidence began to shatter.

"You are right, Terror," she began, but held up a hand to stop him when he would have tried to comfort her with a hug. "But I have confidence in my son. I have to…"

But she could not hold it in any longer. Nello, the wise and strong one who'd always supported Terror and tried to provide aid everyone, finally broke.

"If I'd been there for him…" she sobbed. "If I'd been there, he would still be here!"

"Nello…" Terror began, reaching out to enfold her in his powerful arms, but she rejected his touch, jumping back holding out one hand as the other clenched at her chest, trying to hold together the pieces of her heart.

"No, Terror!" she said in a broken voice, breath rasping as she struggled to get the word out. "If I had stood up to my father, if I had taken him with me, if --"

"Don't live for what-ifs, my love," Terror cut her

off, reaching out and pulling her against his chest. She resisted for a moment, resting her head against his chest and jerking her hands away from him, but his greater strength and arm span overcame her objections.

"Nello," he crooned.

Then she let her tears fly, stopped trying to hold in her pain and suffering, her guilt. She rested her face against his chest as broken sobs exploded from her chest.

"I should have been there," she repeated over and over. "I should have been there for him! I should have taken him home with me!"

"So that your father could have killed him?" Terror asked, as he gripped her shoulders and pulled away from his mate, staring her in her eyes.

He'd had enough of the self-doubt and the pity. It was time to regain order over this situation.

"You don't know…" she began.

"I know," Terror stated with finality. His gaze bore into hers, forcing her to see the truth of his words. "And if you had taken my son away, I would have stormed the gates of the Magic Realm to reclaim you both. If you had taken Torn away from me, *I* would have *died*, Nello. There were times when my only comfort was to look into his face and see you!"

"Terror, I made such a mistake," Nello sobbed, her eyes red and puffy, her face stained with the passing of a thousand bitter tears.

"*We* made mistakes, Nello. They are not exclusive to you. I became so ashamed of what I'd forced on my son, of what was done to him because of me, that I could hardly look him in the eyes. This, after one of the sweetest memories I had of him was when he wrapped his soft, pudgy baby arms around my neck…" His voice broke as he blinked rapidly to hold back the tears. "He put his arms around my neck and said that he loved me, Nello. He said that he loved me and all I could do was stand there, mute, my child clinging to my neck. And all that I could think was that he had no right to love me after I cursed him, tainted him with my blood!"

"No, Terror, no!" Nello exclaimed, her voice rising with intensity as she reached up to cup his cheeks.

"Your father took the darkest parts of me, the blackness of my soul, to create the Reaver!"

"There are no black parts to your soul, Terror," Nello said reassuringly. "My father took a dark part of you to create the Reaver, but what he took was partially your sense of justice and your fighting spirit. There never was any evil in you, Terror, as there is no evil in Torn."

"No evil?" he nearly shouted, after closing his eyes and gulping a breath of air. "No evil in me, Nello? I could not even tell my own child that I loved him, and you say there is no evil in me?"

"Confusion, my love, and guilt and maybe fear, but no evil, Terror! Your son, the Reaver, is made up of qualities that were and are the best of you."

Terror dropped his head at his wife's words. He knew she made sense with her logical mind, but his soul still castigated him for his wrongs.

"You feel him, Terror, because a part of him, a *major* part of him, is from you. You know your son. You feel him every day. You know that he holds no hate for you, that he loves you."

"But he is in pain," Terror whispered as he forced his eyes open.

"He is hurt?" Nello gasped, forgetting for a

moment that if Torn were in any physical pain, nothing and no one would have kept Terror away from his son.

"He is in pain, I can feel it. He is confused and hurt, Nello. Not physically, but the pain is almost as deep."

"We will get to him, Terror. We will bring him home. Soon," Nello stated, regaining her composure and her self-confidence. "We will go together. We will bring our baby home."

"Home." Terror sighed as he wrapped his arms around his mate, still feeling the frantic beat of his heart against his breastbone, but knowing that a resolution was coming, that his child would not suffer very much longer.

But the feel of her soft breasts pressing against the muscled wall of his chest sent his heart racing for a very different reason.

"Nello," he whispered, just before his mate mashed her lips against his. This was no kiss, this was a taking, a sharing of pain, and he understood it was cathartic as well as erotic.

He moaned and parted his mouth as her teeth worried his lower lip, her tongue quick to soothe away the pain, but aggressive in getting what she wanted. Giving in to her demands, he lifted her into his arms and rushed back to the bedchamber, tumbling them both to the center of the bed, reclining and arranging them so easy access to both their bodies were attainable.

Her body rose over his, making him growl as he spied her breasts hanging over his chest.

He had to touch them, to reaffirm that they were his and that he could do just about anything he wanted to do with them.

Nello was his, and soon their child would be

home and they would be one big happy family, a family done right this time.

"Terror," Nello gasped as his hands palmed her breasts, rolling the nipples between his thumb and forefinger.

"Get closer," he growled as he placed her astride his stomach.

He felt his erection surge, his cock throb in time with his heartbeat, his breath rasp from his throat as he felt all of her surround him.

He wanted to be lost in his Nello, surrounded by all the magic and mystery that was uniquely woman, but definitely all Nello.

"Closer," he growled again, and he urged her to bend down, to hang those delectable tits over his mouth.

Nello threw back her head and cried out as his lips attached themselves to her right nipple, sucking the bud deeply into his mouth and the areola around it, into the hot wet heat.

Her hands tangled in his hair, her breathing frantic as she pushed to get closer.

She felt the juices from her sopping cunt leak over his stomach, giving enough lubrication for her hips to begin a desperate slide, the friction teasing her clit as she spread her legs and tried to get closer.

Terror arched up into her slide, adding more friction as the hot wet stickiness covered him. This is what he wanted, he mentally growled as the musky scent of her sex filled his senses. He wanted his Nello a panting, grasping, wanting thing of need; need for him and for what he could do.

His hands slipped down to knead her ass as he pulled from the right nipple and pressed a series of nips and licks to the left.

Her moans were growing more audible, more delicious to his senses as he worked his way up to her neck, biting and sucking at the skin, leaving his marks so that the whole realm would know to whom she belonged.

"Creator, I need you," he rasped into her ear, his tongue lashing out to lave the delicate bit of flesh that made up her lobe. "I need you hot and ready and greedy for my cock. Tell me!"

"I'm ready," Nello whimpered, trying to rise up, but growling as his hands held her in place.

"Tell me you want me!"

"Creator, I want you, Terror," she managed as she struggled to break his hold. Her nerves were on fire, her body a furnace of need, and he was playing these games? How dare he deny her what she wanted, what truly was hers?

"More," he purred as he ground upward as he eased her back, the long hard shaft of his cock nestling between the cheeks of her ass, teasing her with his wicked heat and his thick length.

"Don't fuck with me!" Nello growled, trying to slide back more, writhing as his wiry pubic hair teased the delicate rosebud of her rear passage and her clit bounced along his muscled abs. "Give it to me now!"

"Take it," he urged as he felt the beaded dew of his pre-cum bead up on the head of his cock and slowly began to leak down, mixing with her juices that now covered them both.

He relaxed his hold, and instantly Nello was rearing up, hovering over his cock, her wet, sucking pussy just teasing the purple head.

Reaching down, he grabbed the base, stroking it a few times with the combined lubrication of both their bodies, slicking the way for her, then he waited, his eyes wild and dazed as they bored into hers.

"Oh Creator, Terror…" Then she lowered herself, letting her weight drag her body down, eyes widening as she was parted and filled, and stretched and filled some more.

"Sssss!" Terror hissed as he threw his head back, breaking eye contact with his frantic mate, unable to watch her take what she needed from him and maintain some of his control.

He knew that this session would not last long; they were both filled with too much panic and need. But it was what each of them needed, and because his job was to see to her needs, he would hold on a little longer.

He gritted his teeth as he felt his cock enveloped in the most wonderful, almost painful, wet hot tightness that pulsed and writhed around him.

His hips automatically thrust up, impaling her a bit more, getting that last inch within her sugared walls, driving a wringing cry from her arched throat.

"Nello!" he growled as he forced his eyes open, drinking in the sight of her head tossed back, the feel of her long hair teasing his balls, the helpless sounds she made as she rocked her hips from side to side, circling, grinding him in deeper.

"Move," she managed as she slowly brought her head up, her trembling hands reaching out for his shoulders as her body fell forward, covering him in both lust and longing. "Move for me."

And he moved, slowly at first, still stretching her and making her ride a bit easier for them both. Then his hips were slamming up, pressing deep before a long slow glide out.

"Oh Creator, move for me, Terror," she managed as her body seemed to go boneless and her soft breasts were pushing against his chest, her pebble-hard nipples driving deep.

Fast in, slow out, fast in and a grind.

"Terror!"

Then she was moving, her whole body vibrating as she regained some muscle control and wrapped her hands in his hair, her elbows resting on his chest. She took control, sliding her hips up and down, the feel of his hands on her hips anchoring her and making each movement feel more intense.

Faster and faster they moved, counterpoint to one another until a fast rhythm was established. Then they began to pound at each other, releasing all of the fear and anxiety they felt, taking their emotions out on each other. Harder and faster they moved, driving their nerves taut as their bodies glistened with the sweat of their labors.

Faster and faster, deeper and harder, until the room filled with the sounds of flesh slapping against flesh and the hungry moans and pleas for more. Moving as one determined entity until Nello threw back her head, a loud scream erupting from her throat as the tension broke and her climax was upon her.

"Ter... T... Terro... Terror!" she shrieked as her inner walls clamped tight around his thickness, feeling it swell even further before he too gave his own series of grunts as his cock pulsed within her, releasing its creamy load into her willing body.

"Nell..." he purred, his body quivering, his muscles trembling as she collapsed in his arms.

"Mmm," she answered, sinking deeply into the afterglow and letting all of her cares float away on the warm golden waters in which she now floated.

"We need a bath," he managed, wrapping his arms around her, pulling her closer, not even minding the sticky fluids that covered them both.

"Later," she sighed, snuggling into his neck, her tongue tasting the salty flesh close to her mouth, sleepiness radiating from her body, but it was a contented sort of sleepiness.

"Later," he agreed as he stopped fighting and let the lethargy take him too. "Later." They would have time. They would have everything, their son home where he belonged, their kingdom put to rights, their love. They would have time.

* * *

On the road, Torn took time to examine his leather strops -- uh, pants -- and found them to be the only thing on his body.

Jack's beautifully made coat was gone, his borrowed shirt was gone, even his boots were gone! The only thing he had were the tattered pants and damnable torque.

What can be worse? he thought. Just then, it began to rain.

He jumped as the first drops pelted his body, startling him as they preceded a downpour.

"Does the sky ever not cry here?" he asked, exasperated, then blinked. He was speaking in Sable's language. He was thinking in this twisted, bizarre language.

He looked up at the sky and began to roar with laughter, the rain soaking his body and plastering his hair to his face.

"I have learned something good!" he exclaimed. That his vocabulary was rudimentary at best didn't bother him. He had succeeded at something and he wanted to shout with glee. "I think in this... in these words."

He must have taken some of the language when

he reaved that man in the dark alleyway. Finally, a bit of useful magic that could actually benefit him. Suddenly, the gray sky didn't seem so sad and the world looked a little brighter. Now, to find out where he was.

He turned around, carefully scanning the area, and almost jumped in delight as he discovered something. The path looked familiar. It looked almost like one of the roads Sable had taken while bringing him home for the first time. Had he instinctively headed for safety, Sable's house?

He shook his head. He hadn't a clue, but he smiled as he started off down the road. Things were looking up.

* * *

"So do I walk around calling, 'Here Faeroe, Faeroe, Faeroe'?"

"Not funny, Jillian!" Sable groused as she glared daggers at her friend. "He could be anywhere."

Jillian, Jack, and Sable rode back toward her house, Jase following in his large rusted-out van, filled with the tall, strange-speaking men who carried themselves so much like Torn.

"He'll be fine," Jill assured her as they rounded the bend to her house. "Have faith! He's a big bulletproof boy."

"But he looked so hurt, Jill," Sable shouted over the roar of the engine. "Like he had lost his best friend!"

"He thought he lost you!" Jill shouted back as they pulled the bikes into the garage. "His heart was breaking, Sable."

"He was not --"

"I'm a man. I *know* these things."

"But --"

"Listen to the man," Jack interrupted as he turned off his ignition and kicked the stand into place. "A man in love recognizes a man in love."

All conversation ceased as the van pulled into the drive and a distraught Jase emerged.

"Poor babies," he said worriedly. "I don't think they've ever ridden in a van before. Do you think they're third-world?"

He peered back into the van before opening the side doors.

Inside, three green-faced men sat, wide-eyed, as if their world was slowly spiraling out of control and taking their stomachs along for the ride.

"You do think they will be okay, don't you?" Jase asked worriedly. "I think the shortest one is kind of cute, but I don't do puking men."

Jill exploded into laughter, Jack shook his head as he glared at Jase, and Sable stepped forward cautiously.

"Torn?" she asked as the one who appeared to be the leader seemed to shake himself out of his misery and focus on her.

"Torn," he repeated as he looked around him and made to exit the van.

He seemed most relieved as his feet touched firm earth. He turned and motioned for his fellow warriors to exit, noting that there was no apparent danger.

"You tell me," Sable said as she stepped closer to him, her face showing determination. "Find him."

"Find him," Mace repeated slowly as he stared at the small, red-haired female. She appeared to be angry for some reason, but he knew not why. It had something to do with Torn, so he was sticking near. She could be a witch, just like the last redhead Torn had fallen in with.

"Out!" he called to his men as they were taking their time in exiting the strange transport. "We have things to do. We must find Torn and report to Terror."

"Terror?" Jill asked as he stepped close to Sable, noting that the tall one immediately turned his attention to him. Kind of like a hawk watching its prey.

"Make him look at me like that," Jase demanded as he stared at Mace in awe. "He looks so butch."

The creaking of the van's shocks announced the other two as they crawled out and looked around the garage.

"They're talking terror, Sable!" Jill said again. "I think you'd better find out what they want and what they know."

"Me?"

"Well, you speak Faeroe. I speak fairy and I don't think they'd be interested in a strip club."

Sable glowered at Jill, then turned to face the big one again. "Sable!" she shouted, pointing to her chest. "Sable!"

Mace looked at the woman as if she had lost her mind.

"Is she hostile?" Joz asked, his sable hair ragged and strewn around his head from his nervous fingers, as he moved beside his commander. "Should I take action?"

"Not yet," Mace advised. "We had better observe these beings. They may lead us to Torn."

"You said his name again!" Sable called out, stepping close to the man, her desperation making her bold. "Find him! Find Torn!"

"Maybe we should contact Terror," Del said, shaking off the unpleasant experience of enclosed high-speed travel. "He needs to be updated."

"What are they talking about?" Jill whispered as

Jack and Jase flanked them, a guard of sorts.

Before any opinions could be formulated, the tall one reached into a pouch at his side and produced a little glowing ball.

"If this is sex like in *Cocoon*," Jase purred, "me first!"

"Jase," Jack growled, finally speaking. "This is serious."

They all watched as the orb in his palm began to grow and pulse, a bright blue-white star in his hand. It grew in strength until suddenly it exploded, filling the garage with a warm glow.

"Report!" the voice bellowed, coming from nowhere and everywhere.

"Oh shit," Jase mumbled as he flinched and jerked his head around, searching for the voice.

Jack gasped and Jill took a step closer to Sable, but all waited to see what would happen next.

"Torn is here. The Reaver was spotted," Mace said quietly. "We have come in contact with some... natives who seem to know of him."

"What happened to my son?" Terror asked, his voice barely controlled. "Where is he?"

"We do not know, Lord." Mace repeated. "We arrived in some sort of disturbance and the Reaver took off soon after. We shall track him now."

"What is that place like?"

"It is... savage," Mace said quietly, not knowing how else to describe this place.

"I am on my way."

"But, my Lord --"

"I am on my way! Detain the natives. We will learn what we can from them and then we will find my son."

There was a flash and the light burned away,

leaving four humans looking shocked and confused and three grim-looking warriors.

"He is coming," Mace said, and Del and Joz nodded.

"What was that?" Jase asked, finally getting his breath back. "On second thought, I don't want to know. Later, guys. I'm out of here."

But before he could move, a tall beefy man stood in his way, barring the exit. "Well, maybe I'm not," he said as his attempts to leave were blocked at every turn.

"Well, I'm going in," Sable announced as she glowered at the three large men taking over her garage but giving her no information on Torn.

She turned to enter through the kitchen door, but Mace stood in her way, his mouth set and his eyes grim.

"Look, buster," she snarled as she approached and slammed her finger into his chest. "I have no idea where you came from or what you are, but until you help me find Torn, you are not going anywhere and neither am I!"

Each word was punctuated with a jab. Her emotions were raw and frustration rode her every move.

He blinked at her. Wasn't she afraid? Did she not know what he was capable of doing?

"Move it!" she screamed, making all the men jump. "I'm cold and hungry and I don't know where Torn is! *So* I'm going to find a way to find him and bring him home. You are not going to stop me."

She sniffed as she walked around the man, who still looked at her in confusion, as he didn't understand a word she'd said beyond Torn's name, but reading her determination.

"Fiery, are these creatures not?" Del asked as he stared at the stupefied look on his commander's face.

"She is… different," Mace allowed as he turned to follow the woman into the house, leaving the herding of the other males to his men.

* * *

"Tomorrow," Nello said as she threw objects into a leather bag. "Tomorrow morning, Terror. We retrieve our child tomorrow."

"Yes, Nello, My One," Terror said as he watched his wife gather her mystical implements, paying no heed to the woman who lingered in his doorway. "Tomorrow."

* * *

"Tomorrow!" the servant reported to her mistress. "They leave tomorrow."

"Then I will have to be there with them, won't I?" Zultha laughed, the anticipation of revenge making her mouth water. "Tomorrow, they all will pay."

* * *

Torn walked along the dark, winding road, grateful that he could see clearly. If it weren't for his training and the magic flowing through his veins, he wouldn't have found his way this far.

Walking was tedious, but he could not go to his Sable on wings. That would frighten her before he had a chance to explain what was happening. And more than anything, he wanted Sable to understand him, to not fear him, to love him as he loved her.

He sighed and shivered a bit as the rain -- he remembered the word -- continued to fall, coating his nearly nude body with the cold, clear drops.

Water from the sky, he thought as his long mane of hair stuck to his body, and the torn pants threatened to slide down his narrow hips. It had to be magic.

He closed his eyes, tossing his head back, flinging sprinkles of body-warmed water around. His face turned up to the dark gray heavens, he ignored the river of water flowing down his deep golden chest, through the hills and valleys created by his hard muscles, and concentrated.

His bare feet sank into warm earth as he spread his arms and began to test this planet for energy, magic or human, and the creatures who inhabited this place. And as he freed a tendril of energy, he gasped as white lightning flared through his mind, forcing him to his knees. Groaning, he buried his fists into his hair as the images, the feelings, the aura of this place poured through him.

It was awful! Crying! There were people crying out in anguish, mothers, fathers, children, they all screamed! The trees cried as they were torn from their Mother Earth, the ground screamed out its anguish as it was torn up and plowed over. The seas shrieked their agony as the life within them boiled in a liquid prison, caused by pollution and chemicals dumped there. The very air was anguished as things were forced into it, breaking down its natural composition and leaving it poisoned.

But it was the cries of the people that hurt the worse!

Small people, large people, hungry people and well-to-do people! In countries where they spoke strange languages, there was fighting and death. In large, teeming, overpopulated cities, people with no homes languished in poverty while the city dwellers looked right through them. Sickness ran rampant, killing diseases with no known cure and no way to control them, spread out among the population, striking young and old alike.

There was so much pain! He felt the change begin in him, felt his skin prickle and tingle, but he knew that now was not the time! He fought it, fought it with every bit of power in his body. It was too much! It was too much for a lone Reaver to handle! There was too much to fix and no clear answers how to go about even beginning.

He moaned as he lowered his forehead to the earth, the rich nurturing earth, and prayed for the pain to stop. "Please!" he groaned as wave after wave of need poured through him. Everyone needed him, needed something, and he wasn't sure he could help without destroying himself.

"Please, stop!" he nearly screamed as a fresh wave of dark energy ripped through his body.

Was there no end to the pain, no way to help these people? Then as his mind began to explode with his desire to help and his Reaver's instincts to protect and defend, he heard a new voice.

This voice was raised in song, a song of the future, a song of hope.

His body began to tremble as he focused his energy there, determined to find where this soothing melody came from and how it could aid the people who were still screaming in his head. He turned inward, shutting down his body as his energy regrouped itself and went seeking.

"It's them," he breathed as the pain eased a bit. "It's them!"

Indeed, it was the people of this planet. There was hope here, he realized, there was magic in these new voices. These were the voices that soothed the anguish in those around them. It came from the weak and infirm, the healthy and the wealthy, the poor and the knowledgeable and the ignorant. Inside many of the people here, no matter what their circumstances, there was a seed of hope, a kernel of pride, love for themselves and for others. Torn concentrated on this feeling, this oneness with self, and felt the urge to let the beast take over pass away.

Slowly, he stopped rocking and lifted his mud-splattered face. The wrinkles of pain in his forehead eased and his breathing became regular. Even the tingling of his skin eased as he concentrated and focused on this new delightful sound.

Slowly, he pushed himself to his feet, covered in the earth that had caused him so much pain and then lifted his spirit. It was the people in this place that eased his suffering and rejuvenated him, that was the true magic of this realm.

Hands trembling, he focused more of this energy, feeling it come from many people, searching for one person.

Surely if there was goodness being broadcast, his Sable would be one of the main people emitting such a wonderful magical vibe.

He again closed his eyes, searching, when again; he was suddenly knocked to his knees.

Terror! He felt Terror!

Tightening in his grip on the energies he felt flow from his father and… his mother, he locked in on their location.

If his parents were here, something was dreadfully wrong, and he had to right it. Turning south, he began to jog, eyes closed as his feet moved him over the dark swampy land, letting his magic be his guide.

* * *

"Sit!" Sable growled to the men who now invaded her kitchen, examining everything like they had never seen an appliance before. If they were like Torn, likely they never had.

The three men looked at her oddly, then began to consult each other.

"What did she say?" Del asked as he stared at the two older men. "Could you understand her?"

"That garbled nonsense was speech?" Joz asked, and was answered with a glare from Mace.

"We need to keep an eye on these people until Terror arrives. Especially the female. She looks to know more than the rest and could be dangerous, although I feel she is not a threat to Torn."

"But this place… it's so strange." Joz sighed as he again looked around the small room, noting the position of each man and the female in particular. "And Torn has no judgment when it comes to women! Remember the witch he almost mated?"

"And you know a lot, puppy?" Del snarled as he cuffed Joz on the back of the head. "Now pay attention. Watch and learn."

Del knew Mace had a plan, and he would ensure that the rest of the recon party would follow his moves.

"Sit!" Sable snarled again, pointing to a chair and watching the men.

"Sit?" the large black-haired one said as he stared between her and the chair in question.

"Sit." Sable signed again, deciding that a visual approach would be better.

Pulling out a chair, she gingerly sat, showing them with slow motions what was expected of them. That done, she repeated again in a firm voice, "Sit!"

"For God's sake, Sable!" Jill cried out, torn between exasperation and humor. "They aren't puppies in here for training. They're men."

"Well, can you do better?" she snapped as the

three men stood watching her.

"Yes!" Jill all but laughed and Jack groaned, thinking he might have to pull his partner's butt out of the fire.

He walked over and tapped the largest one on the arm and pointed to the chair.

"Sit," he said as he demonstrated, wiggling his bottom and pointing to it and then the chair.

A look of comprehension filled the big one's face as he too wiggled his butt and pointed to the chair.

Nodding, Jill said "Sit" again, and Joz wiggled his bottom again and sat.

"Success!" Jill shouted to Sable, who snorted, as the other men followed suit. But the loud cracking of wood had them all turning as the three men, with three identical expression of horror on their faces, fell through the flimsy wooden chairs and landed on their tushies on the hard floor.

"Sit?" Joz snarled, glaring at the man.

"Well, they're a bit larger than Torn," Jill allowed as he watched three prime hunks of male flesh bounce on their leather-clad bottoms.

"Only about a foot," Jack added as he walked forward and offered the red-haired man a hand up.

"Oh my, aren't they?" Jase sighed as he tried to get an unobtrusive view of the men's spread legs and massive chests as they glared at Jill.

"I believe they are trying to kill us," Joz said as he glared at the small man who had showed them the true meaning of "sit."

"This 'sit' is a trick that can be used to gain advantage in battle," Del decided as he took the hand offered by the tall, dark-skinned bald man.

"More than likely, the chair was too weak," Mace decided as he too rose to his feet, but without assistance. "These men are so small, Joz. The seats were probably sized for the female."

"My kitchen set," Sable moaned as she mentally tallied up the price of new chairs.

"Well, they *are* rather large," Jack agreed with Jill as he helped heave the redhead to his feet and stepped back.

Jill tried to assist the brawny large one, but the apparent leader rose to his feet without help.

"Living room." Sable sighed as she pointed the way. "The couch can hold them. It's heavy-duty and has a solid wood frame."

They all tromped to the living room, the three foreign men looking around curiously, Jack and Jill wondering what was going to happen next, and Jase still stealing peeks at the men.

Hey, they were eye candy, and he'd just discovered that his eyes had a big sweet tooth!

"Sit!" Sable said again and pointed to the couch.

Obediently yet cautiously, the three men complied, wiggling their butts before sitting, then sighed when the seat held.

"Now what?" Jill asked as he took a seat on his favorite chair, leaving Jase to gawk in peace and Jack to perch on the arm of the chair, his hands stroking Jill's back lightly.

Sable began to pace.

"Now we wait," Sable said. "From the way they herded us in here, they want us to stay put. I have a feeling they want Torn to come here and maybe they're bringing help to find him."

"How do you figure that?" Jase asked, snapping out of his lust-induced daze.

"Female instincts," she said. "Besides, the dark-haired one looked concerned when I mentioned his name, not angrily, just anxious."

"You think?" Jase asked, doubt evident in his voice.

"I pray," Sable said as she looked at the three men. "Because if they harm Torn, I'll have to kill all three of them, and that's a lot of killing."

The determined look in her eyes proved that she meant every word, and the three men prayed right along with her.

If she tried to harm them and they retaliated, they'd have to get involved. And each of the humans knew if that happened, no one would make it out alive.

* * *

Zultha's servant hurried with news for her mistress. This would be the final time she returned to this vile cave. The woman could die, for all that she cared, and she prayed that it would happen soon.

"What news?" the mad one asked as she watched her servant scurry into the cavern.

Zultha, her red hair matted to her head and her clothes dirty with accumulated grime and filth, was the perfect picture of the Queen of the Insane. Her eyes glittered in her madness, more frightening because of the small child's voice that came from the mouth of that viper. Her mind was almost totally broken and it showed.

"They leave within a few hours, Lady," the servant said as she dropped to her knees and held her breath. The odor coming from her mistress was decidedly rank.

"I will need a disguise," Zultha said as she smiled down at the lowly woman who served her. "Something low-class and tasteless," she added. "Like what you are wearing."

Without a word, the servant stripped the deep

brown cloak from her body and laid it at her mistress's feet, her thin shoulders quivering with fear and uncertainty as well as total self-defeat.

"Thank you," Zultha purred as she stared at the garment.

"Lady," she answered as she tried to huddle into a small ball, so as not to draw her mistress' unwanted attentions.

"You may leave," Zultha said quietly as she stared at the human waste at her feet. Nodding, the servant scurried out, her thin shift no protection from the cold air in the cavern, but she paid no heed.

Turning to one of her guards, Zultha smiled at the man.

"Kill her quick," she ordered. "She did, after all, find out what I wanted to know." Silently, the guard disappeared, blending in with the shadows. He had no expression on his face, but inside, he was thinking, *Are we all so expendable, Lady? Is this a taste of your rewards?*

* * *

She's going to kill me, the servant thought as she scurried from the cavern. *Before the sun rises, I shall be dead.*

As she ran toward the relative safety of the castle to prepare for her murder, tears ran down her face. She knew her death was inevitable. Her fate was sealed the first time she'd laid eyes on Zultha. Broken both mentally and spiritually, she raced toward the castle. So be it! If she were to die, she would at least get a small amount of revenge.

Nello would know what to do when she found her body. The true Lord would be notified and Zultha would not get away with destroying all that was innocent and pure, like she'd destroyed her servant.

Chapter Nine

Terror paced as he waited for his entourage to gather. This group included his precious Nello, a healer, and his assistant.

Everyone knew the risks yet were happy to go retrieve the young prince. He had touched so many of their lives with his gentle nature and kindness that they were willing -- nay, eager -- to help him in his hour of need.

That he was the Reaver shocked and surprised many people, but those chosen to accompany Terror banked their fear of him. They were trying to see him as just Torn, but it was difficult at times.

"Where is the assistant?" Terror grumped.

"Patience," Nello cautioned as they waited outside the transport chamber. "She will arrive soon."

No sooner had the words left her mouth than a small figure, completely swaddled in a cloak, made a shuffling appearance.

"It took long enough," snapped Terror.

"My usual assistant is somewhat troubled," the Healer, a tall white-haired warrior hefting a large leather satchel, said quietly. "So she found me a replacement from the ranks of the acolytes. This one is mute, though a competent worker. Hopefully this task in this new, faraway place will give her a chance to gain some experience that will help us all in the future. She is a quiet efficient worker, though I sense something troubling in her. But my assistant assures me she is the most qualified for this mission."

"I have the perfect thing for her," Nello said suddenly, sensing much confusion and darkness in the woman.

"Nello!" Terror glared as his wife turned and

made to quit the chamber.

"You three go along! I'll be right behind you. I need to gather an amulet for the good Healer's assistant. It is designed to help focus and stabilize… energies. Besides, it will take time to transport all of us to the foreign realm. We have time."

Actually, it was designed to neutralize any dark energy. What she had felt wafting off of the woman was akin to madness! A malevolent spell or just mental instability could cause it. Either way, Nello was taking no chances. She wanted her son home safe without interference from anyone or anything.

"Nello," Terror called out as he raked his hands through his hair. "Come back here!"

The laughing Healer didn't help the situation.

"Let her be, Terror!" he cheerfully advised. "Living alone all of these years has made you forget how to live with a woman. Rule one, they are always correct, even if they are not. Rule two is to always refer back to rule one. Let her follow us. Her amulet may help and it will ease her mind."

"I think I have to," he said with a sigh as he turned toward the chamber. "I need to get to Torn. I feel his… pain."

"He is a part of you," the Healer said. "A very important part. He is of your spirit and your mate's magic. You will feel the connection, Terror. You love him."

"That I do," Terror said, with a smile. "And it is time to bring him home. Time for me to be the father he needs, and failing that, the friend he can count on."

Turning, he entered the chamber, followed by the Healer and the eerily grinning assistant.

* * *

Nello stepped into her private chambers, where

she kept all of her magical implements, and stopped dead.

There was someone sitting in her chair.

The room was very large but sparsely furnished. The small desk and chair were set off to one side as a huge wooden table dominated the room. No one ever sat in her chair. While she was away, Terror had kept this room locked and cleaned, but people very rarely ventured here now that she was back.

But now there was someone sitting in her chair.

"Can I help you?" she asked as she stepped into the room, waving her hand at a torch and watching as it exploded into light. "Do you need my help?"

But the figure did not move.

Detecting no movement, she stepped closer to the figure. It appeared to be asleep, its head laying on top of her desk.

"Hello?" she said again as she approached cautiously and shook the shoulder.

The listless head flopped to the side, exposing one eye, open and cloudy with death. With a small shriek, Nello stepped back as she recognized the lifeless face.

It was the servant! It was the woman who had been seen cleaning the rooms and assisting the Healer...

"What is going on?" she whispered as tears of compassion filled her eyes. "Who did this to you?"

Sending tendrils of her magic seeking, she searched quickly for the source of death. There was trauma, severe trauma to her neck!

She searched deeper and found no other source of death. The woman had been strangled and left in this chamber. But to what purpose? Stepping closer to the body, she stared at it, struggling to reason why someone would do this horrible thing.

There were signs of a struggle, now that she was searching for them. One of the woman's shoes was missing and all she wore was a thin shift that would not keep out the chill of the castle.

Her feet were encrusted with dark earth, one remaining shoe hanging off her foot as if she had kicked and fought her captor. Her hands were clenched into fists as if she had fought to survive. Around her lay scattered papers.

Now that was odd. Nello never left papers on her desk. She liked things neat and orderly.

Using a puff of magic to lift one of the sheets, she reached out and claimed the cream-colored parchment. It was blank. So was the next one and the next one that she retrieved.

She shook her head, about to summon the guards when she saw it. A strand of red hair, *bright* red hair clutched in the woman's fist.

"Where did you get that?" she mused out loud. "What warrior has bright red hair?"

She tentatively reached out and pulled, noticing length of the strand.

"What are you trying to tell me?" she whispered as she noticed the clenched fists.

If she were being strangled, she would have used magic to destroy her attacker. But if she were mortal and of this realm, she would have scratched at the face and hands of her captor.

The woman's hands were tightly fisted, as if she refused to let something go, as if she were trying to give her a clue.

"Long red hair," Nello said as she closely examined the length of the strand. It was by far longer than any warrior she had known, except maybe for

Torn, and his hair was the jet black of his father's.

She sighed as she recalled walking in and seeing her son with that hated torque around his neck, his long hair flying wildly about him, and that red-haired witch gloating as she taunted him…

Red hair! Nello gasped. No one else she could recall had red hair that shade! That is why she could not place a warrior with that hair color! It did not belong to a *warrior*! It belonged to Zultha!

And if this was the servant who assisted the Healer, who'd had accessed to these chambers, who was supposed to be traveling with them to retrieve her son, sitting here practically naked and dead, that meant that someone had taken her place!

Zultha!

Zultha had just traveled through the portal with her mate and the Healer.

Zultha was on her way to that foreign realm where she would meet with her son. Zultha was going to attempt to hurt Torn.

Zultha was *going to die*!

Nello growled her fury then screamed for the guards. She paused for a moment to stare at the woman's body, to wonder who she was and what part she'd played other than warning her about Zultha. Then she was gone, charging through the halls to the transport chamber.

No wonder she had felt darkness on the woman! Not because of a spell, but because the woman was pure evil. And if she harmed one hair on her child's head, she would die screaming!

* * *

Torn was cold, tired, sore, and elated. He had managed to find his way straight to his beloved's home. Filled with pride in his accomplishments, he strode to the front door, wearing the tatters of his pants regally, and knocked on the door.

"What do you want?" an irritated female voice called out. "Who is it?"

"Torn, I am!" he replied as he recognized the voice. "I want you!"

"What?"

"You, I want?" he asked, wondering if he was wording this correctly. This language was so hard to learn…

Before he could complete his thought, the door was flung open and a small warm body launched itself at him. Instinctively moving aside to avoid the attack, as his training led him to do, he was stunned into stillness as Sable's small body hurtled past him and landed at his feet.

"Sable?" he asked as he quickly bent to assist the love of his life to her feet.

"Torn!" Sable cried, not caring that she was on her knees in the mud, not caring that she had just made a spectacle of herself, not even caring that there were now a few new aches to add to the headache she'd developed while dealing with Torn's people.

All she saw was her would-be lover, the man who set her soul on fire, the man she'd feared would never come back to her. "You're alive!"

Not caring about the mud or her oh-so-graceless entrance, Torn reached down and gathered her to him, her breasts pressed against his quivering chest. He had something to tell her and he had to tell her now. Not another moment would go by without him acknowledging how he felt.

"I… I am… I love --"

"Good Lord!" Jill exclaimed as he peered out of the door at the couple on the stoop. "He looks like the

Incredible Hulk! Get him in here before he catches his death!".

"Torn," Sable said as she turned in his arms, her hands moving to frame his face as she gazed into his violet eyes. "You're safe. You're home where you belong."

Home. His eyes watered at her words. He had a place, he was home. He ran his hands slowly up her back, forcing her closer to him as he bent low, his damp hair sliding forward to conceal their faces.

"Sable," he began again, only to be interrupted a second time. And this time, it was a heavy hand on his shoulder that made him pull away from his Sable.

"Jillian," he said, meaning to ask the man to wait, but his words froze in his throat as he saw who it was.

"Mace?" he asked, his eyes wide in shock as he looked up at the captain of his father's personal guard. "*Qua tu vere*?" Why are you here?

"I was sent to retrieve you, Torn," said the big man, his eyes watching him with a hint of fear in them as if he expected Torn to do him harm. His stance appeared almost at ease but was held in lethal readiness that showed his less than trusting nature.

This was not right, Torn thought as he released Sable to stare at Mace. Mace was the man who had befriended him and invited him to join the warriors' ranks. Mace was his mentor when his father was not there to train him, was there to teach him to handle sword and lance. Mace had, on more than one occasion, doled out some sorely needed punishment as well as given him a shoulder to lean on when his isolation became too much. Now Mace, his friend and confidant, appeared to be… afraid.

"So now you fear me?" Torn asked, hurt obvious in his tone even if his words were not understood by all.

"Torn," Mace began, but as Torn stepped closer to him, Mace took one small step back. It was enough to make Torn ponder his decisions to accept these things all over again.

Sighing deeply, he dropped his head, shoulders slumped, and the new pride in which he carried himself faded.

What had he been thinking? Even here on this plane where the people thought him large but normal, he was a freak. There was no getting over the fact that he was different and would always be different. He was deluding himself if he thought people could accept him for what he was. And if Sable could overlook the monster that dwelled within him, how would the people treat *her* for being in the company of one such as he?

"What do you want?" he asked as he seemed to shrink in on himself, defeated before the fight had begun.

"I... it takes some getting used to," Mace said, realizing something had broken in Torn in that moment and knowing that his inadvertent reaction had caused it. "But I have been sent to secure your safety."

"My safety? That is a laugh," Torn stated bitterly as he turned to look at Sable.

"What did you say to him?" Sable growled at Mace.

She too recognized the fact that something had deflated in Torn, that he'd been about to tell her something important that would change her life, and now he'd withdrawn into himself.

"What does she say?" Mace asked Torn, a confused look on his face.

"Stop talking to him!" Sable shouted, pushing

her way in front of Torn and glaring at the oversized man. "I let you into my house and you say something to make my man upset! I want you and your lackeys out!"

"What's going on?" Jill asked as he popped up on the side of Mace, staring at Sable in consternation. "Are you fighting again? Honestly! I can't take you anywhere!"

"He hurt Torn!" Sable cried out, not noticing Torn shaking his head sadly.

She was trying to defend him, but she still had no inkling to what he really was. He was something to be feared, hated, something his own father could barely tolerate.

"Well then, I guess I'm going to have to kick his ass!" Jill said, rolling up his sleeves as he too began to glare at Mace.

* * *

Not liking the way this whole conversation was going, or the heated looks directed at him while he couldn't understand their words, made Mace defensive.

"What are the little man and the spitfire saying?" he asked as he kept his eye on the red-haired man.

"I think we had better move this conversation inside," Jack's deep voice rumbled as he drew the attention of the combatants back toward the house. "Torn is wet and cold, and I don't want to have to kill someone for Jillian's benefit on the front stoop."

"Inside," Torn said to Mace as he motioned toward the house. "We will discuss this inside."

Mace nodded and stepped around the murmuring, glowering red-haired man and past the larger, dark-skinned hairless one. People here were so volatile, he decided as he met the eyes of his first and second.

"Torn has arrived," he said, and the two rose to their feet.

Torn warily made his way into the house, again marveling at the floor coverings as he moved into the living room.

Sable instantly, it seemed, had a towel and was doing her best to smother him, dry him off, and direct him to a chair at the same time.

"Sit!" she said and the three strangers watched, amazed as Torn did not do that embarrassing wiggle before he placed his rump on a chair. So that was the meaning of the word "sit!" One didn't have to do that ridiculous dance before parking their bottom. All three blushed in embarrassment.

"Where were you? Why did you leave? Are you okay?"

Sable shot questions at him even as she sent evil looks at the three men who now stood looking at them.

"Let the man speak," Jack said to Sable as he placed a calming hand on Jill's shoulder, his other hand rubbing the high-strung man's back, easing the heavy muscles that had tightened as he'd moved to defend Torn.

"Men of Terror," he stated as he peeked longingly at Sable. He sighed as he gazed upon what he could never have. No one deserved to be tied to one such as him, two things trapped inside of one body.

"Men of terror?" Sable glared at the three. "They don't look too terrifying to me. In fact, they look like a bunch of overgrown bullies! What did they say to you?"

Sable was still hot about the unknown words that had caused Torn pain. "They have come to take me to Terror," he said. "I must go." It would be better for all concerned if he disappeared right now. He would hurt, but he would bring more pain to Sable if he stayed.

"What?" Sable shrieked and placed her hands on his hips as he stood. "They aren't taking you anywhere!"

"They bring Terror," Torn tried to explain, and didn't understand Jack's growl and Jill's indignant gasp.

"They will do no such thing," Sable shouted, the force of her words and the heat of her anger forcing the three warriors to back up a bit.

How did one battle an unknown element, which happened to be a female one at that?

"They're a bunch of bullies and there will be no terror or fear brought upon you while I'm still alive!"

Torn blinked as he stared at his fierce little warrior. She would defend him to the death, she said. But what did fear have to do with his father?

"Terror is good," he tried again, thinking that maybe Zultha's lies had reached her here on this unknown plane.

"It is not!" she said as she turned to Torn, her heart in her eyes. "It is not good for anyone to be afraid." She turned to the big three again. "And I'll be dammed before they bring fear to you, no matter what they say."

"Fear?" Torn asked, knowing the meaning of that word. "My father… fear?"

"Father?"

"Father?" Jack and Jill chimed in together, disbelief in their voices.

"Father… Terror," Torn said as he tried to find the bridge between their two languages. Why would they think that his father was fear?

"Wait!" Sable cried out suddenly, bringing everyone's eyes on her. "Child abuse?"

"He ain't no child, honey!" Jill snickered, only to be elbowed into silence by Jack.

"Abuse?" Torn said, realization dawning. "No! Father is Terror."

"His father is that bad?" Sable breathed, wondering what could terrify a man who turned into a giant flying cat with black angel's wings. Did he turn into a floating lion?

"Terror is Father! Torn, I am," Torn explained, looking at Sable and willing her to understand as he thumbed his chest. "Terror, he is. And Mace, he is," he said, pointing to the man who had made him cringe. "Del, he is." He indicated to the man roughly the same size as the first one. "Joz, he is," he said finally, pointing to the largest of the three. "Terror's men. Father's men."

"Well, that's a relief," Sable said, relieved, pictures of fire-breathing felines banished from her mind. "Now tell them to go away. You're mine and I'm not giving you back."

There was a pleasant smile on her face as she said this, dismissing the men at a glance.

"I need… go," Torn said at last, sinking into himself again.

"No! Torn, no!" Sable said, her smile leaving as she sat on the couch beside him. "I just found you again. I can't let you go."

"What does the female say?" Mace asked, looking at Sable, uncertainty still in his eyes.

Clearly this female was no good for the lad. She was trying to get him to do something he didn't want to. He understood the body language, Torn sadly shaking his head as he gazed at her and the set to her stubborn chin. He had to get him out of this place before he was corrupted.

"Nothing that concerns you, Mace," Torn said as he tried to stop the pain he felt welling up in his heart.

"Nothing… A few days with these creatures and already you show no respect for your teachers," Mace growled, causing Torn to sit up at attention and Jack to move forward.

Del, whose hand went to his scabbard, and Joz, who moved beside him countered the move.

Not one to let his partner face danger alone, Jill again got a pugnacious look on his face as he stepped forward. This battle would be well and truly met.

"Stop it!" Sable shouted as she leapt to her feet. "All of you!"

Her heart was breaking. Didn't they understand? Torn said he had to go. Silence fell as Torn rose and took Sable's hands in his.

"I don't want… go!" he said passionately, his eyes tearing up as he stared at the woman who almost made him believe he was lovable. Worthy of love. "Have to! Not safe, not safe… you!"

"I don't care! Stay with me! What can be so dangerous?" she cried out. "What?"

"Me," he answered solemnly.

"Oh, come on, Torn! You aren't going to hurt me!"

"But the others will!" he said with conviction.

"Them?" She pointed to the trio who watched them curiously.

"No! Others!" He pointed toward the door.

"People? Other people? Torn, they don't have to know!"

"Know what I am? They will know! I cannot… hide!"

He looked imploringly into her eyes, begging for understanding, but she held fast to her dreams.

"What are you?"

"What am I?"

"What are you, Torn? What is that thing you turned into? Why are they taking you away from me?"

Tears began to break free of her control. They poured down, crystalline drops of grief that left their trail of sorrow down her face, splattering on the floor, even as her heart shattered into a million pieces.

"I am… Reaver."

* * *

Terror stepped out of the void and into… hell.

"What is this place?" he asked as he stared dumbfounded at the metal boxes that moved on big black wheels and the so very tiny people who rode in them.

There was a loud clashing in the air, a klaxon of horns, and talking people moving about in a manner the likes of which he had never seen before.

The men, if you wanted to call the swordless knarks who dressed in soft fibers, not the tough animal skins of warriors, looked feeble and weak, not worthy for a true solider at all. A few stared gape-mouthed at his party, the giant white-haired healer and his assistant, in wonder.

"Torn was in danger because of… these people?" he asked, incredulously.

"They may have hidden dangers," offered the Healer as he too shook his head at the strange people and their devices.

"What? They will gnaw on his ankles until he yields?" Terror snorted.

"Um, well, their danger may be a bit more subtle," the Healer said as he shook his head at Terror.

"Like a certain child who appeared to be a dreamer, but held within him a nightmare."

Snarling in rage, Terror turned toward his old friend.

"If you ever call my son a nightmare again, I will pull your tongue out of your mouth and shove it up your ass!"

Startled, the Healer backed up, but held his ground. "You deny that the child is cursed? That he carries darkness within him?"

"That darkness is there because he purges it from people! Torn is *my child* and the son of *my heart*! I have lost so many years out of fear, Fal. So many wasted years because I believed that I had cursed him. All the time *I* was the one cursed. I let my misgivings take him away from me for so many years, and I will not sit back and let someone defame his name. He is *my child*, Healer! Watch your words!"

Nodding, Fal turned again to the people moving swiftly around them. The sky was dark and there were stars out, but there was a damp chill in the air.

"Very well, Terror. Let us see to your son. Maybe these hidden dangers will become more apparent to us as we search. No one is to be underestimated."

"I agree," he said as he too turned to observe the people and the quickly emptying streets. "But this is still a strange place inhabited by strange-looking people. Can you not see how short they are?"

"Size isn't everything," Fal said as he nodded to his assistant. "Let us be off."

"Nello will soon follow," Terror said as he halted the procession. "She needs to track us."

"Can she not follow the collar on Torn?" Fal asked.

"Yes," Terror said quietly as he closed his eyes

and had to fight a sudden urge to cry.

"What is it?" Fal had not missed the paleness of Terror's face.

"My son! He is in pain. He needs me."

Without a word, they were off, the cloaked assistant following behind. No one noticed her long red hair or her warped smile. But she moved swiftly, staying behind the men, biding her time, waiting for her chance.

* * *

"What is a Reaver, Torn?" Sable asked, her eyes searching. "What are you?"

"Reaver kill... evil," he said looking into her eyes. "It takes evil."

"Takes evil?"

"Inside! In me! It is inside me." He pointed to his chest, staring deeply into her eyes, willing her to understand, to know the meaning of his words.

"You take evil inside you?"

"Evil, hurt, pain. It is all... inside... me."

"Criminy! I get it!" Everyone in the room turned to stare at Jill as he sat up in excitement. "Remember I told you I felt purged, cleansed inside? Torn did it. He took my pain away and I think it is with him, inside him, Sable."

He turned to face Jack who now had a stunned look on his face.

"You all right then?" Jill asked as he examined his mate, as the revelation took him as well.

"Yes, the pain. I have... *had* a lot of darkness in my past. After Torn... reaved me, I guess, it all seemed not as important. I could suddenly get past it and not just deal with it. Is that what a Reaver does, Torn? Do you take away the pain so that a person is... free?"

Nodding vigorously, Torn smiled sadly at the

two men before turning to face Sable once again.

"Reaver takes pain, takes hurt."

"I can live with that, Torn," Sable said softly and sniffled. "I just can't take life without you."

"Reaver is… not only inside, Sable. Reaver is… ugly." He searched for the word to let her know how distasteful his second form was to others, how hideous he appeared to himself, how he could never accept the part of him that dwelled within.

He snorted in disgust as he seemed to sink into himself again. His gaze dropped as if he were ashamed of ever thinking that something could come of an infatuation with Sable. His desolate sighs seemed to echo within his body as defeat settled like a heavy mantle around him.

"There is nothing ugly in you, Torn," Sable denied as she slipped to her knees in front of him. "In you, I only see goodness and light."

"I see… *saw* your face." He struggled with the words. "Here, I have not…" His eyebrows twisted as he fought to find the words. "Not enough control. There is much evil -- no, pain -- here. I change when… I change."

He ran frustrated hands through his hair as he thought of the futility of his situation.

"Better if I… go."

"I was surprised, Torn." Sable took his hands and pulled them gently from his hair, bringing his gaze back to hers. "I have never seen anything like you before. But I truly don't care, Torn. I don't care. You can grow three heads and I'll love each one of them."

"Depends on where they're located," Jill murmured, then winced as Jack whacked him.

"Look into my heart," Sable urged. "You will know if I lie."

Staring into her face, her dear familiar face, Torn fought the urge to use his powers, just to see. But the truth of her words showed brightly in her face. She really was not afraid of him.

He blinked then sat up, eyes still glued to her visage.

"I love you, Torn. I'm jealous of everyone who comes near you; I would fight to keep you near me. I love you!"

"Sable," he began and almost automatically his face began to lower toward hers. "You love…"

"*At vort, Torn!*" What did you do, Torn!

He jerked his head up and turned to his father's soldiers and Mace's frowning glower.

"Why do you dally with that woman? She may be fair of face, but remember, so was Zultha. What can you offer this woman? Better you leave with us now. Your father should have received my signal and is probably already here. Do not waste her time with this foolishness."

Torn pulled away from Sable, who glared at the tall man who'd spoken so harshly to her Torn.

"Better I go," he said, again regret shining in his eyes as he eased Sable to her feet and rose to stand beside her. "Mace is correct."

"Mace can kiss my ass! What did he say?" Sable demanded in frustration as she planted her fists on her hips and glared for all the she was worth.

"He reminds me I have no place… here."

"You *have* a place," she yelled, still glaring at Mace. "Tell him I said it is in my bed."

Blushing, Torn translated her words to the others and looked down, not wanting to see the laughter in their eyes.

Who would want to bed a man so full of the taint

of others, a monster in a place where monsters were common?

But instead of laughter, Mace took a deep breath, one of admiration.

"What did you do to the lady, Torn, to get such devotion out of her? She looks to take us all on in defense of you."

Torn raised his head, blinked at the threat emanating from Sable. She indeed looked as if she were going to bite Mace's head off and hand it back to him. *That* was how much she wanted him; that she would take on the fiercest of warriors for him.

"I… love her," Torn explained. "She feels it."

"Then what are you waiting for? Go and take her to her bed!" Mace decreed. "We shall wait, and when your father returns, we may be able to take her with you."

Although Mace had begun to loathe this place, its strange water falling from the sky and the weird way the people spoke, he had to admire the changes he saw in Torn.

Although he still seemed untried and youthful, there did seem to be more confidence in him. He still couldn't believe that Torn, quiet bashful Torn, had been in a street brawl. He still couldn't believe that Torn was the Reaver, but he had seen this phenomenon for himself. And although he was wary of the power the Reaver held, the young man standing before him was just Torn.

"What did he say?" Sable asked, and Jack and Jill leaned closer to hear.

"He said to take you to bed."

"As if I needed his permission," Sable sniffed, before she took his hand and pulled him to the back bedroom.

"Jack, Jill, get them out of here."

"With pleasure!" Jill jumped to his feet and pointed toward the door. "Let's go, boys!"

"Go with them, please," Torn translated as Sable pulled him closer to her bed and their ultimate enjoyment. "Sable doesn't need witnesses."

The other two looked at Mace for guidance, but the man nodded. "Follow the loud one and the larger one," Mace ordered. "Torn needs his privacy."

"But we are to protect him," Joz protested quietly.

"We can't protect him from his heart," Del said quietly as he motioned the larger man toward the door. "If he can't take her with him, he has to deal with the fallout. Love is tricky, Joz. There is no saving you from your emotions. Better you learn that now."

Nodding, the trio of men followed Jill and Jack out of the house.

"Take them to the gym, then?" Jill asked. "Or maybe we should just take them back to our place."

"Why not? You already caused a riot at the pub. The apartment would be safer and we won't have to answer too many questions."

"That was not me," Jill defended. "That was Torn. Who knew he could dance like that?"

"The whole of Scotland, by now." Jack sighed as he motioned the men toward the garage.

"What about them, then?" Jill asked. "Someone is bound to notice us taking these guys into our flat. We do have a lot of curious neighbors."

"We'll tell everyone they're from… Egypt. Yeah, that will explain it! Egyptian friends who have come for an art show or something."

"Egypt it is," Jill agreed, thinking about the eyes that would pop when they walked in with the well-muscled men. "I can see tickets to Africa being snapped up right now."

"I'll take a one-way!" Jase piped in helpfully from the back, and then shrugged as his friends groaned.

Chapter Ten

"You are so filthy!" Sable giggled as she led Torn into the bathroom down the hall from her bedroom.

"Filthy," he agreed, staring at the rapidly drying mud that flaked off his body and realized he was starting to itch.

"We have to clean you up a bit."

"Clean." He nodded. That was reasonable. Cleanliness was good when you were ready to take someone to bed. It saved the bed linens.

Smiling at the man who gently took her commands, Sable pulled him into the bathroom and snapped on the lights.

Torn watched her, amused, as she bustled about, pulling towels out of a closet, shifting through an impressive collection of what he assumed were bathing soaps in oddly shaped bottles, and finally turning the shower on so that the hot water steamed up the air around them.

"Come on," she encouraged as she pulled him toward the shower, then jerked back the curtain and gestured for him to enter.

Showers were one of Torn's favorite things on this realm. *If water was going to fall from the sky, it should fall warm and be controllable*, he thought.

But he moved forward and stepped into the tub, sighing as the steam warmed his body and the hot water sluiced down his skin. He closed his eyes and stepped deeper into the shower, letting the water wash over his face and soak his hair.

But when he felt a naked body press against his back, his eyes jerked open in surprise.

"Sable!" Was she getting in with him?

"Torn!" She smiled at the look on his face.

He was confused. He thought he would get clean and then go and service his chosen. It was a job he would enjoy, but he never thought she would become this intimate, this involved.

"Someone has to wash your back, baby," she murmured as she held up the bottle in her hand.

But his eyes were not on the bottle, or anything else she'd brought into the shower, for that matter.

Sable was... Sable was... Naked! Beautifully, gloriously, wonderfully naked!

His violet eyes darkened to a smoky gray as he stared hungrily at the rounded curves, highlighted perfectly by the water on her body.

Oh, the water! It flowed along her body, soaking her skin, giving her a sensual, sultry look even as it glistened on the thin, curly hair covering her mound. His eyes lovingly traced every drop as he ran his finger from the tip of a hardening nipple down to where it slid over the tight curve of her calf.

He shuddered in the water as he felt his body tense and harden. His cock rose as blood rushed downward. He felt a thump against his stomach and looked down to see the head of his cock hitting his abs just over his navel. His skin tingled from more than the hot water and he had to bite his lip to hold in a low, hungry growl.

He wanted her! He wanted to push her against the hard shiny-squared wall and thrust his cock deep inside her cunt. He wanted to hear her scream as he drove himself in as deep as possible, feel her nails scratch and claw at his back as he pounded into her flesh, forcing her surrender.

He wanted her *bad*.

Then he forced his eyes up.

Her face was a study in confidence and curiosity,

a burning look in her eyes, her full lips slightly parted as her breath rasped, merging with the sounds of the falling water.

She looked hot and horny as hell!

Then he started, eyes widening in shock as he realized that she was staring right at him!

He drew this reaction from a woman? His small body? His less than perfect physique?

Damn, she was hot and horny over him, maybe as hot as he was over her! Creator, when did his luck change?

"Back?" he finally replied, forcing his brain to function even though he felt like an animal in heat.

"But I would really like to scrub something lower, and in the front," she purred as she flipped her thumb over the cap and popped it open.

The smell of passion -- vanilla in this language, filled the humid air, making his nose twitch as he recognized the smell that she often wore.

Then she squeezed a sudsy white substance in her palm, much different than the usual bar soap he used.

Wait! Something lower and in the front?

He looked down to his throbbing and neglected cock, and a slow smile crossed his face. She could go lower than that, but it wouldn't be much fun. He gazed back up at her face only to see her drop the bottle and rub her palms together, creating a thick, rich foam that he could only imagine encasing his cock.

"May I?" she asked as she licked her lips, staring at his straining erection and trying hard to be polite and not scare the man.

It had been years for her, and she was feeling distinctively… hungry.

Mute, all he could do was nod as she stepped

closer, the water plastering her cropped hair to her delicately shaped skull. She looked so small and dainty, but there was such… passion flowing through her. Even without using his abilities, he could read desire pouring off of her. He held his breath, watching to her hands, and they moved closer and closer to their prize.

"Ung, Sable!" he gasped, almost going up on his toes as her hands gently reached out and drew his erection down from his stomach.

Her hands encircled and stroked carefully, twisting on the upstroke and tightening on the downstroke, tempting him to lose all control.

"You are so big," she praised, her eyes growing fever-bright and her breathing quickening as she held that magnificent piece of meat in her hands. "So thick and strong!"

His hands went to her shoulders then he gasped in wonder at the soft feel of her skin.

Lubricated by the water, his hands glided up and down her arms, feeling the muscles work as she caressed him in turn. But he wanted to touch more, to feel more, to experience more.

"Sable, may… I…" He didn't have the words. But he was not at a loss for action.

His hand dropped down and gently cupped one breast, hefting its slight weight and drawing a cry from her lips as his thumb rubbed across the tip of her nipple.

Sable groaned and leaned into his touch, encouraging him more. "Yes, Torn. Just like that."

Then her other breast was given the same sensual treatment.

"Anything you want," she urged as one hand left his thick cock and slid around his lean waist, dropping down to grip one firm ass cheek.

That was it! Her words gave him the freedom to do what he wished. And he did so want to do a lot to the body that drew him from the first time he'd laid eyes on her.

Pulling her tight against his chest, he dropped his head and took that temptingly full bottom lip in his teeth, carefully nipping with his fangs, sending sharp pleasure-pain to her nerves, before he used his tongue to enter the sweet heaven of her mouth.

His hands were given free rein as they spread across her back, pressing her closer as one dropped to her thigh, bringing that leg up so that he trembled with the feel of her pressed even closer than before.

"Oh yes!" She gasped as she released him and wrapped both hands around his neck, opening her body to his possession, to her pleasure, to their mutual satisfaction.

Her hips began a slow grinding motion, desperate to get closer to his cock, now all soaped and slippery and ready for her. But Torn was not done playing.

Sliding his hands under her arms, he lifted her up, her breasts right at mouth level so he could easily...

"Ohh! I love that!" Sable moaned. "Suck my nipples, Torn."

Grinning, he sucked in the tender fruit, pulling it deep within the cavern of his mouth and laving it with his tongue.

Her body squirmed, sliding against the water and the soap now liberally covering the front of him. But, God, did it feel wonderful!

Growling, Torn switched nipples, giving the second the same attention as the first, easily holding her in place.

"More! Please, Torn, more!" she panted, her hands leaving his shoulders and tangling in his thick hair, tugging it as she urged him onward.

Soon, that was not enough for him. Not nearly enough to ease the hunger that had grown over the days as he'd watched her parade around in that perfect body, her aggressive attitude, and fought his natural urges.

No more.

"Torn take… now!" he growled as he released her nipple with a *pop*. "Now, Sable!"

"Yes, Torn! Now!" Sable breathed, clinging to him as he shifted their weight and lifted her even closer.

"Guide," he breathed into her neck, his tongue lapping at the water that still flowed over them both. "Guide Torn."

Frantically, she reached for him, arching to get his cock where she wanted it. The base of his thick member in hand, she tentatively lifted her other leg, grinning when he moved to assist, and wrapped it around his waist. Now she was riding his body; not the part she wanted to be riding on, but pretty damn close.

Her eyes closed as a full-body tremor racked her, her senses spiked, her juices flowed down to become mist in the water, creating a hot, wet environment any thrusting cock would enjoy.

Then he was positioned at the mouth of her cunt, hot, hard, and throbbing, silky smooth and a wonderfully soft texture that no human had ever been able to recreate.

He was almost there.

"Now! *Please!*"

Torn gritted his teeth and he felt his muscles

bulge as he fought to maintain his hold on his woman and keep enough control as to not thrust inside like a rabid beast. But the feel of her, dripping down and coating his cock, was too much.

"Sable," he breathed one last time, then surged upwards.

"Yes!" Sable's ecstatic cry echoed around the stall as she felt Torn's hardness demanded entrance, parting her and burrowing out a place for itself.

His sigh was more a groan as he felt her folds part and grant him entrance. He was home! Nothing had ever felt this good. That other woman; she was *nothing* compared to what he felt just by being with his Sable. And now that they were fully connected, he vowed no other would usurp his place here, with her, inside of her, being one with her.

He leaned back against the wall and just basked in the glory of being deep within her. But the grunts and wiggles she made were growing too hard to ignore.

Her legs tightened around his waist, the heels of her feet digging into his ass, urging him to move. She wiggled and ground herself on his cock, the muscles gripping his base, the internal walls massaging and clenching around his flesh.

"Damn it! Move, you big oversized… Oh! Yes! You great big oversized god! *Yes!*"

Torn tightened his grip on her waist, lifting her up an inch or so, then slammed her down, hard!

"You can be my god!" she shrieked as he repeated the move, much to her delight. Her toes curled as her thighs trembled. Fire shot through her cunt as the soft hairs at his base rubbed her clit the right way. Torn might not know squat about her world, but the man knew how to fuck!

"Again!" she pleaded, her head dropping back as she began to ride the magnificent beast she'd found for herself. "Harder! *Harder*!"

Smiling outright now, Torn began to thrust in earnest, angling his cockhead to strike her most sensitive spots.

He noted her reaction and tried to strike that spot over and over again, arching his hips to get more of himself inside.

"Torn!" she bellowed as her nails broke the skin on his shoulders.

He grunted at the pleasure-pain and added a bounce to his movements.

"Ah! Ah! Ah!"

Sable couldn't think! Her mind was lost in a lust-filled haze. Her body was taut, swimming in the erotic sensations that were flowing through her. He was too good to be true! This kind of loving only took place between the pages of a romance novel -- maybe an erotic novel, but stuff like this didn't happen in real life.

Yet here she was, crying out, screaming, groaning and screeching, sounding like a cat in heat while the sexiest man she had ever come in contact with was driving his cock hard, deep and fast within her body.

"Yes!"

Suddenly, she stiffened. She knew one more thrust, one more bounce, one more jiggle, and she would explode.

"Please!" she managed as her head lolled on her shoulders. "Please, make me come!"

The lustful surrender he saw in her eyes was his breaking point.

"Sable!" he bellowed as he jerked her to his chest,

bent his knees, and thrust upward with everything he had.

"Torn!"

Then she was flying, her body jerking as unbelievable waves of climatic delight tore through her body. She panted, her eyes opening wide as his hands clenched around her hips and he gave in to his own pleasure. It was the most erotic thing she had ever seen.

Without another word, his face went lax, his breathing almost nonexistent, and the muscles in his jaws stood out in stark relief. He shouted once, tossing his head to the side, then he rapidly thrust hard, three times, slamming even deeper than before. His hands clenched, his eyes shot open, and she felt his cock swell even bigger. Then a glowing white light flared up around them both, blinding and yet filled with emotion.

"*Sable!*"

Her name was ripped from his throat as his whole body began to shake as spurt after spurt of his white-hot seed filled her to overflowing.

As the tension in his body eased, so did the light, which left Torn a devastated, shaking mass of muscle, leaning against the wall for support, trying to hold her even closer than she was now.

"Torn… love… Sable," he panted, one word with each breath.

"Torn," she breathed. "You are my world."

She lowered shaky legs to the floor of the stall, legs that refused to support her weight, so Torn kept a tight grip on her waist.

"The water is going to be cold soon," she added, her voice trembling like her knees. Funny, she hadn't noticed the drop in temperature before.

"We… dirty." He gestured to the mud still streaking his body and the bodily fluids glistening on them both.

"So we hurry and wash." Sable grinned and reached far down for the shower gel, almost falling as her body decided that balance wasn't really necessary at this point.

But Torn held her safe until she grabbed the elusive bottle and a bath puff sitting on the built-in soap dish.

Silently, she covered the puff in foam and began to gently wash his chest. Torn had never felt so loved.

"Torn… I love you," he repeated, and noted the sly grin spreading across her face.

"Not as much as I love you," she replied smugly as the strength returned to her legs and she set about washing her man. "I'm not running and screaming because you turned into a lightning rod, and believe me, most women would be screaming now."

"Torn no hurt," he said indignantly as he rose up to his full height then turned and presented her with his back. "Torn protector!"

"You certainly are," she agreed as she ran the soapy puff over the mountains of muscles that made up his back. "And you're mine. All mine."

"Torn is Sable's." There was finality in his words.

"And don't you forget it!"

They enjoyed the rest of the shower and Sable discovered a few new places on his body that made his huge dick dance to the rhythm she set.

And Torn let her. He really was the perfect mate.

* * *

Contentment. Complete and utter contentment!

He'd never felt that before, and he doubted anything would ever feel that good again. Torn felt a smile spread across his lips as the slight weight of Sable pressed him deeper into the sheets.

Sable was perfection. There was no sense of going through the motions to please him; she genuinely wanted to make him feel…

Loved!

The voice of his inner demon seemed content as well. The stuff Sable had done, that she'd taught him…

He purred at the memory.

* * *

"Again, stud?" Sable giggled as she nestled under his chin, shivering at the velvety texture of his skin on her sensitive body.

"I like again, Sable," Torn whispered as he cuddled her closer, bending to brush a kiss against the tangled mass of bright red close-cropped hair on her head.

"Oh, I think I like it, too." She chuckled as she pulled away far enough to begin kissing down his chest.

She paused at one masculine nipple to tease it into a sharp point with her tongue before her lips resumed their tantalizing travels again, toward his navel.

She smiled as she thought about the shower incident.

That was the most amazing… outrageous… unbelievable act of wanton carnality she'd ever been a party to! She wanted to do it again.

After scrubbing down in the tepid water, their bodies rubbing close in the shower stall, she pulled the dazed man out and into the steamy bathroom. A quick application of towels and they headed to the bedroom for some much-needed sleep.

But that's not what happened, exactly. Torn

spied her lotion and whispered, "Massage," which happened to be one of the most powerful words in the human language.

Where he'd learned it was anyone's guess, but the man sure knew what he was doing there, too! He started with her front, gently massaging the small red marks made with his mouth, frowning as he examined them.

"Torn sorry," he whispered, looking so sad she felt guilty for having fair skin. "It's okay, Torn," she reassured him. "It's a small reminder and I'm proud to have the marks."

He looked at her with such wonder in his eyes that she couldn't resist taking the lotion and applying it to his chest, watching as his eyes widened in wonder. He'd never had a massage before, it seemed, and she set out to see to that oversight. But his body was too delectable. She wound up dropping the lotion onto the bed and running her hands all over him, pressing on the spots she knew would drive him wild.

Torn, for his part, laid back, eyes wide in amazement as his woman painted his body in tiny nibbles and long licks. As the licks went lower and lower, his body got hotter and hotter, and he just knew they would need another shower after this.

Sable giggled, but it was a low, erotic sound as her tongue traced the cobblestones of his stomach then dipped into his navel.

Torn jerked as he felt fire shoot through his veins. His hands found themselves tangled in her short hair, urging her lower.

"Not until I'm ready," Sable purred, laughing at his frustrated groans.

He had a damn hot body. She loved the taste and feel of it, and she knew he was enjoying what she was doing. Proof was hitting her under the chin.

"Sable --"

"Not yet!" She bypassed his groin altogether to part his legs and place kisses along the sensitive skin of his inner thigh.

"Mmm." He arched into her touch, spreading his legs wider, showing her where he needed her touch the most.

Sable sat back and stared at the wanton sprawl before her and licked her lips.

His thick cock was lying against his stomach, his heavy balls lay just beneath, all framed by a soft nest of curly black hair.

His thighs were muscular pillars, golden brown in color and the best example of masculine perfection she had ever seen.

His chest heaved with every breath he took and she marveled that she controlled all that strength.

His arms slowly lifted, reaching for her as his eyes turned that smoky gray, pleading with her to finish what she started.

Relishing her power, she slowly shook her head and ran her fingers along the throbbing shaft of his cock.

"Pretty, pretty piece," she murmured, running her fingers along the head, rubbing through the beads of moisture there and lovingly rubbing them into his skin. "Pretty, pretty and all for me."

She was so engrossed in her game that she never noticed the predatory look that crossed his face.

Before she could even think to squeak, Torn rose up and grabbed her around her waist.

The world shifted on its axis and she found herself lying flat on her back, her limbs spread wide, her mouth open in shock.

"Torn play, too!"

Then he shifted over her, his long hair dragging over her body, catching and dragging against her hard nipples, making her sensitive skin all the more sensitive. But it was the sight of her mate, her man, that stole her breath away.

"*Vernt ta Orge*," he growled, low and dangerous as his eyes glittered, a hint of red bleeding into the stormy gray orbs. "*My mate*," he growled as something that lived deep inside of him began to break free.

Sable could only watch in aroused awe as Torn rose above her, proud and strong. "Mine!" he repeated in English, though his meaning before was perfectly clear.

"Yours," Sable soothed, feeling the urgency build up in her mate and wanting to ease it, but at the same time she wanted to see it build. She reached up a hand and caressed his smooth cheek, felt the muscles there clench and jump with tension.

Torn had never felt this level of want, this level of need, and yet it was tempered by an extreme level of protective instincts. No one would ever lay a hand on her. She was his and his alone.

That dark place deep inside him reached, swirling to life, and it felt right, this darkness. He would kill anyone who dared touch her! A low growl rumbled, filled the air, and he realized that it was bubbling up from his throat. And that it felt good, it felt like letting go.

Then he felt it, that gentle touch against his face. He snapped his head down, his attention on… her.

The smell of her, the feel of her, the taste of her he could feel in his mouth. His mate. His woman. His Sable.

He lowered his head and gave in to the need to

taste her, to run his tongue along her neck, to feel the rapid tattoo of her heart, to smell the arousal that poured off of her in waves. Then he had to have more, wanted to taste more, wanted to cover his body in the pure essence of her.

Sable moaned and arched her neck, tilting her head to the side, a blatant act of submission on her part.

Seeing that, the anxiousness in him eased and the growl became a low rumble. *Sable*!

Her scent enfolded him, as her skin… so soft.

His eyes zeroed in on her nipples, dark berries that pointed toward him, inviting his tongue to forage, to play.

Sable shuddered under her mate's touch. She never knew this side of Torn existed. All the time she'd known him, he had been gentle and sweet. This was different. This was a turn-on. She felt hot wetness seeping down to soak her curls and made her clit throb. His lips wrapped around her nub, sucking as his tongue laved the swelling tip.

"Torn!" she gasped as her hands dove through his silky curls, rubbing his scalp, encouraging him to suck harder.

Her body began to tremble with this new desire, the emotions within her began to swirl and churn. Her back arched off the bed, pushing toward this source of pleasure and her low moan filled the room with sound.

"Suck it harder," she groaned, pulling at his hair. "Please, baby."

Grunting, delighting in the pleasure-pain at his scalp, Torn left her nipple and moved toward the other, treating it to the same delicious torment.

"Lower," Sable gasped as she parted her legs, creating a space for him while encouraging his lower explorations.

Torn almost purred as he gave in to his mate's wants, and he licked and nipped at the skin of her stomach until he reached the small indention of her navel.

Once there, he nipped and licked at it, making her shiver in unexpected pleasure. Who knew that a navel could be so erotic? Maybe it was the man, she decided, then all thought left as he reached lower.

Torn trembled as he got closer to the sweet, musky smell of his mate, closer to the source of her desire. His hot hands grasped her thighs firmly, spreading them further, exposing the weeping pussy.

She was beautiful, a golden-drenched rose, delicate lips lightly furred and parting as they throbbed in desire and spread to expose the pale, milky seed of lust that fueled her drive.

Her clit was beautiful to him; it called for fingers and tongue. It begged to be manipulated until his mate was nothing more than a pile of wanton, screaming passion, clawing at him and wanting more.

The imagery was enough to almost cause his control to slip and his vibrating cock to explode.

Moaning, he closed his eyes and fought to give his body time to ease, to not just slam into her as deeply and as roughly as he could, to fulfill both of their fantasies there and now.

But he slowed down, lowered his head, inhaling deeply to draw in her scent, to mark himself as belonging to no one but her. Then he rested his elbows inside her widely spread thighs, and lowered his head. His thumb ran lightly over her clit's wet, silky surface.

She hissed as every muscle in her body tightened in reaction. "God, Torn!"

With that glorious cry of hers ringing in his ears,

Torn growled and buried his face in her cunt.

"Ahh!"

Her thighs clamped around his head, holding him in place as she writhed under his touch.

"Sable," he murmured against her hot flesh as his tongue parted her folds and spread her juices around. His hands moved up to take her thighs again, to spread them further apart so that he could move his mouth lower.

With relish, he began to enjoy his mate, to slurp in her juices, to purr in delight at the growing sensation of warmth deep in his chest.

This was right. He was home; he was where he wanted to be.

Shaking his face and growling softly, he closed his eyes and gave in to his need. More Sable, sweet Sable, *perfect* Sable.

Sable threw her head back and wailed her pleasure to the heavens. Wave after wave of ecstasy flowed from her clit to her hungry walls that seemed so empty. It shot up her spine and tightened her nipples and made her back arch. It left her body in a wanton sprawl as her fingers ripped at her sheets, and her feet slipped on the bed as she tried to find purchase with her heels.

This was amazing! This was perfect. This was Torn.

Her hips bucked upward, forcing more movement, more pressure from his mouth even as his hands fought to hold her still so he could partake of his special feast. But soon that was not enough.

His cock, swollen and throbbing in his need, begged to be bathed in the soothing moisture that flowed from his mate. He knew that only burying himself in her heat would assuage the lust that had taken over. Growling, he jerked himself up and spread her thighs wide, pulling her legs on top of his shoulders.

"Mine!" he rumbled as he positioned the head of his cock against her weeping opening.

"Yours! Yours, Torn!" she managed, then sucked in a deep breath as she felt the wide broad head of his cock part her. "Ah… ah… *yes*!"

The solid heat of him, the wide breadth of him, the grunts and growls that rolled from his throat made her cry out loudly.

"Ah… Torn! Harder, baby! Harder!"

Tightening his grip on her waist, he pulled her into each of his thrusts, his teeth gritted and his eyes narrowed as pleasure spiked up and down his spine. "*Ja kerien tu sont*!" I'll give you what you want.

He leaned over, almost bending her in half and took her mouth in a fierce kiss.

His lips dominated hers, forced her submission then invaded the sweet recesses of her mouth, sliding in and pulling out, mimicking the smooth deep glide of his cock straining at her pussy walls.

Her scream of pleasure was muffled inside his mouth and he greedily swallowed her cries and sought to force more of them from her.

Shudders took both of them and a pale white glow began to emanate from his body, filling her with power and causing mini explosions along her straining pussy and tightening the muscles of her stomach.

Again and again he slammed himself home and the intensity of the light grew.

There was a wailing in the air and Sable found herself stunned to realize that it was coming from her mouth! Her eyes grew wide as the pleasure doubled, then tripled, then threatened to take her sanity. She jerked her head back, almost afraid of this extreme passion, this all-consuming feeling, and then she gasped as she caught sight of her mate.

Throwing his head back and ignoring the tendrils that clung to both of their flesh, Torn arched his back and roared as a massive set of black wings exploded from his back.

Feathers fell around them as Torn gave a shout and began to move faster, deeper, harder than before.

His cock swelled impossibly wide inside her, going deep enough to push against her soul as he opened solid red eyes, eyes that were fierce and passionate and filled with love… for her.

It was too much! Sensory overload!

Her body doubled up and stilled, locked in position as a screaming orgasm tore through her.

"Torn!" she shrieked, then her inner walls clamped down on her mate, marking him as hers, demanding that he give up his seed to her hungry body.

"*Griths!*" he screamed, his tri-toned voice higher yet deeper than she had ever heard as he dropped low over her and began a series of rapid-fire lunges that slammed against her sweet spot, increasing the intensity of her climax, dragging it out, even as it brought him to his own apex.

"Sable!"

Then he was there!

He felt his balls slam up to the base of his cock, felt the tingling that began low in his spine slide along his stomach and his legs, felt the almost burning sensation as his hot seed forced its way through his cock.

He felt the wave of heat as his skin darkened to midnight before flashing back to its gold tones, felt his whole body come alive as spurt after spurt of his seed exploded through his vibrating cock.

"Grrrr!" He growled, his mouth dropping to her neck, his teeth clamping sharply on the soft, sensitive skin there, then the sensations were too much for his swollen cockhead.

He exploded, a white-hot gush of passion that flooded her gripping sheath, spurt after spurt of bone-melting pleasure that sapped the strength from his bones and turned his muscles to water.

His hips continued to thrust in reflex as he collapsed on top of her heaving body.

"Sable," he breathed again, as he felt his black angel's wings flutter down to envelop them both in their downy soft haven.

"Torn," she gasped, trying to slow the rapid beat of her heart as her hands traveled up his back, one buried in the wildly mussed hair, the other tracing the oddly spongy skin where wing met back.

He shivered in response, his whole body tightening around her and a deep purr escaped his mouth.

"That… that was…" Sighing, she closed her eyes, bereft of words.

Torn lifted his head, staring at her face, wondering if his changed appearance had frightened her. Never had he had a partial transformation before, never in all the times he pleasured his own self or the one time he was with Zultha.

Maybe because you finally let go, that inner voice purred, replete in its freedom and the sexual act.

His thoughts turned away from that voice as he stared down at his mate, watched her eyes blink once then slid open slowly.

"Sable?"

Sable stared up into his eyes, now a deep purple, and said the only thing she could say.

"Again! I wanna go again!"

* * *

Terror paused as his eyes widened. A sudden flush of color filled and reddened his body, making him gasp for breath.

"Terror?"

"We have got to be near the place," Terror whispered as he stumbled, and a heartfelt sigh left his chest. "Oh yeah, this has got to be the place."

"And you know this because?" the Healer asked as he stared at Terror in some concern.

"Because I think he just got laid."

"Really?"

"Oh yeah. And this time, he enjoyed the feeling! A lot!"

Behind them, a low growl erupted from the assistant, barely heard over the talking of the two men.

"Oh, yeah," Terror chuckled, a very masculine chuckle as he peered over at his healer. "He is not faking it this time."

He didn't hear the indignant squeak behind him.

"Oh! There goes another one," he gasped as his knees began to wobble. "You know, I love the feeling of this bond between us, but I sure as hell hope it ends soon. I kind of feel funny experiencing my son's orgasms! But at least there seems to be plenty of them. I am glad that he found someone for release. If he had mated that cold bitch Zultha, he never would have experienced this."

The Healer nodded in agreement as the party moved on. Falling behind, the assistant stomped her feet and mumbled under her breath, the anger pouring off of her in palpable waves.

Chapter Eleven

"Lift, two, three, four, five, six, seven, eight! Push, two, three, four, five, six, seven, eight!"

"Wrong song, Jill."

"Push-ups and sit-ups, bending and stretching, ahhh, feels good!"

"Not much better." Jack sighed as they made their way through the dark streets and toward their complex.

This trip had been… interesting so far, to say the least.

First, they'd had to drop off Jase at his apartment, and convincing the other man to stay there had not been easy. But with promises of picking him up the next day, they accomplished their goal and were now driving down deserted streets that seemed to fascinate the trio in back… when they were not turning green in the face from the drive.

In the backseat, the three intrepid warriors were disgusted at being ordered away by their charge.

"Terror is not going to like this," Joz said sadly as he watched as the other two being jostled around in the "van."

"And what of Torn?"

"He will do what he must," Mace replied as he tried to hold in his last meal. These people were insane, traveling at these speeds in these magical carts.

He looked out the window, blanching, as the scenery flew by. The trees blurred and the ground was no more than a dark haze. He could hardly make out the forms of Terror, the Healer, and his assistant as they sped past…

"Terror?"

At his words, Mace and Del turned toward the

direction he was pointing.

Jack fought to steady the wheel as the three men in the back suddenly leapt to their feet, clanging their heads on the ceiling of the van, then began to shout in that strange language.

As the van swerved on the thankfully empty road, Jack rapidly gained control only to have the side doors explode as the tall one and the muscular one forced them open.

"What the fuck?" Jack bellowed as the three men leapt to the ground and took off running back toward Jase's apartment.

"Damn it!" Jill gasped, one hand on the "oh-shit" handle, the other over his heart. "They've gone AWOL!"

"Not on my shift," Jack growled as he shut down the engine and pocketed the keys. "You coming?" he asked, shooting a look over his shoulder as he stared at his partner.

"For this, I better be coming later, man!"

Then they were both off, chasing after the rapidly retreating forms of the three men they were supposed to keep out of trouble.

* * *

Mace, Del, and Joz jogged to the spot where they'd passed Terror and his party. They needed to connect with their leader to inform him of the goings-on in this place. So intent were they on their quarry that they never noticed the small cloaked figure that seemed to suddenly appear out of nowhere! It was quite a shock when she let out a small scream, as they were inches from plowing her over, then found themselves suspended a full foot off of the ground.

The cloaked woman stood there, dark hair flying from around her hooded cloak, her eyes spitting violet fury as she suspended the warriors easily. One hand was extended and the other clutched a long dagger that glowed eerily with her power.

"Nello!" Mace barked, halting his struggles against the magical barrier holding him aloft.

"Mace?" Nello gasped, then quickly lowered her hand, dropping the men gently to their feet. "Where? Where is my son?"

"Back there!" Mace pointed in the direction they were running. "We saw Terror and were trying to intercept him to inform him about the redheaded woman."

"I know all about the redheaded woman," Nello snarled. "And the witch will be dead by my hand before this realm's sun rises for the day!"

Then she took a good look around her, noting a few parked metal wagons and the lack of patrols wandering the streets.

"Do they have day here?" she asked, hesitant to use any more of her magic in this strange place.

"I have no idea!" Mace answered as he and his men looked sheepishly around. "But they do have water that flows from the sky."

"Water? From the sky? What madness is that?"

"I wish I knew," Del said with a laugh. "But it is cold and quite disconcerting."

"I can imagine." Nello sighed as she again turned to survey the area around her, and then froze as her eyes narrowed in anger.

"They rush us!" she snarled, and again that hand was raised, this time, catching Jack and Jill completely unawares as they were suspended above the ground.

"Saints preserve us!" Jill gasped as he was suddenly caught in an immovable force and his feet left the ground.

"Shit!" was Jack's eloquent contribution as he floated beside his partner.

"Nello," Mace called out. "They are friends."

"Friends?" she asked as she began to lower her guard, then blinked twice, her eyes riveted to the two strange men. "They have been touched by Torn!"

"Reaved?" Mace asked, shock on his face. He could feel no taint in the two, but then what magical gifts he possessed were small and inconsequential.

"No, not reaved as there is no dark residue, but... he has... lightened them."

"Put me down, you insane hussy!" Jill took the opportunity to bellow as his stomach threatened to turn itself inside out. "This is why I was never into birds, Jack!" he added, turning to his mate. "Too damn hormonal!"

"*Knart?*" What? Nello and company asked en masse.

"My God, she's one of them," Jill breathed, and he began to let go of his worry. "She must know Torn!"

"Torn?" Nello asked, smiling as she lowered her hand and let the men drop to their feet.

These men were strange, she decided as she stepped closer to get a good look. They were plenty big enough to be of the warrior caste, but they were just so short! If this was an example of the masculinity in this realm, then Torn must really feel at home, she decided as she examined the two carefully. Their words were strange, but she had the cure for that.

Jack and Jill stared at the woman -- who they assumed had hefted them up into the air without breaking a sweat -- tossed back the hood of her cloak and faced them clearly.

"My God!" Jack gasped. "You look like Torn!"

And she did, from her long, curling purple hair

to the glittering violet eyes. This was a female version of their fey friend.

Jill just gaped.

But then the woman stepped close to him. Raising one delicate hand, she gently caressed the side of Jill's face.

Jill smiled as he felt a flash of warm heat flow through his body, searching his mind, then it gently withdrew.

"Where is my son?" she asked in perfect but slightly accented English.

"How did you…"

"Forgive the intrusion, but I pulled the knowledge from your mind. I would have asked permission, but we haven't the time. Where is my son?"

"Torn is your son? But you don't look old enough to have kids!"

At that, Nello blinked twice and smiled, but turned the conversation back to important matters.

"My son? He is in danger and I must help him as he has helped you in some way."

"Danger?" Jack growled as he turned to look at the three men. "Can you make them understand?"

Nodding, Nello turned and shot a pale white bolt into the bodies of the three guardsmen. Joz, Mace, and Del gasped as the magic entered their bodies, then turned to Nello in shock. First, she'd spoken this strange language, and then she'd touched them with her magic! To what purpose?

"They understand," Nello said as she turned to Jack. "My son?"

"Is she in danger?" Jack asked, eyes flat as he stared at the woman. Magical or no, if they endangered Sable…

"Who? The redheaded bitch who tried to murder my child?" Nello growled as her eyes narrowed at Jack. Maybe she was wrong! Maybe these men were the instruments of evil! "You protect Zultha?"

"Who?"

Nello's anger eased as quickly as it rose as she turned toward her men for conformation.

"Has Zultha reached my son?"

"Not since we were ordered away, My Lady," Mace said. "I believe he refers to the red-haired witch with whom Torn is enamored."

"Red-haired --"

"Sable!" Jack growled. "Is Sable in danger?"

"Two of them?" Nello asked. "Two red-haired women?"

"Damn it, is my friend in danger?"

At Jill's outburst, they all turned toward the shorter, bristling man.

"And I know you can understand me because she" -- he pointed to Nello --"did that voodoo thing!"

"Sable is the wench that Torn fancies," Mace explained. "If she is with Torn, then yes, she is in danger."

"I refuse to believe that Torn would --" Jack began, only to be cut off by Nello.

"It is good you defend my son, but the danger does not lie with him, but with the one who sent him here."

"Wait!" Jill interrupted. "He was sent here?"

"Why, do you think he would abandon his family on a whim?"

"Never mind that!" Jack interrupted. "What danger to Sable?"

"Ah, we have no time for this!" Nello glared at the two men. "I need to get to my son!"

"You can protect Sable?"

"Yes!"

"We'll take you there."

Nodding, Jack grabbed Jill by the arm and turned back toward the van. He wanted his girl safe.

"I guess they aren't faeries after all," Jill mumbled as they dashed toward the van, Nello and the three henchmen following.

"I don't care what they are," Jack said as they approached the van. "I just want Sable safe."

"And Torn," Jill added. "Sable will never be happy without Torn."

"I know." Jack nodded at his partner. "And that's what scares me."

* * *

"This must be the place," Terror decided as he followed the feelings of giddiness back to this dwelling. "Curious, these people's dwellings."

"They are short and not very defendable, are they?" Despite his vocation, the Healer was still a warrior at heart.

His assistant said nothing.

"I suppose we should go right in," Terror said, looking dubiously at the not too stout door. "I don't think we should bother with announcing ourselves."

"How true."

Shrugging off the unsettling feeling of his son's orgasms -- there went another one! -- he braced himself before charging the door. Two swift kicks and the wood splintered like so many practice boards in his arena, easily and without much effort.

Before anyone dwelling inside could investigate, Terror rushed the entranceway, wary of magical traps and skilled warriors, but only found a neat sitting area, a small fireplace, and one screaming, red-haired woman holding a round wooden... staff?

"Get the fuck out!" Sable screamed as she lunged through the room and attacked the home invaders.

She'd been on her way to the kitchen for a drink when she heard the telltale sounds and leapt into action.

She'd heard about stuff like this, these invasion robberies, and she was going to protect her own! Especially with Torn near comatose with pleasure after their last romp. It just wasn't fair!

Instinctively, Terror leapt back, sliding into a defensive position, but before they could blink, a dark streak shot through the room, grabbing the red-haired wench, pushing her behind it, and took up a defensive position before her. It all happened so quickly Terror didn't have time to react or even blink.

When the blur settled, there stood the partially nude figure of his son positioning to launch an attack.

"Torn?" he gasped, easing himself to a standing position, not sure that the quick moving raven was actually his son.

"Father?" he asked in his strange lilting language, his violet eyes confused, but slowly clearing as he beheld a sight he thought he would never see again. "Father!"

Technically he'd known his father was coming; Mace, Joz and Del had told him so. But to actually see him, knowing all the things that had happened leading up to this event, it was overwhelming.

"*Torn!*"

Then Terror raced across the room, pulling his son into his arms, holding onto him like he would never let him go!

"Oh, my son," Terror breathed as he embraced his lost child. "I thought I would never hold you. I thought I would never get the chance to tell you how much I love you."

Torn was too choked up to speak as a few stray tears made silvery tracks down his face.

Then Terror pulled back, his large hands framing his son's face as he rested forehead against forehead, and stared deeply in his son's eyes.

"I am never letting you go again!"

Then he was pulling his son to his chest again, lost to the world around them as he vowed to protect his offspring with his very life.

A throat clearing behind him caused him to pull away slightly to stare at the redheaded wench who'd attempted to attack him earlier.

"Torn, who is this?" he asked, pulling himself back from the emotional reunion, to stare at the one obviously responsible for his son being half-naked and smelling of sex. Smelling strongly of sex, he decided as his other senses engaged and he peeled himself away from his son's sticky, sweaty body.

"Sable," he replied as he faced his chosen and offered up a hand to her.

"Torn, I take it you know these guys?"

Her voice was wary, and who could blame her. These oversized warrior… people had just kicked in her door and invaded her house. And even worse, they'd destroyed the excellent lethargic sexual afterglow she and Torn had just entered into.

They'd taken her by surprise and she *really* hated surprises of the destructive nature. Still, she trusted Torn, so she placed her hand in his and allowed him to draw her close.

She became self-consciously aware she was dressed in only the large T-shirt she'd dragged on before she grabbed her baseball bat and reacted. It only came to mid-thigh, but when you were defending yourself and property, decorum rarely came into play. When she discovered that all eyes were on her, the man who hugged Torn -- the tall silver-haired man who accompanied them, even the eyes of the hooded person who huddled behind them in the door, she tugged at the hem, wishing she had a long paper bag to hide in.

"Father," he said in his lyrical language, "this is Sable."

Then turning to his chosen, he smiled and said in his accented English, "Sable, this is Father."

"Father?"

She stared from Torn's grinning face to Terror's curious one, and back again.

"I don't see much of a resemblance."

But then maybe there was! Though Torn was several inches shorter -- okay, about a foot shorter -- than the man he'd introduced as his father, they had the same strong, sturdy build. As he stepped closer to her, for a better look, she assumed, she decided they both moved with the same languid grace.

"Torn," Terror said as he watched her catalog the similarities and differences between father and son, "she is small."

"Well, so am I," Torn returned. He chuckled, drawing Sable to his side and wrapping one large arm around her, pulling her close.

"What did he say?" Sable asked, looking puzzled at the amused expression on both father and son's faces.

"He commented on your tiny stature," he answered with a grin. Then he pointed to the door.

"Father, why did you not knock?"

"Knock?"

Terror felt a blush stain his cheeks as he looked shamefaced. "It was in the way of what I wanted," he answered finally then turned back to glare at his healer and dare him to say anything.

But Fal intelligently kept his mouth shut and his snickers to a minimum.

"Somebody is going to fix my door," Sable growled as a draft blew through the house and sent goose bumps running up her legs. She realized she was angry about the invasion, something she forgot in meeting these people.

"My damn good English oak door that cost me a pretty penny!" More than angry, she realized. She was enraged!

"Haven't these people ever heard of a phone call? Or knocking? You don't just barge into someone's home without asking permission! And to destroy my property? Just who do you think you are?"

Even Terror took a step back at her sudden and unexpected anger, not understanding what she was saying, but knowing she wasn't happy.

By now, Sable was pointing at the door and bellowing, her eyes narrowed as she stared at the man who professed to be Torn's daddy.

"If my door doesn't get fixed soon, there will be serious consequences and repercussions."

Finished, she stared at Terror, making sure her point was taken, even if he didn't understand a thing she'd said. Anger was making her chest heave and her face fill with bright color. She never realized what a pretty picture she made in her anger.

"Magnificent," Terror breathed, giving his son an all too male smile. "Absolutely breathtaking. You have managed to find a jewel in this strange place."

"Thank you, Father."

"Now please tell me you understand what she just said."

"I do. The language here is kind of like Dervish, but with a bit of Knishtol."

"Very good, son. But I don't have your talent for languages, so can you please tell me what that was about? I understand she is angry with me about something but am not quite sure what that something is."

"Her entrance door."

"Yes?"

"You broke it."

"I did."

"She is angry about that."

"So have her workmen fix it. There has to be some laborers in this manor." "Things don't work that way here. She has to pay someone to do the work."

"Odd."

"A lot of things here are odd. And the men are so small I feel like a giant."

"I saw," Terror commented, then turned his attention to the woman again. "Tell her I will make recompense for her door. I will send laborers to repair it as well. It is the least I can do for having inconvenienced her. And it would be a fitting gift for having her protect you until I could find you and bring you back home again."

"Home?"

"Yes, Torn. I have come to take you home with me. I have wasted so much of my time with you feeling guilty that I will spend the rest of my days making it up to you. So go and gather what you need, and we will be off."

"But Father --"

"And I am sure your mother would love to give

her, this Sable, her thanks as well."

"But Father --"

"So hurry, explain to the female so we can be off."

Feeling his distress, Sable stepped in front of Torn and glared at the man. She had no idea what his father was saying, but it was causing Torn discomfort, and *that* she wouldn't put up with. If only she could speak that damn language!

"But Father," Torn said again, stepping forward and staring straight into his father's eyes. "I am not going back. I am staying here, with Sable."

"Fal, there is something wrong with my son. Please come here and examine him."

Torn blinked at his father's steady words, and then shook his head, amusement in every line of his body.

Turning to Sable, he whispered, "Please, beloved, clothing?"

Sable looked down at her half-exposed body, then nodded and rushed off to get something on. But she was not going for beauty queen. She was going to grab the first pair of sweats and get back out there. Something told her she didn't want to leave Torn alone very long with his people.

As she left the room, the assistant glared after the red-haired woman. What was so special about that skinny harlot? What did Torn even see in her? The strange one was just a weak imitation of her, Zultha thought as she watched the small one exit the room.

"Fal," Terror called again, and the Healer motioned for his assistant to advance with him.

"Father, there is nothing wrong with me." Torn sighed as he rolled his eyes, a Jill move that he found effective and telling.

"After Fal checks you for magical spells, we will discuss this."

"*No!*"

At his refusal, everyone stopped dead and turned shocked eyes to the heir. No one, absolutely no one, told Terror no.

"What did you say to me, Torn?"

"I said no, Father. No, I am not leaving Sable, and no, I will not submit to any magical examination. No."

"You tell me no?"

"I tell you no."

Terror became angry. "What has this place done to you, my son? What has this place, these people, *that woman*, turned you into?"

"They have done nothing to me, Father," Torn said, shaking his head at the man who refused to try to understand.

"They must have done something, and I want Fal to discover what it is."

"There is nothing wrong with me!" Now Torn felt angry. "There is nothing wrong with me, there are no spells being cast to keep me here! I want to stay here. I want to stay with Sable."

"So it is the witch," Terror said grimly."

"Watch your tone, Father," Torn growled, his voice deepening, taking on the multi-hued tones of the Reaver. "That is the woman I love."

As soon as the words crossed his lips, he felt a smile take hold and he couldn't stop it. He loved Sable. He was capable of love! If he felt that emotion, then he was safe from the pit. He had something to live for.

He realized that *this* was what his inner voice, the voice of the Reaver and his conscience, was telling him.

He loved Sable. And she loved him back. Maybe he was worthy of that love after all.

"You take that tone with me?" his father growled back, for once not concerned with the beast that dwelled within his son's body.

"I take that tone with anyone who interferes in my life! I love that woman and I will stay here to protect her!"

"Gentlemen." Fal stepped forward, trying to ease the tension between the father and the son. "We all need to calm down."

"I *am* calm!" Terror shouted as he glared at his ungrateful brat of a child.

"So am I!" Torn shot back. "And I am not leaving her, period!"

At this point Zultha was fuming. Torn had never spoken of her like that. He had never shown any type of backbone whatsoever!

He'd even *talked* his father into their mating instead of standing up and arguing him down. He hadn't defended her as he now did that washed-out weak version of herself! Sable, he called her. He risked much to be with this Sable.

And seeing him here and unharmed let her know it would not be as easy to trap this Torn as it had been to trap the milksop Torn who'd lived back in their realm.

But she wanted him to hurt, her mind screamed at her. She wanted him in pain! She wanted him to suffer! Here, he had too many people, too many powerful people protecting him. And Nello was soon to follow.

Her time was running short, she realized. Nello alone would prevent her from seeking her justice. She would protect her son, and Zultha was not up to the physical standards to take on a full-grown warrior like Terror in his prime.

Then there was Torn himself. With this new attitude, there would be no way to find a weakness in him to exploit.

Or was there?

There was such passion in his eyes when he spoke of the little washed-out copy, such passion. He openly admitted he loved that thing, and he was going against his father's wishes to be with her.

Even now, she thought, as she watched him step right up to his father and make his demands, he showed his passion for that thing.

"It will kill me to leave her!" Torn bellowed at his father, ignoring Fal's restraining hand.

The weakness, she decided, a sinister smirk spreading across her face.

As the men argued, Zultha took the opportunity to follow the redheaded thing back where she'd disappeared deeper into the house.

She paused at every closed door, leaning against it slightly to listen for sounds of movement. The pendant around her neck gave off no warning of magic being worked, so she knew the female wasn't a witch and that Nello was nowhere nearby. She still had time to alter her plans and make Torn hurt.

As she paused at one door to the rear of the manor, she smiled as the means made themselves known.

"Stupid men breaking my door and upsetting my Torn," Sable muttered as she sat on her bed to yank on thick socks and her runners. She wanted to be totally covered when she confronted the invasion party, as she thought of Torn's people, and find out what the hell they were doing to her man.

She shot to her feet, anxious to get back out into the living room, then jerked to a halt, a shriek of fright caught in her throat.

That hooded person was standing in her bedroom door, towering over her. "What…"

"Hello, means," Zultha purred in her tongue as she slipped the hood of her robe back and revealed her grinning superior countenance.

"*Where is she*?"

* * *

"Nello!" Terror turned as his mate burst into the room with five men, three of his guard and two he had never seen.

"The assistant! Where is she?"

The men turned to watch each other, confusion written plainly on their faces as they halted their heated discussion and looked around the room.

"The assistant?"

Before Terror could utter another word, they heard a loud feminine shriek and the sound of a body hitting the floor, followed by the crash of breaking furniture. En masse, they all turned and raced toward the hallway that led deeper into the house, tangling up with each other as Terror and Torn got stuck trying to force their bulk through the hall at the same time.

"Move!" Jack bellowed, slamming into them, knocking them down, but it solved the human blockage holding up progress. Another scream spurred them all to untangle and move faster.

Torn was the first to enter the room, followed by Jack and Terror with Nello pushing her way through.

"Sable!" Torn bellowed as he stared at the mess of what was once a very neat and tidy bedroom. Then turning to his father, he fisted his hands in his father's vest, dragging the shocked man closer to him as his eyes began to swirl and change into a glowing demonic red.

"What did you bring into my house?"

* * *

"What do you want?" Sable snapped as she stared at the Amazon blocking her way. She didn't like the unsavory look on that woman's face. In fact, her whole demeanor was downright frightening. It seemed this chick was surrounded by an aura of madness.

She recalled her days of volunteering at hospitals, helping psych patients on the mental ward play in the bright primary colors. There had been one woman there who the doctors swore could be rehabilitated. She didn't know why, but she was always disturbed by the mere presence of the woman.

One day, the Scary One, as she referred to her, walked over to her and whispered in her ear, "You are fated to die."

"What?" she asked, not believing what the woman was calmly saying.

"You are going to die screaming," she added in a singsong voice. "I have seen it. They told me last night that you would die. And that they would eat your soul and drink your screams, and bathe in your blood and misery."

She stopped volunteering soon after that, but she never forgot the feeling of madness that surrounded that woman. She still had nightmares about it.

And now, she was getting the same vibe from the Amazon who blocked her bedroom door. The woman didn't say anything, but her smile got wider as she stepped into the room, spreading her arms out, preventing a quick escape.

"What is this?" Sable demanded as she stalked up to the woman, intent on pushing her away and getting back to Torn. She didn't have time for foolish games of superiority, and this woman was getting on her nerves, going where she was not invited. But as she stepped closer, the woman shot out one hand and slapped her soundly across the face.

"Oh, no, you don't!" Sable snarled as she stared into the woman's smirking face. That's why it was so easy to ball up her fist and let it fly straight at the Amazon's stomach, doubling her over to Sable-height and bringing her into the perfect position to slam that same fist across the right side of her face. The woman let out a shriek as she toppled to the floor.

"You don't come in my house and pull some shit like that!" Sable growled as she drew back her foot to kick the woman out of the doorway.

But the woman, snarling in her rage, reached out and caught Sable's foot, jerking her heel up and taking her off balance. Sable tumbled to the floor on her butt but rolled to the side as the woman used her grip to try and pull her in closer.

"I don't think so!" Sable bellowed as she reached out her hand and caught the leg of an accent table. She yanked it to her, sending a small statue of a metal dragon falling to the floor and brought it over her head, crashing it down on the crazy one's back. Shrieking, the woman let her go and they both rolled to their feet.

"Now, it's on." Sable said grimly as the woman glared at her, *how dare you strike your better*, written all over her face. But before she could move, the woman reached into the folds of her cloak then tossed some powder into Sable's face.

"Poison!" Sable gasped as fire burned her eyes and nose, as her lungs began to seize.

Stumbling away from her murderer, she tripped

to her window, struggling to get it open when all her arms wanted to do was grab her throat and make the burning stop. She forced one hand away, pounding at the glass, slamming it with all her strength until the pane shattered, slicing her hand and arm but letting in the precious air. It wasn't enough. She saw the blackness at the edge of her vision closing in and struggled to stay aware, but to no avail.

As the powder overcame her, she heard the hissing laughter of the crazed one and the sound of her window being shattered, then knew that all was lost.

Chapter Twelve

"Torn!" Nello snapped as she slapped her son on the arm, drawing his attention. "Now is not the time! We have to save that young woman."

"Who?" Torn roared, releasing his father and turning to his mother. "Who has taken my Sable?"

"Zultha."

"The witch is dead!" Torn vowed as he looked wildly around the room, trying to catch some sense of where the witch had gone.

"I can find her," Nello said, trying to calm her son.

"Who are all these people?" Jack asked, fear and anger evident in his voice.

"Where the hell is Sable?" Jill added, his eyes going to the woman. "You said you could protect her!"

"Who are these men, Nello, and what are they saying?" Terror demanded, eyeing Jack and Jill with suspicion.

"What do you mean, Zultha?" Fal demanded. "What has happened to my assistant?"

"Enough!" Nello roared, glaring at the men in the room who growled and demanded, but were acting like a bunch of children. Without thinking, she lifted her hands and two white balls of power struck Terror and the Healer, gifting them with the knowledge of the language. She reached out to Torn but he shook his head. He understood enough to express himself and understand what was going on around him.

Terror blinked as a thousand sounds filled his head, then settled to a low hum. Then he jerked his head toward the taller of the two new men. He could understand his words clearly now.

"What happened to Sable?"

So the wench's name was Sable. "Zultha happened. That is why I was in such a rush to get here."

"Impossible!" Fal stated, shaking his head. "I saw my assistant hours before we were to travel to this realm, and it was my assistant who carried my belongings."

"Fal, I believe I found your assistant dead in my library," Nello said, not unkindly.

"What?" Disbelief was in his voice, his heart saddened by the loss.

"Someone strangled her, but in her hands, she clutched lengths of long red hair. I believe she knew she was going to die and left a message for me. She had to be one of Zultha's people."

"But I've known my assistant for years, Nello. I can't believe she would betray the realm!"

"Has she been acting funny?"

"She disappears for hours, but that is normal behavior for her. I never suspected --"

"We waste time!" Torn interrupted as he walked to the window, his presence growing with every step, his anger mounting with every second passed. "I must find her!"

"We will," Nello soothed, placing her hand on her son's arm again. "We will bring her home."

"Damn right, you will," Jack growled, and the guards placed hands on their weapons. "You promised she would be safe."

"I will do everything I can do to make her safe."

"Then do *something*!" Jill yelled. "We're standing here arguing and holding our limp dicks while that bitch, whoever she is, makes off with Sable! We have to do something."

"Zultha is protected by my father's amulet."

"Your father?" Jack yelped, incredulous. "Your father gave her the means to hurt your son through Sable?" Jack was no fool. He knew the only reason to take Sable was to get to Torn. It was something he'd feared for the longest.

"Nice family," Jill added, still waiting anxiously for some kind of good news. "So your daddy gave her some jewelry. What good is that going to do us?"

"I can track it," Nello said calmly, watching the faces of the men.

"Well, then what are you waiting for? Get to tracking!"

"We will retrieve the woman," Terror said as he glared at the men. "Then we will take Torn and go."

"I am staying, Father," Torn said, still concentrating on tearing up what was left of the room. His anger was growing and it needed release.

"Torn --"

"Enough!" Nello snapped. "First we find Sable, then you can argue with your father!"

"Father?" Jack and Jill both exclaimed, staring from Torn to Terror. There was a slight family resemblance, but it definitely was small, mostly in the build.

"Later!" Nello almost screeched as she stepped to the window beside her son and closed her eyes in concentration. "I need silence."

There was silence. But Creator knew how long it would last, Nello thought as she sent her magic out seeking, seeking... seeking...

Where was she?

* * *

Where am I? was the first thought in Sable's brain as she began to regain consciousness. The second was that she was in extreme of pain and wished only to go back to sleep. The third was that it was going to rain. Again. That made her open her eyes.

"What the..." she muttered, drawing the attention of the person who stood above her, wrapped in a voluminous cloak. When the figured turned toward her, it all came flooding back with a vengeance.

Zultha sneered as she watched awareness dawn in the copy's eyes. She snorted as she ran one finger over the swollen area of her eye. She had never been struck before, and to have this little worm of an imposter be the one to deliver that blow... The witch would suffer!

"Well, well, well," Sable drawled as she placed her hands on the cold hard ground and forced herself to her knees. "Looks like beauty got one blow in on the beast."

Zultha couldn't understand her words, but she understood the tones all too well. Narrowing her eyes in anger, she lifted one foot, ready to deliver a blow that would wipe that smirk off her face.

Sable had a second to see the foot flying in her direction, then dropped both hands. The smile left Zultha's face as Sable neatly caught her foot. She had a second to look shocked before Sable smirked even harder... then yanked that foot with all her might and shoved it backwards.

Zultha shrieked as her free leg shifted forward, then flew up in the air. She hit the ground with a satisfying *crunch* that Sable had no time to savor. She was up and running before Zultha's ass bounced once, not that she was making much progress as woozy as she still was. But the ground was rocky, hard and unfamiliar. *How far could that woman have taken her?* Sable thought. *She was on foot, for goodness sake!* She had to have taken her out through the window because

Sable knew if she'd tried to get her by Torn, he'd have stopped her.

Breath heaving in the cool night air, Sable was grateful for the sweats and tennis shoes as the terrain grew rougher and the night grew colder. Who was that lunatic, anyway? She huffed as she ran, arms churning and lungs burning.

Suddenly the terrain changed, and instead of rocky ground, there was softer gravel and then that too gave way to a line of trees. Sable knew where she was! She was at the cliffs near her home.

Even as she rejoiced that she was only a few miles from home, she felt a frisson of unease before a shadow overtook her. She slid to a halt, just nearing the trees when the shadow formed itself into that psycho bitch again. Man she was fast. She moved as fast as Torn, Sable decided. But what did she want?

Zultha growled as she approached the copy that had dared to do her person harm yet again! Did she not realize that she was a princess, that she was worthy of nothing but adoration, respect and honor? Maybe it was time to teach that harlot a lesson.

"You would do well not to strike your betters," Zultha said, taking a step closer to her prey.

"What are you saying?" Sable was tired of being the prey in this game of cat and mouse. "What do you want?"

"I do not understand your savage words, copy. But I do so long to hear your screams of pain."

Before Sable could move, Zultha had her trapped within her arms, then surrounded by a rope that seemed to come from that never-ending space in that damn cloak.

"Time to play," she whispered, enjoying the widening of her copy's eyes, the smell of fear that filled the air. One perk about being such a delicate princess was the nose to smell such delicious scents.

"I know how to make Torn suffer," Zultha said in her singsong voice. "I know how to make him pay."

"Torn?" That was the only thing Sable understood as she was being dragged through the woods.

"You are not fit to speak his name," Zultha said, still in that surreal tone. "But that does not matter now. I know how to make Torn pay for what he did to me and my father. How he will weep and wail when he finds your body! How I will rejoice to see the Reaver brought low."

"Reaver?" Sable managed as she stumbled over a root, nearly falling on her face. In fact, the only thing that kept her face from smacking into the rough ground was the leash that the bitch managed to fashion with another length of rope, the same leash she was using to drag her through the trees. She struggled to make it back to her feet, to climb to her knees, but the woman just kept dragging her and speaking in that damnable language.

"The Reaver hasn't the power to find us and the only one who does is Nello. And Nello isn't here, little copy. By the time he finds your corpse, I will make my way back to Terror and then I will kill him. This is so easy! I wonder why I hadn't thought of it before? But there is the Reaver to consider."

"Torn is the Reaver," Sable said out loud, trying to piece together the mishmash of sounds, trying to buy some time, trying to gain her feet because she was not liking the direction this Amazon was taking her.

They were getting closer to the cliffs and the rocky bottom that meant nothing but an excruciatingly painful death for her.

"And the Reaver will weep black tears for you," Zultha added with a dreamy smile on her face as she easily dragged the copy, who'd sought to be her rival, closer to her doom.

"And I will go back to the realm and kill Nello. Then I will take the crown and everyone will love me. I will have what is mine. No one will be able to take it from me. I will have what is rightfully mine, all mine, all mine, all mine…"

* * *

As soon as Nello pointed in the right direction, Torn was off, followed closely by Terror, who refused to leave his son again, not when he needed him. After they saved the wench, they could go home and leave this place behind.

Nello was at her mate's side, refusing to leave him to this task alone. That, and she wanted to kill the red-haired witch herself and meet the woman her son professed to love.

Mace, Joz, and Del had returned to the realm to tell of what was happening and to seek out other spies.

Master Healer Fal traveled with his leader and his family, praying to the Creator that his services would not be needed.

Jack and Jill were along for the ride. They had to be. Jack had refused to drive them to the woman who had stolen Sable unless they both went along.

Terror relented after Nello explained the speed of the animated metal carriage.

Now Terror was praying to the Creator that he would not lose his dinner and his dignity in the insane thing.

"That way," Nello pointed, leaning over the driver's seat giving directions to Jack. "They are not far now!"

"Isn't that the park with the cliffs?" Jillian asked, his eyes growing wide with fright as he deduced the only reason for a kidnapper to take her hostage to the cliffs.

"Zultha is mad enough to want to kill Sable," Nello said softly as she prayed that the metal contraption would move a little faster.

Torn was just as anxious. The only reason he had not taken to the skies in his Reaver form was because he was afraid he couldn't pinpoint her location as his mother could. That, and from the sky he could miss the pair of females in the trees that hid much of the ground from his view.

He waited as his mother directed them, waited and felt the caged animal within him cry out for release and the justice it would bring.

"So his ex really has a head trip," Jill whispered, his hands knotting in his lap. He didn't know what he'd do if he lost Sable. And Jack... Jack would be inconsolable.

Nello just wished she'd been there from the beginning; then she could have put an end to Zultha's game to hurt her family even before it had begun. She had many regrets, and they were rising to the surface, making themselves known as the road they traveled flash past in a blur.

"There!" Nello suddenly cried out as she felt a spike of protective magic from the amulet. "She is under attack, though not of a magical kind."

"Sable would fight," Jack said, pride in his voice. "She's always been a fighter."

"She gives us precious time we need to get to her," Nello said with a smile, glad that Torn had managed to find such a woman.

Terror's opinion of the strange beings hadn't

changed much, but he felt a little admiration for the female. She was so tiny, he thought as he fought back his gag reflex, to be facing one as large as Zultha. Their women were almost as large as their men, and in this realm that made her practically a giant.

Torn said nothing, just sat there and wallowed in his anger, the voice inside his head screaming for vengeance. Once again the two beings that made up Torn were in complete agreement.

"Where are these cliffs?" Terror asked, then swallowed hard.

"Why? It's not like you really want to help Sable anyway. You just want to get her away from your son." Jill's tone was hard and filled with anger.

"I wish no harm to the female," Terror said yet again. The argument with his son had flared up as they'd left the manor, and the two men had felt the need to get involved. "But this is not my son's place."

"You harm Sable by taking away the one thing she needs more than anything. And you do the same harm to your son as well."

"I do no such thing!" Terror growled, and regretted it as his stomach rebelled.

"What do you want to know about the cliffs?" Jill interrupted the tirade. There was no use in arguing with a brick wall.

"Strategy," Terror answered shortly. "If I had no magic and no conceivable means of killing a person without drawing attention to myself, I would toss them over a cliff and make it look like an accident."

"That's what I thought." Jill sighed as he turned to Jack. "Isn't there a shortcut to the cliffs?"

"What if you're both wrong?" Jack asked as they entered the timberline of the park. "Nello has the magic GPS system."

"But we would be following!" Jill protested. "We would get there too late. It's better to cut her off, to stop her before she's actually able to toss Sable over."

"You think like a warrior," Terror complimented Jill reluctantly.

"Several generations of Highlander blood in these veins, lad." Jill rolled his eyes over his shoulder at Terror. "And don't you be forgettin' it," he added in his exaggerated brogue.

"I don't know..." Jack trailed off, looking uncertain. Jill had made several valid points, but Nello had the magic.

"Trust me." Jill looked into his partner's eyes.

"I do, but..."

"Trust in me!" Jill growled with intensity. "Go to the cliffs."

Nodding and praying that he wasn't making a mistake, Jack cut the wheel hard to the right and sped toward the little-used maintenance road that led to the cliffs.

God, Jill thought. *Don't make me be too late!*

* * *

Zultha smiled as she saw the end of her journey and the beginning of her bright and glorious future, just up ahead. She looked back at her imposter, finally subdued after being dragged several miles over roots and tree branches that littered the ground.

This was fun.

"End of the line?" Sable managed as she forced her eyes to open and her body to respond instead of endure.

"I know not what you say, copy." Zultha giggled, her eyes almost beautiful, in an eerie way, as she looked down almost kindly at her captive. "But soon it will be time for a minor parting of the ways."

She sighed and dropped the rope leash as she surveyed the area before the cliffs. "Such a beautiful sight, my copy," she muttered, dropping onto the ground next to Sable.

"Princesses were not meant to touch the hard bare earth, but for you I make an exception. You are not a worthy opponent, my copy, my shadow, but even you have to see the beauty in this view."

She reached down to where Sable had been lying on her stomach and forced her head up.

The moon sure was pretty, Sable decided as she wearily closed her eyes. Then she narrowed her eyes in anger.

Why was she eyeing the moon and waiting for her final curtain call when she had a real live superhero cat/bird/flying thing in her life? Just where the hell was Torn? He was supposed to take care of evil, wasn't he? Well they didn't get any more evil than this… this crazy bitch holding her head up.

"I am right here, Sable."

Sable and Zultha jerked around at the sound of that tri-toned voice. They both knew there was only one being that could produce that sound.

"Torn!" they both cried out, Zultha in anger and Sable in great delight… and more than a little relief.

"Release her!" the Reaver demanded as a huge shadow blocked out the light of the moon, hinting at the large creature creating it.

As they both watched, huge black angel wings snapped open and the frightening apparition of the Reaver stepped into their view.

"No!" Zultha bellowed. "Why do you always ruin my plans?" Her face was red in her anger as she jumped to her feet, hauling Sable's body before her.

"Because you plan such poorly executed ones," a

light female voice said from behind the frightening apparition. Nello stepped around her son, narrowed violet eyes snapping.

"No, no, no, no, no, no, *no!*" Zultha screamed as she looked wildly around her. Before she could make a move back the way she'd come, none other than Terror himself, bearing his huge broadsword, stepped forward, blocking that avenue of escape.

To the right, two angry-looking warrior types stepped out, and to the left, the Healer Fal made his presence known, his huge sword in his hands.

"What else can go wrong?" Zultha screamed, her eyes roiling wildly as she searched around her again and again, looking for an opening. Then the sky seemed to open up and pour… water? Yes! Water fell down on her, ruining her vision as well as her cloak. She screeched as the first drops hit her.

"What kind of place is this realm?" she bellowed as intelligent thoughts receded and the madness took over once more.

"I don't know what you're all saying, but it's about time you got here," Sable managed, sighing and sagging in Zultha's arms.

Torn was here. Torn would make everything all right again.

"No!" Zultha screamed. "This is not fair. You ruined my plans! You seek to rob me of my vengeance."

"Will you tell that bitch to shut up?" Jill and Sable bellowed in unison.

Sable had to chuckle at their perfect timing. She might not be able to see Jillian, but she sure heard him. All of her family was there to protect her.

"You never stood a chance," she told Zultha with a chuckle. Zultha suddenly became aware of the one she held in her hands. When Sable's chuckles became full-blown laughs, Zultha snapped.

"How dare you mock me?" she roared as she struggled to stare at her copy through the blinding water falling from the sky. But awareness gleamed for a moment, and a thought was born.

If she had to fight to see them, then *they* had to fight to see *her*. Vengeance would be hers, after all.

"Die and burn little copy!" she cackled as Sable felt her muscles tense. "And grieve, Torn. Grieve your pathetic life away."

Mindless of the danger that surrounded her, Zultha barreled to her right, directly at the strange warriors. Before they could react, the giant female holding their Sable broke between the two of them, veering off and aimed right for the cliffs… and the bitch wasn't slowing down!

"No!" the Reaver bellowed as he took off after the madwoman, using all the strength and speed in his body.

"No! Torn!" Sable screamed as she realized what Zultha intended. The crazy bitch was going to toss her off the cliff and suicide right along with her!

Time seemed to move in slow motion as Torn tore after Zultha.

Zultha stumbled, slowing herself down, but quickly recovered, moving closer to the cliffs.

Then the unspeakable happened. The princess tripped.

In the mud.

In the mud that sent her sliding closer and closer to her goal.

"*Die!*" Zultha shrieked as she fell partially on top of Sable, crunching her body as they both slid headfirst over the cliff.

"Sable!" Jack bellowed as he struggled to his feet, racing toward the cliff even though he knew in his mind it was too late to save her.

"Zultha! No!" Nello screamed as Terror used his breath for running, even though his warrior's mind was already calculating how many seconds they would be too late to save the women.

"Beloved!" the Reaver gasped. He raced ahead, only to watched the two women slide over the cliff, and then just like that, they were gone.

* * *

She was falling! With a mouthful of mud and gravel, she was falling!

I should be scared, Sable thought as she felt the evil bitch's arms tighten around her aching body even more. *I should be afraid of dying, watching my life flash before my eyes, should be screaming*. But she was silent, grateful for the moments she'd spent with Torn.

This is so seriously fucked up, she thought as the bottom literally dropped out of her world.

* * *

They saw a streak, a huge black streak, racing through the driving rain before it dove without hesitation over the cliff.

"*Sable!*" Torn thought as he leapt over the edge. His beloved was all that was on his mind, his beloved and his determination to reach her!

He pulled his wings in tight as he tried to make his descent faster, willed the forces to push his body down with greater speed.

There! Just ahead, he made out the flapping cloak and a wild tangle of red hair, the pale flash of skin.

It was them!

Sucking his breath in deeper, making his body more streamlined, he urged himself faster and faster, closer and closer!

But still too far away and the ground was coming fast!

He raced and reached, then… There! He was an arm's length away. Straining, he reached farther and snagged the trailing leash. Taking what the Creator offered him, the Reaver tightened his hold on the rope and jerked up as he snapped his wings open.

He hadn't accounted for the rain.

It soaked his wings, making them heavier, weighing him down. His wings slowed his descent, but it was a fight to slow them down faster, to hold onto both his chosen and the screaming witch who was wrapped so tightly around her. Dozens of solutions spilled through his head in a split second. What could he do?

You know what you have to do, his inner beast growled at him.

"But we have to save her soul! We just can't let her die!"

So I guess you have a decision to make, the inner voice rumbled. *Do you live for others, for their views of you, or do you live for yourself? What will make you happy? Trying to reave the soul of that madwoman, or saving the one who keeps you the abyss?*

A shadowy view of the dark cauldron that was his soul appeared before his mind's eye.

You choose, hero, the Reaver sneered.

The voice made sense, Torn thought. But the voice was evil, as was his dark soul and all the dark souls he'd consumed. The Reaver spoke of truth!

But how could the dark speak of the light? Did not the dark twist the light into what it could force others to believe?

But to let Sable die…

We can't let Sable die. Without Sable, there was no Torn. Without Torn, there was no Reaver. Without Reaver, there was nothing. He would kill them both!

He couldn't let Sable die! Without Sable, there was nothing, there was no reason for being. But could Torn let a woman die?

The ground raced closer and closer; the time for his decision was at hand. Torn did the only thing he could do.

* * *

A piercing scream reached the white-faced people standing on the cliff as they looked down into its darkness, struggling to see if the unthinkable had happened.

"He… he… failed," Jill moaned, hot tears falling, mingling with the cold rain that continued to soak them to the skin.

"No!" Terror gasped. "This can't be!" His son loved that woman so much he'd willingly dived over the cliff in an effort to save her, knowing that if he couldn't pull up in time, it would be the death of them all. His son loved that woman so much…

At this thought, he was struck mute. His son *loved*. His son had found the woman he'd dreamed of, and Terror had refused to listen to him, only wanting to take his son home and try to make up for the years of his perceived neglect. All the while his son had needed him, and he was too selfish -- still -- to pay attention, thinking *his* way was the only way.

Terror fell to his knees in the wet earth, knowing that if his son loved his Sable as he loved Nello, he would make no effort to pull up out of that dive. His son was lost to him, and this time forever.

Nello just stared over the cliff, shock plainly written on her face.

"Torn," she managed through a tight throat and burning eyes. Again, she was too late to save her son. She stumbled back from the cliff just as Jill threw himself into Jack's arms, his sobs ringing out over the cliff.

Fal looked on, pitying all the parties involved in this... this... situation. It wasn't fair; to find happiness and have it all stripped away. What damage would this do to Terror and Nello? What would this do to the realm?

As he cleared his throat and stepped forward to do his job as healer, a huge gust of wind threw him backward and landed him on his ass as his feet slipped in the thick mud.

"What...?"

He looked up, and just as the waters from the sky began to taper off, he was struck by the most magnificent sight he had ever seen!

There, hovering above, wings flapping like mad, the Reaver forced his way up over the edge of the cliff and flopped onto the muddy ground.

And in his hands -- Creator, in his hands, was the small, red-haired woman.

"Sable!" Jack roared, then he was racing toward his friend, dragging his crying partner behind him.

"Impossible!" the Healer whispered as he rose to his feet and approached the couple, disbelief in his eyes. "Impossible!"

"Anything is possible!" Terror managed as he made his way to his son and his female. "Anything at all, Healer. He is my son."

"Our son," Nello added as her sad tears transformed into tears of delight.

And from the ground, Sable commented. "Have I ever told you how much I hate the rain?"

Even though she smiled, there was pain in her eyes and in her voice.

"Heal her," the Reaver gasped, his tri-toned voice sounding weak as he fought to breathe. As he lay there protectively over his mate, his skin began to lighten and his muscles to grow more compact.

Slowly as they all watched, the wings furled close to his body and melded his back. The whipping tail retreated back into his body and the clawed hands morphed into something more human. The Reaver withdrew, sliding back within his body, leaving only the panting man behind.

"We have got to get them to shelter," the Healer shouted, his training taking over as he visually assessed his patients. "We have to get them warm and dry, and I will work on the female. She is the less sturdy of the two."

No one argued as Terror descended on his son, hefting him up in his arms and holding him close to his heart.

"I'll not leave Sable," Torn managed, though he was too weak to lift his head from his father's chest.

"Then I will visit you here," Terror decided. "And I will learn the strange ways of this even stranger place."

Following in Jack's arms, Sable managed to gasp through the pain in her chest, "Now, can someone tell me who that bitch was? I hate being almost killed by some chick who won't even tell me her name!"

Epilogue

"I can't believe all is right with the world," Sable whispered as she wiggled deeper into the thick covers on the bed and snuggled closer into the body spooning her from behind.

They had all gone -- Terror, Jack, Jill, Nello, and the big blond healer, but Sable knew they were nearby.

"All is well. You are in my arms," Torn replied as he squeezed her tighter, fear still making him keep her close. He never wanted to see her come as close to death as he had out on that cliff.

Sable sighed as she recalled the frightening ride in the back of the van with Jack cursing and swearing at every pothole, Terror holding onto his son, turning green in the face, the platinum blond healer hovering over her, and Jill and Nello talking over the level of distress in the small rolling box.

Then things were a bit of a blur as the big blond began blowing powders in her face and chanting. After the third puff of green dust, she blacked out, only to be awakened later by the same man cataloging her injuries in halting English.

"Bad cut on your right hand. Three broken ribs. Scrapes and slices on your hands and legs and face. Knees skinless. All in all, I say you are lucky to be alive."

"Torn won't let me die," she managed, before seeing his smile as her eyes closed again.

The next time she woke up, the woman was in the bathroom with her. Well, the woman was in a hot bath, holding her in the same water as she sponged much of Scotland off her body.

"Who…"

"I am Torn's mother."

"You're Nello? For a moment, I thought his mother was the one who tried to kill me."

"No," Nello said with a laugh. "That was the woman he was going to mate."

"The one who sent him here?"

"Yes."

There was silence for a few minutes, except for the sound of water splashing, then, "He doesn't have any other psychotic women at home that might try to come here and kill me, does he?"

"No," Nello assured her. "But would you leave him if he did?"

"Nah." Sable sighed as she decided that having the woman wash her was like being bathed by a nurse. Usually, the nurses didn't climb into the tub with you, but the woman was very clinical about how she moved the sponge. So that was all right, she supposed, unless they practiced some weird lover's mother/lover sex ritual. That, she would have to take a pass on. "But I would have you teach me some magic to keep them away from my man."

"Human," Nello remonstrated with a smile, "you can't be taught magic. You have it or you don't."

"I guess I need to learn to use a sword then."

"Sable, you have magic!" Nello chuckled as she squeezed the sponge over the younger woman's face.

"But... No, I don't."

"It is different than what I was born with, or from any of the realms I have traveled through in the past, but it is there."

"What magic?"

"The magic that taught my son he is worth being loved and that made him love you in return."

Sable contemplated that for a moment.

"That wasn't magic. That was just meant to be."

"Sure," Nello agreed. *Stubborn woman*, she thought. *Just perfect for my son*.

* * *

At that moment, Torn was sitting in the living room, speaking to his father about serious matters.

"You could feel that?" he gasped, amazed and slightly embarrassed.

"Yes. And it probably was right because I didn't feel it when you were with Zultha."

Torn blushed as Fal snickered. Jack and Jill shook their heads at Torn and wondered what Sable would think of this new development.

"Maybe it is temporary." Torn said hopefully at his father's amused yet miserable look.

"I pray it so. There are just some things in your life I need not know about."

The others roared with laughter and Torn blushed, hanging his head as he peered at his father through a long fall of curly black hair.

"So, how did you manage it?" his father finally asked.

"What?"

"How did you actually kill that woman without attempting to cleanse her soul?"

"She was dead the moment she touched Sable," Jill growled. "I would have killed her myself."

"I before you," Torn said, then shook his hair back and looked, clear-eyed at his father. "Father, I had no choice."

"But I thought that the Reaver couldn't --"

"Father," Torn interrupted, a new strength in his voice. "I am the Reaver."

"But --"

"We are one and the same. By dividing us, I sought to keep the dark and the light separate in my soul. But as I struggled to hold both of them, the evil one and my beloved, from death, I realized there can be no dark without the light and that light does not exist without the dark."

"You have finally accepted all parts of you," Terror said with pride as he stared at his son and the man he had turned into.

"I did myself harm in trying to separate the two. No one is all good or all evil. If we were, there would be no balance and only chaos would follow."

"Chaotic is watching all of you go over the cliff," Fal put in as he recalled the despair they'd all felt, assuming that Torn, Sable, and Zultha were lost.

"Out of chaos, from great destruction, comes our greatest and most positive change."

Everyone looked over at Jill, surprised that such eloquence had come from the mouth of the talkative one.

"What? I'm not just another pretty face, you know!" he groused until Jack pulled him into his arms and gave him a tight squeeze.

"You are all more than what you seem," Terror agreed, recalling the bravery of the two strange men who'd stood up to dangers they knew nothing about, all for the love of a friend. Then he turned to Fal, who had once been afraid of his son, but now treated him like the old Torn... albeit, with a lot more respect. And he looked at himself. It had almost taken a disaster to teach him to listen, to really listen, but finally the lesson was learned. "We are all more than what we seem."

"And I am a complete man, Father," Torn added with a small smile. "A man complete with his woman at his side."

"I understand," Terror said with a sigh, then he

let out a huff of laughter. "As I am complete with your mother."

Nodding in understanding, Torn felt joy as he knew his father now understood how important Sable was to him, and how much he owed her for coming to the rescue of his only son.

Torn would be staying here, in this realm with his Sable. And he would finally have the peace he'd had wanted his entire life.

"You will visit!" Torn demanded as he stared at his father and smiled. He loved the man so much, and now that love was freely returned. No more guilt clouded his father's eyes.

"As will you. Your mother will miss you, Torn… son," he amended. "You better not break her heart."

"I will not. And you are welcome anywhere Sable and I make a home. And our home will always include Jack and Jill."

"As if there was ever any doubt," Jill called out from the sanctuary of his lover's arms.

"And I still have a job to do," Torn stated simply, his inner monster agreeing wholeheartedly.

"A job?" Now Terror was confused.

"I am the Reaver, Father. For that purpose I was created, and for that purpose I shall continue."

"I don't want you harming yourself, Torn!" His father was adamant that his son kept the personal peace he had wrought for himself.

"It is who I am, Father. It is what I was designed for. I cleanse souls. I reave the ones that can't be mended. But now that I have discovered balance, there is no danger to me of either side winning."

Torn seemed content with his answer, Terror decided, and gave one stiff nod. "I just wish, son…"

"I know," Torn said with a smile as he heard the

bathroom door open. Then all his attention was on his mother, who was hauling his beloved into the bedroom.

Within seconds, he was on his feet and following his beautiful beloved. She would make it all right. She would make everything all right.

"Guess that ends this conversation," Terror said as he faced the trio of men still awake and in the room with him. "What now?"

"Well, Nello spelled the door and fixed it," Jill said as he started to turn toward the door but instead fixed his eyes on the window and the new day that was dawning. "And dawn is cracking." He snickered. "So I guess we go and get some sleep."

"I don't want to intrude."

"Man, you break in her door without a fare-thee-well, and now you're concerned about overstepping your manners? You tall people are funny!"

Even Jack had to hold in a shout of laughter at that one, but recovered himself enough to add, "But you are family now. And Sable has enough guest rooms to hold us all."

"But…"

"The place where my thighs meet," Jill chuckled as he rose to his feet, pulling his partner with him. "And I have it on good authority that mine is extremely cute."

Which caused all in the room to have a great laugh.

Soon, Jack and Jill had pointed out all the guest rooms, seen to everyone's comfort, escorted Nello to her mate as she exited the bedroom, and were soon closing the doors and making for their own bed.

"I love it that she keeps a room for us." Jill sighed as he stripped off his still-damp clothing and tumbled into bed. A shower could wait until tomorrow. He was surprised he still had his eyes open.

"I love it that they're all safe," Jack added.

"Still believe they aren't fairies, love?" Jill asked as his partner climbed into bed and pulled him against his smooth, strong chest. God, he loved this man of his!

"They're from a different realm, whatever that is," Jack allowed, recalling the explanations they'd received from Torn and Terror that night.

"Hon, Sable fell in love. They're going to live happily ever after. The big bad witch is dead! If that ain't a fairy tale ending, I don't know what is!"

Jack was silent. What could he say to that?

* * *

In the master bedroom, Sable snuggled deeper into her lover's arms and let sleep overcome her. She had her hero in her arms, they were all safe, she was healed, and the bad guy had gone bye-bye.

Torn, on the other hand, buried his face in her hair and breathed in her scent.

He was still shaken as he recalled the look on Zultha's face as he'd gripped that rope leash and used his tail to whip at her hands, breaking them, forcing her to let go.

He recalled the terror in her wide eyes, the open mouth that shouted out in fear at the realization of her own impending death. He recalled all of it as he held on tighter to his Sable, his center.

We are one, brother, the hissing voice chanted, filling the dark recesses of his mind.

We are one.

It would be a while before he closed his eyes in sleep. Because something else occurred to him, the thing that made his body quake in fear. Zultha's death? He'd enjoyed it.

Outtakes
Bonus scenes that didn't quite make the final cut

First Zultha and Torn Bedroom Scene
Take One

Grinning, she stepped forward, allowing one hand to brush his chest as she stared into his purple eyes, reading the hunger that dwelled there.

"I have what you need."

Then her hands were pulling his loose tunic over his head, her nails scratching at his nipples as she ripped the hapless garment from his body.

"You know what I need?" Torn questioned, a smile in his voice.

Torn was no virgin, untried in the ways of love sport. But he'd held his urges back with his mate, both to quell the small warning voice that was always with him and to honor her parents. He would show she who would be his mate all due respect.

But apparently, Zultha was more than ready to take this step.

"I know what men like," she whispered, her tongue lashing out to lap at his lips. "I know what men need."

Taking a step back from her bewildered lover, she smiled an evil smirk, eyes narrowed as she ran her tongue over her lips.

Torn gulped as his eyes widened. Was he going to get… Yes! She was licking her lips and staring at his crotch! He was getting a BLOW JOB!

Torn sat up, eagerness painted on every feature of his face.

She turned her back to him, but paused to sling her hair around to stare into his face, her eyes glittering though a curtain of silky red.

Oh boy! He was getting a BLOW JOB!

Then she spun back around… and he realized he *wasn't* getting a blow job!

"WHY?" he bellowed to the sky, falling to his knees in anguish! "Why? Creator, why?"

But then he noticed she was holding something in her hands.

A remote to a strange thing called television and a six-pack of beer! And not just any beer, the imported stuff!

"You do love me!" Torn cried. He crawled over to her on his hands and knees when he discovered what else she was holding.

She'd magically produced a porterhouse steak, a pound of western fries, and a programming guide that had the Porn Boy Channel and TTPN, The Tractor Pull Network, all paid for and programmed in the remote.

"You know it, baby," she purred, blinking sweetly down at her man.

"We'll get hitched tomorrow, right after the three o'clock tractor pull and *When Triplets Attack with Dildos*," he said, already playing with the programming on the remote.

"No rush, dear," Zultha crooned as she reached behind her and pulled out a butcher knife.

"You are the greatest!" he exclaimed happily… between bites.

Looking at him, then the size of the knife, she shrugged and tossed it over her shoulder then walked to the closet to find something better.

"Most women don't appreciate the finer things."

"Uh-huh," she murmured absently, bent over and tossing things around.

Finally, she came up with a blowtorch, took one

look at the size of the man, then shook her head. *That* one went over her shoulder, too.

"I mean, food and porn," he gushed.

"Yeah, baby!" she said, then stood up with the biggest missile launcher ever to grace that realm. "Take your time."

She carefully aimed at the man who was torn between ripping into the food as if he hadn't been fed in ages and gluing his eyes to a wide-screen TV that showed two women licking each other's breasts and reaching for a rather large, um, toy to share. "Take your time…"

Blam!

Never Argue with the Author

"Please, Stephanie! Don't make me do it!"

Hush, Torn. I know what's best.

"But I'm shy!"

You're not that shy. I saw what you did in that dream last night! And I'm your creator, for goodness' sake! I really didn't need to see that, Torn.

"But you needed to see to describe my size correctly," he grumbled, tossing a few locks of hair behind his head. "I had to do it! It was a mercy orgy!"

Yeah, right!

"It was! I bet this is punishment! You're punishing me! I know you are!"

I am not! I could never punish you, Torn! You are my baby! So stop it with the watery, wobbly purple eyes. That crap stopped working after the first time you gave me writer's block.

"But --"

No buts, Torn! And I'm tired of having this argument. Get out there and do what I told you to do!

"But --"

But nothing! Or do I have to call in the secret weapons?

"You don't mean…"

Yes! I'll bring in Ani, and Patti, and Jen wanted you in that thong, and then Liz and Bree wanted to try that tag-team spanking, and Shi and Diane wanted to try that hot wax, and Sahara wanted to use that new riding crop, and… Torn? Where are you going… Oh! Now you decide to strip like I told you! Never listen to the author, but when I start bringing in other writers, then we do all sorts of things to cooperate.

"But I'm taking my clothes off now! See? I'm stripping! Down to the undies!"

Noo! Can't listen to the one who knows what's best! Bring in a bunch of rabid women with stress to work off and no end to research in sexual torture, and then you fall in line!

"Stephanie? Steph? Flash?"

That does it! Where's a cliff? I feel the need to have you fall off something. Hmm…

"Mama. NOOOOOOO!"

I wonder if a man can survive without having sex for more than half a book.

"For the love of the Creator, no! Please, Stephanie!"

Zultha? I think I should give you special powers…

"Please?"

Sable? How about a yeast infection?

"What did I do? Punish Torn!"

"Sable! Et tu, Bruté?"

Stop it! You don't speak English anyway! Sable, back to the woods where you'll be dragged, kicking and screaming. Torn, back to the strip club. Grind and thrust, and grind and thrust… Damn, he's good. I think I've got a frozen quarter around here somewhere…

The Cliff Scene

"*Sable*!" Torn thought as he leapt over the edge. His beloved was all that was on his mind, his beloved and his determination to reach her!

He pulled his wings in tight as he tried to make his descent faster, willed the forces to push his body down with greater speed.

There! Just ahead, he made out the flapping cloak and a wild tangle of red hair, the pale flash of skin.

It was them!

Sucking his breath in deeper, making his body more streamlined, he urged himself faster and faster, closer and closer!

But still too far away and the ground was coming fast!

He raced and reached, then… There! He was an arm's length away. Straining, he reached out farther and…

"Oops." Torn overshot his target by a foot.

Rising to his feet, he looked out at the readers and said… "Damn. I missed. How did that happen?"

He turned back to look over the edge of the cliff, then at the assorted heroes and shrugged his shoulders. He looked at the readers again, tossing hanks of soft, wet hair over his shoulder.

"Um, Medic?"

Queen of the Insane

"What news?" the mad one asked as she watched her servant scurry into the cavern.

Zultha, her red hair matted to her head and her

clothes dirty with accumulated grime and filth, was the perfect picture of the Queen of the Insane. Her eyes glittered in her madness, more frightening because of the…

"Wait? What do you mean matted hair? Dirty clothes? What's wrong with you people? I mean, do you know what I'm worth? I have enough money and power to buy and sell you a million times over, you skinny tart! Dirty hair? Funky clothes? I mean, what turnip truck did you fall from? Have you seen this script? And don't go callin' any of your friends, either! We got nothing but space and opportunity here, woman! Bring it on! You know what? You're not worth even a second of my time! *Wardrobe*! I need bottled water and I want it like yesterday! And get my agent on the phone! Dirty hair, my ass! My hair is insured by Lloyd's of London! Screw this crap! I'm so outta here!"

With that, Zultha stormed off the set, leaving a cast of bewildered minor actors and cast members… thus ensuring her painful demise in the end.

Note to everyone else: Don't mess with the author! Take notes!

Nodding, the masses comply…

Stephanie Burke

Stephanie is a *USA Today* bestselling, multi published, multi award-winning author, Master Costumer, handicapped, wife, and mother of two.

From sex-shifting, shape-shifting dragons to undersea worlds, sexually confused elemental Fey and homo-erotic mysteries, all the way to pastel-challenged urban sprites, Stephanie has done it all, and hopes to do more.

Stephanie is an orator on her favorite subjects of writing and world-building, a sometime teacher when you feed her enough tea and donuts, an anime nut, a costumer, and a frequent guest of various sci-fi and writing cons where she can be found leading panel discussions or researching varied legends and theories to improve her writing skills.

Stephanie is known for her love of the outrageous, strong female characters, believable worlds, male characters filled with depth, and multi-cultural stories that make the reader sit up and take notice.

More books by Stephanie at Changeling: changelingpress.com/stephanie-burke-a-30

Changeling Press E-Books

More Sci-Fi, Fantasy, Paranormal, and BDSM adventures available in e-book format for immediate download at ChangelingPress.com -- Werewolves, Vampires, Dragons, Shapeshifters and more -- Erotic Tales from the edge of your imagination.

What are E-Books?

E-books, or electronic books, are books designed to be read in digital format -- on your desktop or laptop computer, notebook, tablet, Smart Phone, or any electronic e-book reader.

Where can I get Changeling Press E-Books?

Changeling Press e-books are available at ChangelingPress.com, Amazon, Apple Books, Barnes & Noble, and Kobo/Walmart.

Changeling Press, LLC

ChangelingPress.com

www.ingramcontent.com/pod-product-compliance
Lightning Source LLC
Chambersburg PA
CBHW051525260626
47170CB00003B/794